Wrecked Lives

(Vidas Destrozadas)

A Story of Survival

Donald R. Wraith

Published by Clink Street Publishing 2021

Copyright © 2021

First edition.

ISBN
978-1-914498-03-9 Paperback
978-1-914498-04-6 Ebook

Contents

Prologue

During the 16ᵗʰ Century, exploration to the New World provided Spain with huge amounts of gold and silver. However, maintaining new colonies was costly, and had to be financed by this treasure, as well as funding Spain's many conflicts between other countries. At this time Spain fought the Turks and the French, and from 1568 the Netherlands where, due to invasion, a rebellion began a long war of independence throughout that country. From 1587 to 1604 Spain also fought the English.

Spain's desire for exploration and thirst for world glory provided many politicians the opportunity to increase their wealth and status. One such person was Antonio de Mendoza, the Spanish viceroy who controlled the conquered lands of New Spain (Mexico). He sent out explorers to scour the New World for Native American treasure. They had heard persistent tales of fantastic wealth and treasures, one of which was called the Seven Golden Cities of Cíbola. So, in 1540 Mendoza dispatched Francisco Vázquez de Coronado to follow up on these reports, where he encountered many Zuni Pueblos from which the original legend was inspired. Eventually, the legend proved false, and the expedition turned out to be a ruinous misadventure for all those involved. However, many tales came back from those adventures, inspiring others to follow. Perhaps the following was just such a tale…

Chapter 1
1540 – New Mexico

Dense foliage of the tropical forest floor was being rapidly hacked away by sharp cutlasses and broadswords, wielded by panicking Spanish sailors and conquistadors. They painstakingly cleared a rough path through the undergrowth, in a desperate attempt to flee the forest and get back to their ship. From a group of twelve expeditionary men, only ten remained. They were escaping from a mob of angry natives, following an unfortunate incident at their tribal camp, in what started out as a peaceful fact-finding mission. Although they had a few minutes head start, the Spaniards could hear screams of hate and revenge coming from the chasing warriors. The natives seemed to be getting closer and closer, and the Spaniards faced certain torture and excruciating death should they be caught, like the two men who were last to leave the camp. They heard terrible cries of agony as the two men were captured, and that mental image spurred the fleeing Spaniards on. Sweat and blood poured from faces, arms and bare legs as broken foliage lashed and tore at their flesh. The pain was relieved only by adrenaline soaring through their bodies as they used all of their natural instincts to survive. In single file, the men raced on for what seemed an eternity, with no end to the forest undergrowth.

Suddenly, an arrow flew through the forest and embedded

itself into the last man's leg. As he fell, he grabbed the man in front, and the two men crashed to the floor. A lone native appeared, took aim with another arrow, and was just about to let loose when… Bang! One of the sailors ahead of them fired a pistol, sending the native flying backwards into the undergrowth. The man with the pistol shouted at the two tangled men trying to recover.

'Venga! Amigos, there is no time to waste… we must hurry or be captured'

The wounded man was lifted by his shipmate, and the two men struggled on, following the path created by the leading group. Emile, the injured man, winced as he limped agonisingly onwards, but he summoned enough breath to thank his shipmate.

'Gracias Miguel for stopping with me… I owe you my life my friend'

'Forget it Emile, we do not have much time before they catch us and then we will both be sorry for stopping'

The two men entwined their arms to ease the searing pain from the wound on Emile's leg and managed to continue. A few hundred feet later a clearing appeared just before a wide river where their ship was anchored. However, they also knew it would be the place where the natives could get a clear shot at them.

Dawn was rising fast and the group realised they would be easy targets for arrows and spears as daylight spread.

'We have to run as fast as we can Emile, try to ignore the pain.' As the two men staggered across the open ground, the chasing natives came to the edge of the clearing and quickly formed a line for a final salvo at the Spaniards. Emile looked over his shoulder and could see them taking aim. He realised it would only be seconds before they felt the arrows penetrate their bodies.

There was a pause…

Andalucía, Spain 1588

'Que pasa? Que pasa?' a boy's voice bellowed as he urged his grandfather to continue the tale. The old man, Emile Rodriguez, paused during his storytelling and stared motionless into space, his mind reliving every moment of that dreadful day in 1540.

He was a young crew member on one of the ships for explorer Francisco Vázquez de Coronado, whose mission was to discover new lands and riches in the Americas for Spain. Emile's patrol had been sent out to explore the Gulf Coast Bay area of Ochuse, when they had stumbled across a Zuni Indian village. After several days at the Zuni camp trying to glean information out of the tribe, Coronado's men noticed by accident, hordes of artefacts in a large tent on the edge of the camp. In the dead of night, they took several of the artefacts, including items of gold as potential evidence of Cibola. Just as the last of the men was leaving, one of the Zuni Indians saw them, and quickly raised the alarm. The Spaniards had to force their way out of the village, and two of the men formed a rear-guard to delay the Indians. Shots were fired by the Spaniards, killing three natives, which delayed them. However, it wasn't long before the natives regrouped, and the two men were overpowered and savagely ripped apart.

Returning to his grandson's plea, Emile, with his lean weathered features and long swept back grey hair, turned and looked into the keen eyes of the fourteen-year-old boy. For several seconds he just stared at Juan Carlos Rodriguez, a small skinny lad looking much younger than his age. He had short black wavy hair, olive skin, and his bare legs and arms were covered in cuts and bruises from his antics on the family farm.

'So, Juan Carlos, you want to know what happened next?' Emile quizzed annoyingly.

'Si, grandpapa! What happened next, were the men killed?'

A wry smile appeared on Emile's face and he grabbed the boy in his strong arms.

'Well… the ship was alerted by the crew and the canons fired several times, which scared the chasing natives so much that they couldn't release their arrows or spears… ha ha ha!'

He laughed loudly, and playfully tickled and teased the boy.

When they had both calmed down, Juan Carlos enquired.

'Grandfather… is… is that how you hurt your leg?'

Emile looked down at his withered leg, and grabbing his wooden crutch, eased himself from his chair.

'Si, Juan Carlos… It was my leg the arrow hit, and it has never healed properly.'

Seeing the worried look on Juan's face, Emile span around on his good leg and hopped around the room.

'But I still have my good leg and two strong arms my boy… and my share of the spoils we took from the natives helped me set up this farm, so all is well.'

Juan Carlos sat at the table, his head cradled in his hands, as he beamed and admired the many stories his grandfather had told him.

'How I wish I could be like you, grandpapa, the adventures you have been on, and the many places you have seen.' He paused thoughtfully. 'I want to do that! I want to go to sea like you.'

Juan Carlos then spent the rest of the day dreaming about life at sea and distant lands. Pretending to be a brave Spanish sailor, he attacked bushes and trees with a wooden sword, and chased the chickens in the yard.

All this time, Juan's mother Francesca listened, whilst preparing the late evening meal for the family in their small farm cottage. It was surrounded by a few acres of mixed olive, arable and goat grazing fields. They also cured their own ibérico ham in cool mountain caves from wild pigs that roamed the oak pastures. Francesca was in her early thirties, and she was a slim, beautiful Spanish woman with long wavy black hair tied back to make her many chores easier. She wore a simple, full-length dress and tunic, with an apron wrapped around her small waist. Her shoes were a simple '*chopine*' style used as a patten, clog, or overshoe to protect the shoes and dress from mud and street soil. Looking at Emile, she sighed loudly and felt dismayed and disappointed with the old man.

'You fill that boy's head with too much rubbish, and no good will come of it.'

Francesca and her husband wanted Juan Carlos to stay on the farm, and perhaps take it over one day. He was their only son, and together, with their daughter Maria aged five, she wanted to keep them at home where she knew they would be safe. Nevertheless, she was concerned that although isolated from large towns and cities, she knew that young men were being recruited by the military from all parts of Spain. She also knew of the dangers of such a life because of her father's many tales since returning home. Young men dreamt of seeking fame and fortune in distant lands, fueled by stories of those who had returned with treasures and fascinating stories, and Juan Carlos was no different.

The Granada province of Andalusia, where Juan's family lived was particularly beautiful, where lush valleys contrasted against dry, arid mountain ranges. Where seasonal rains captured by the mountains, provided water for rivers and lakes that made certain areas very fertile, and much sought after by wealthy landowners.

Their farm house was a simple single-storey building

of timber and stone with one main room for cooking and living. Bedrooms were added over the years as the family grew bigger, and animals were kept in a wooden barn or shack adjacent the house. During this period, peasant farmers could only become tenants on estates owned by wealthy landowners, although generations of the same family lived and worked on the same farms. Many of the long-established traditional farming techniques had been the mainstay of the local economy for centuries, but a large portion of their produce was exacted by landowners, and what little extra they produced was sold at local markets. Because of the hard lifestyle and rural poverty, many families were discouraged from farming, which provoked migration to Spain's cities and colonies of the New World.

Chapter 2
1588 – Historical Note

King Philip II of Spain was married to Mary, daughter of England's Henry VIII and Spain's Catherine of Aragon. Mary eventually became Queen of England in 1553 and as a devout Catholic, she was perfect for Philip's world plans, in which he considered himself to be King of England as well as Spain. This was emphasised in 1555 when Pope Paul IV issued a papal bill recognising Philip and Mary as rightful King and Queen of Ireland. However, Philip eventually deserted Mary, and in 1558 she became ill and died. This resulted in her half-sister Elizabeth, daughter of Henry VIII and Anne Boleyn, becoming Queen of England in 1558, and Elizabeth re-established the Protestant church set up by her father. This angered both Philip and the Catholic Church, so in 1587 Philip obtained backing from Pope Sixtus V to invade England and re-establish Catholicism. The invasion was proclaimed to be a Catholic crusade, and Philip ordered an "Invincible Armada" to conquer England.

Work started on the Armada in 1587, and Alvaro de Bazan, Marquis of Santa Cruz, was the Spanish naval commander commissioned to plan the invasion. The Armada was to leave the port of Lisbon, and then collect an invasion army from the Spanish territory in the Netherlands. The combined force would then invade England's southern coastline. The giant Spanish invasion fleet was completed by 1587 and was due originally to have sailed shortly afterwards, but the English captain Sir Francis Drake's daring raid on the port of Cadiz earlier in the year delayed the Armada's departure until May 1588. Apart from 130 ships, the Armada carried 2500 guns and 30,000 men, two-thirds of these men were soldiers.

Although Santa Cruz was a very able commander was much admired by his staff, unfortunately, he died in February 1588. Philip then appointed the 7th Duke of Medina Sidonia as his replacement, even though he had no naval experience of any sort. Philip demanded total support for the invasion and he realised he would require divine favour from the church. So, Philip summoned all those taking part in the task force to confession and contrition before sailing, and several priests were to accompany the Armada. Further injunctions were made against swearing, blaspheming, whoring, brawling and gambling, although to enforce such rulings proved difficult.

The winter passed, April came, and the preparation for the Great Armada had been going on in every port throughout Spain. Philip had to gather as many ships as possible to achieve a formidable invasion force, and many ships were requisitioned when they sailed into Spanish ports, regardless of their owners' rights and wishes. However, before making the hazardous voyage to England, many ships required repairing or adapting to make them suitable for the voyage. Castles were added to merchant trading vessels, at the front and the rear (forecastle and aftercastle) and at the top of the mast. The Spanish fought with their fleets as if on land, discharging arrows and hand cannons, while the crews grappled the enemy ships so that soldiers could board and try to capture them by conducting hand to hand fighting. The main Spanish fighting vessels were galleons, sailing ships that rode high out of the water, although their height and broad beam made these ships awkward to sail. Other ships included galleys, galleasses, zebras, patches, and caravels. Sturdy Baltic Urcas were used as supply ships, whilst others also used oars for added manoeuvrability. Caravels, for instance, were fast sailing vessels whose lateen (triangular) sails gave them speed and the capacity for sailing to windward.

To make a ship seaworthy took many tradesmen, including carpenters, pitch-melters, blacksmiths, coopers and shipwrights. Ships were constructed of oak for the keel, pine for the masts and other timber for the hull and decking. As the building of the Armada gathered pace, ships congregated in major ports such as Cadiz and Lisbon, where final loading of provisions, weapons and men took place. The Armada consisted of several "squadrons" of ships, and each had its own commander with a single overall commander in charge of the Armada. One such squadron was the Andalucía squadron, whose commander was Don Pedro de Valdes. His flagship was the *Nuestra Señora del Rosario*, and his squadron consisted of 11 ships in total. The ships gathered in the port of Malaga in southern Spain, before moving onto Cadiz, and then Lisbon.

In the 16th Century, Malaga was usually dominated by foreign merchants that attracted many trading ships. Wine and raisins became the main commodity of exports, although silk textiles were still important as it was linked closely to the Moorish part of the population. Trading encouraged new infrastructures to be built, including roadways from nearby towns such as Antequera and Velez. These links proved invaluable as more and more ships arrived in Malaga, and for a few weeks, the port became a frenzy of activity. Merchants, tradesmen, soldiers, sailors and farmers mingled with each other in an effort to supply the warships with enough provisions, equipment and men to make the long voyage to England. So, let the story begin…

Chapter 3
Spain – Granada Province

During the early summer of 1588, Juan Carlos' father, Alfredo Rodriguez, and his sister Maria, arrived at the family farm on their open cart pulled by an ageing mule. Alfredo, in his late thirties, and of average height with dark, trimmed hair and beard. He was lean and strong from heavy manual work on the farm, which he managed with his father-in-law Emile. Peasant farmers such as these wore simple, loose cotton clothing due to heavy work and hot temperatures. They had just returned from the port of Malaga where they had sold their produce at the local markets, bringing back much-needed money and provisions. Carrying some of the provisions into the cottage, Alfredo's demeanour had an air of excitement, and his sweaty face beamed in unguarded pleasure. The rest of the household waited eagerly for the reason behind this great joy.

'I have sold everything… all the livestock, olives, preserves, jamón ibérico… everything!'

As he dashed about excitedly bringing in more of the provisions, he continued with his news.

'I could have easily sold more… and I received a good price too.'

Francesca wiped her hands on a cloth and began to load the provisions into household storage boxes and cupboards.

She was keen to know more, but was always wary of disappointment.

'Why is this Alfredo? The markets may have been good to us since the ships came, but we have always struggled to make a really good profit.'

Without a further word, Alfredo placed a bag of coins onto the table, and then lifted Francesca up in his arms, spinning her around the room. Francesca was a little shocked and surprised at the sudden burst of energy during a very hot day, but soon became swamped with the euphoria and the pair danced and laughed around the house. They were quickly joined by Juan Carlos and Maria in a makeshift family dance, whilst Emile sat at the table clapping and stamping his good leg. After a few moments they stopped, as they were all out of breath, and the family slumped onto chairs around the old kitchen table. Once they had regained their breath, Alfredo began to explain.

'Soldiers have now arrived at the port along with more ships, because they are preparing to leave very soon. They are stocking up with fresh food, and traders were struggling to find enough provisions for all the ships.'

Juan Carlos was always fascinated with any news of warships and was very keen to know more.

'How many more ships are there father? Did they have many cannons? How many soldiers are there? Can we go and see them?'

Juan Carlos had been many times to the port with his father, and often watched the ships being repaired, but there were never any soldiers at the port, only crew and tradesmen. Francesca scowled at the boy and was afraid of the consequences of the news, all because his grandfather had filled his head with so many stories.

'Keep quiet Juan Carlos! We only need to know how

much money we have made, and if our provisions will last for the next few weeks.'

Ignoring his wife, Alfredo explained.

'After many delays, the ships are finally ready to sail to England, and they will be leaving very soon.'

The family conversations buzzed for the rest of the day and early evening, yet there was tension building in the Rodriguez family home. Francesca could sense that this latest news would excite the male members of the family, and she dreaded the two men filling Juan Carlos's head with thoughts of excitement and adventure. She knew it would not take much to convince him to go and see the ships for himself, and she had to make him see the dangers in doing so. Over dinner that evening, Alfredo, Emile and Juan Carlos discussed in detail the events of the day, and when Maria had been taken to bed, Alfredo continued.

'People were talking at the port today about the amount of timber needed to repair some of the ships for the long sea voyage. There have been many heavy carts loaded with oak beams brought into the city, and everywhere is full of workers and soldiers.'

Emile realised the urgency of the work.

'They have to sail now, during the summer, if they want to get to England, because the weather in those seas can become very bad in winter. All this work is good news for many farmers like us, because it will provide much needed money for their families Alfredo. We must take more produce before they leave.'

Francesca, who was busy clearing the dishes, looked up in dismay.

'Yes, but for how long? Those ships will go soon and the workers will move away, and we will have to struggle again to make ends meet. It could also mean that many families

will lose their loved ones when men are needed to sail those ships or become soldiers.'

She paused and sighed before continuing.

'Spain is always fighting with someone, and how many men will come back from this war? We all know families who have lost fathers or sons, and I don't want it to happen to my family.'

She stared angrily at Emile and pointed to his leg.

'Papa… you of all people should know what dangers there are for young men… Just look how you ended up?'

Emile flushed red in the face, but eased himself around on his chair to face her, and angrily replied.

'But I survived, didn't I? The trouble is Francesca, you don't know the desire and passion young men have for adventure, and no matter what you women say, or how much you try to dissuade them, they will always find a way to satisfy their curiosity.'

Francesca stood up abruptly and shouted selective Spanish obscenities at her father, and then hurriedly began clearing the table, whether they had finished eating or not. As she raced around the room, she snapped.

'I will not have Juan Carlos have his head filled with stupid stories…he is only fourteen, it is too young. If he has to go… then he can wait until he is at least twenty.'

Emile knew his daughter could be feisty and short-tempered, but he had always led a sailor's life and did not like being tied down on a farm. He also found a release from telling his grandson about his adventures. Emile turned his back on Francesca, winked at Juan Carlos and whispered to him.

'I was thirteen when I ran off to sea my boy, and I loved every minute.'

Finally, Alfredo interrupted them, attempting to broker some peace.

'Enough! Enough! Nobody is going anywhere! The ships will be gone in a few days, and by now they will have gathered all the men they need. We will probably not see another warship for a long time.'

Alfredo stood up and placed a friendly arm around the waist of Francesca, and in a softer voice, he whispered.

'As for making 'ends meet,' we have always managed to survive, and we will continue to do so, even when the work goes quiet my love.'

Francesca shrugged her shoulders and poured water from a wooden bucket into a bowl, ensuring to splash her husband. Alfredo realised that it would be quite dark before she would calm down.

That night as he lay in bed, Juan Carlos could not sleep for thinking about the ships and what his father had said. He had little time to decide if he was going to see them, and worried that he might not get another chance. Eventually, he made up his mind to go and see the ships before they leave, and he spent most of the night thinking of a plan to get to the port on his own. He realised that the next day would be Sunday, the day his family went to church in the village, and afterwards they nearly always had lunch with relatives, as it was a traditional pastime in many parts of Spain. He decided that in the morning, he would pretend to be ill, and by the time his family returned home, he would be long gone. Juan Carlos also decided that if the ships had already sailed, then he would return home and accept his punishment, but at least he would have tried.

The morning light came slowly for Juan Carlos, who was eager to start his adventure, and he could not wait for his family to go to church. As a teenager, this was to be the first time he had ever seriously disobeyed his parents. There have always been arguments and tantrums, especially where his grandfather was concerned, but this decision could possibly tear his family apart. He could not face telling his parents, as he knew they would not approve, and they would prevent him from going. His passions and desires were raised now, and he knew the time was right.

With the onset of summer, the sun rose quickly, spreading its warm fingers of light throughout the farm house, and the family was beginning to stir. The first to rise was Maria, who shared the bedroom with Juan Carlos, and she burst out of bed and rushed into her parent's room, which was the signal for Francesca to get up and start breakfast. In order for his plan to work, Juan Carlos had to stay in bed and make an effort to feign illness. A little later, his mother poked her head through his bedroom door.

'Juan Carlos! Get up or we will be late for church'

He pretends to be asleep, and attempts a moan of discomfort in an effort to appear convincing. Noticing this, Francesca walks over to his bed, touches his forehead to see if there was any sign of fever.

'You do not have a fever Juan Carlos, so what is the matter? Perhaps you have eaten something bad.'

Francesca knew her family well, and it was not like any of them to become ill in this way. She was always careful with the food they ate, and water came from a small, but clear mountain stream that very rarely ran dry. She decided to leave him in bed until he felt better, and returned to the kitchen where she spoke to Alfredo.

'Juan Carlos is feeling a little unwell. There is no fever, but I think he should remain in bed, and my father should stay with him today. If he is no better tonight, I will gather herbs to ease his stomach.'

For the next hour or so the family prepared for the journey into the village, Francesca took some food to add to the lunch with their relatives, and Alfredo harnessed the mule to the cart. When everything was ready, they washed and put on their Sunday best clothes for church. Emile was pleased that he was asked to stay, as he was never keen on the long church services, although he did like the opportunity to tell his stories at lunch with relatives and friends in the village.

Juan Carlos watched his family leave, eager for them to go, and once they had drifted from view, he quickly got dressed. He then took out a small travel pack from under his bed, and climbed out of a window, hoping his grandfather would not see him. As he cleared the corner of the house, a strong hand grabbed his arm.

'Ouch!'

He stopped suddenly, and Juan Carlos looked up into the face of his grandfather.

'Grandpapa, please, please let me go...You know I have to see the ships before they sail.'

Emile held Juan Carlos firm by the arm and looked sternly at him.

'And you know your mother will be worried and heart-broken if you go to the port.'

Emile paused...

'Are you sure this is what you want?'

Juan Carlos winced in the tight grip of his grandfather, but he was determined to go and he twisted and turned as he tried to get free.

'I know they will be hurt, but I will regret not trying grandpapa. This might be my only chance, and anyway... father said they have all the men they need, and I will probably not go with them... It's just...I have to see them... I have to go now.'

Reluctantly, Emile released his grip on Juan Carlos, and the boy ran off.

'Thank you! Thank you, grandpapa...I will be back I promise.'

Juan Carlos ran across familiar fields and rugged countryside, towards the port of Malaga. After a short while, he stopped to catch his breath, before walking along rough tracks leading to El Chorro Gorge. It was a spectacularly long canyon in an area surrounded by forests, lakes and limestone cliffs. The Gorge was carved out by the River Guadalhorce, before reaching the Mediterranean Sea west of Malaga City. He followed the river on a well-worn track, not suitable for carts, but popular with villagers travelling to and from the city. As he walked along the undulating track, Juan Carlos wondered about the sights he would see at the port. Later he stopped for a break at a mountain stream as it cascaded into the main river, and he gulped at the cool water to quench his thirst. It was about midday and the sun was getting hotter, he knew there were another three or four hours before he would reach the port. He slowed to a walk and thought about what he had done, but was pleased with himself that his plan had worked. He'd taken with him a small travel bundle which included some clothes, coins he'd been collecting, a small knife, bread, cheese and a few of his mother's preserved olives, although they always made him thirsty.

By mid-afternoon, the clear blue skies began to quickly cloud over, as rain clouds began to form. Juan Carlos knew he had to shelter, although he didn't want to go to anyone's house or farm, as the news would soon get back to his family. So, he sheltered in one of the many small caves carved out of weathered limestone along the river bank, often used by goat herders. As the storm arrived, heavy rain formed a curtain at the entrance to the cave, and he watched as a sudden deluge caused the river level to rise almost immediately. Parts of the bank were swept into the river, and he became a little anxious that the water would enter the cave. He crouched into the highest corner of the cave, and clutched at his belongings, he then watched and waited as the storm raged on for the rest of the day. As the last of the daylight faded, Juan Carlos realised he would have to spend the night there, and he hoped that the storm would have also delayed the ships from sailing. As the storm began to ease, summer temperatures returned, the cave became warmer and Juan Carlos began to relax. He drifted off to sleep to the sound of insects and frogs buzzing, which was a pleasant and reassuringly familiar sound.

Back at the farm:

Alfredo, Francesca and daughter Maria returned late from their day at the local village. It was mid-afternoon, the prevailing wind had begun to blow, and Alfredo sensed a storm was coming. As soon as they were inside the farm-house, Francesca asked Emile how Juan Carlos was, and if his stomach pains had eased a little. Emile instantly looked pained and dreaded the moment.

'I am afraid he was not ill, and he has gone to see the ships.'

Emile said in a forceful but reticent voice.

'I tried to stop him, but he was too quick, and I cannot run with this leg'

He gesticulated towards his damaged leg, which they all knew was troublesome for him, yet that did not prevent Francesca from scowling at him. Although she was angry towards her father, she knew it was useless to prevent a very agile boy from doing whatever he wanted. Alfredo was silent but very angry, and he looked outside to see if it was too late to go after him.

'There is a storm coming, it looks bad, and it would be too dangerous to chase after him now.'

Alfredo and daughter Maria consoled Francesca, and Alfredo reassured her.

'Juan Carlos would probably be close to the city by now, and he knows many families where he could shelter with for the night.'

He added reassuringly.

'I will go and find him first light Francesca, he has probably followed the river track, and he will be severely punished when I find him.'

Alfredo walked across the room and took Emile to one side away from Francesca.

'Emile, did you know about this? Juan Carlos tells you everything.'

Emile looked sheepishly at Alfredo.

'No Alfredo! I did not know he would run away like this. He knew how much it would hurt his mother, but I do understand why he did it.'

Alfredo was not sure about his reply and turned to thoughtfully stare out of the window, but the storm was now upon them and he knew it would be useless to go and look for him. He then went over to Francesca and comforted her as she wept and cradled Maria to her bosom.

'Francesca, it's too dangerous to go now, but I will take the mule and with luck, I will stop him from doing anything stupid. Please have faith that all will be well.'

Francesca started to cry, turned her back on Alfredo, and whisked Maria off to her bedroom.

Chapter 4
Spain – Port of Malaga

The next day, Juan Carlos was pleased to see that the storm had passed, with the sun was shining in a clear blue sky. After eating some of the food from his pack, he set off along the track. He could not believe how much damage the storm had done, as the rising waters had washed large sections of the bank and track away. With the water in the gorge remaining high, he struggled at first to get back on solid ground, and several times he slipped and almost fell into the rushing water. He could see that there was a lot of broken branches and tree roots bobbing in and out of the strong currents, and for two hours he painstakingly picked his way through the gorge. Eventually, he came through the gorge safely and joined the coast road leading down the hill to the sea, it was a magical sight. In the distance he could clearly see the whole of the coast, and he could make out at least eight large ships anchored in the bay. If the journey had made him tired, then this spectacle of timber and sail had re-energised him, and he ran off down the road leading into the city.

Juan Carlos had been to Malaga and the port before, but always with his father or relatives, as he was never allowed to go anywhere on his own. The busy city seemed a little daunting without adults, so he quickly raced around people and obstacles until he came to the port. Upon arrival, he immediately noticed a change in the air, which was far different from that of the countryside. He could smell the sea, fresh fish and treated timbers of the ships moored in the harbour, with their oiled canvasses, ropes and fresh pitch between weathered timber joints. There were so many people, and quite a few different accents and dialects he had never heard before. Juan Carlos had never seen the port as busy as this, and he was amazed at the sight of so many huge ships. As he wandered along the quayside, he tried to pluck up the courage to talk to a boy of his own age, who was loading supplies onto one of the larger ships. A pile of cargo was stacked on the wooden quayside before being manhandled onto each of the docked ships via narrow gangplanks. He noted the skills required carrying each package, whilst maintaining a balance along a steep narrow track of wood, and it was impressive to watch. Juan Carlos was about to approach the boy but stopped, because a cargo net was being raised across the quayside high above the boy's head. Suddenly, a small wooden crate, precariously nestled on the edge of the net, came loose and hurtled to the quayside heading straight for the youth. Without any thought for himself, Juan Carlos lunged at the boy and bowled him out of the way, just as the crate crashed to the floor. From the splintered remains, its cargo of cannonballs rolled off the quayside and into the dock.

As the two boys came to a halt, Juan Carlos helped the confused lad to his feet, pleased neither of them was hurt. Neither realised it, but they could have easily fallen in the space between the ship and the quayside. The dazed young man was trying to come to terms with the incident, and as he checked himself for any injury, he looked at the shattered crate, and then at Juan Carlos. His bemused face then turned into a huge sharp grin.

'Gracias señor that was a very good thing you have done.'

'No problem,' Juan Carlos replied, trying not to show any fear. 'I was only passing by and saw the crate falling… there was no time to say anything… Are you alright?'

'I am thanks to you my friend.'

Juan Carlos brushed himself down and saw this as a great opportunity.

'Do you work on these ships?'

The boy, who was possibly one or two years older than Juan Carlos, wiped his brow with a grubby rag, smiled, then turned to Juan Carlos. Realising he was being addressed by a youth of similar age, he placed one hand on Juan Carlos's shoulder and pointed towards the large ship he was loading supplies on to.

'See this ship, señor?'

Juan Carlos had never been close to such a large ship before, and he gulped in admiration at the magnificence of it.

'Yes, I do… it is wonderful'

'Well, this is my ship, and I am one of the crew… She is called *Barca de Amburgo* and we will soon be sailing to England.'

Juan Carlos turned to his new friend, and with growing confidence enquired.

'Can we be friends? Can I join your ship? My name is Juan Carlos, and I come from the hills over there.' He pointed behind him.

The young man followed Juan Carlos's directions to the hills beyond the docks and replied assuredly.

'Of course, we can be friends Juan Carlos, my name is Paulo Mauritio and the captain is Diego Mauritio, my uncle. He is taking me to England, we will unload the supplies and then he will take me back to my family in Hamburg. Unfortunately, he is not here at the moment, although I am sure he will take another crew member on the journey, as we have lots of soldiers and animals to look after.'

Juan Carlos looked puzzled and didn't really understand everything he said.

'Animals? What kind of animals?'

'Oh! We have to carry horses and mules for the soldiers… but of course they all smell really bad. Ha! Ha! Ha!'

Paulo pinched his nose with his fingers, pulled a twisted expression, and the boys laughed hysterically for several minutes. Eventually, they shook hands, smiled at each other, and were really pleased to have become instant friends. As they sat on bales of sailcloth, Juan Carlos's curiosity rose.

'Can you tell me more about the ships Paulo?'

Paulo was only too pleased to impart some of his knowledge onto Juan Carlos.

'Si, Juan Carlos… to begin with the *Barca de Amburgo* is part of many supply ships belonging to Admiral Juan Gómez de Medina, and we will soon sail to England with his flagship *El Gran Grifon*.'

'What is a flagship?' Juan Carlos quizzed

'Ah! It is the boss ship of all the other supply ships…we have to take our orders from the boss, to make sure all the Spanish warships has all it needs to battle with the English.'

Juan Carlos looked up and down at the large ship, and noticed the fine display of cannons along the vessel, and he queried.

'But this looks like a warship? It has so many cannons.'

'Si!' replied Paulo proudly 'She has 23 cannons, and we can take care of ourselves because we carry a lot more equipment and supplies than the warships… no one will attack us.' He said fearlessly. The two boys gazed up at the huge ship, and revelled in how busy the ship was with all the cargo being stowed away. Teams of crewmen were scampering up and down the rigging, checking ropes and sails.

'What about all those other ships? Do you know their names too?

'But of course, I do, I watched them all come into port and I have spoken to some of the crew when they came ashore.'

Paulo paused and whispered to Juan Carlos.

'Do you see that warehouse over there?' Paulo pointed behind Juan Carlos to a tall wooden building on the edge of the harbour quayside.

'You must go there, climb up the stairs and wait for me, I have to finish this work here, but I will meet you in a short while, you can see all the ships from there.'

The two boys quickly parted and Juan Carlos headed for the warehouse. Paulo meanwhile, returned to his duties loading the supplies onto the ship, he was pleased to have found a new friend the same age, and he was determined to convince his uncle to take him on board.

An hour later, Paulo met Juan Carlos inside the warehouse on one of the upper levels, and Juan Carlos had found a very good viewing point overlooking the harbour. Paulo smiled as he approached Juan Carlos.

'Excellent Juan Carlos, this is the place I would have chosen to view the ships... You can see all of them from here.'

Juan Carlos was still awestruck at the number of ships gathered in the bay, he had only ever seen one or two smaller merchant ships, but now there were ten or more ships of all sizes.

'Tell me, Paulo, do you really know all of their names?'

'Maybe not all of them mi amigo, but I know the main ones... we shall start with the furthest over there.'

Paulo pointed out across the bay to a magnificently large ship with four masts as it anchored at the western entrance, it was surrounded by slightly smaller, but equally impressive ships, providing an overall collection of sailing vessels that filled the whole bay.

'That one is called *Nuestra Señora del Rosario*, with 46 cannons, it is the flagship of Don Pedro de Valdés, who is the commander of the Andalusia Squadron. This port of Malaga is their home.'

Juan Carlos interrupted.

'What is a squadron?'

At first, Paulo did not like being interrupted, but understood that there was much that his new friend did not know.

'There will be many ships going to England, and I am told that to control them they have been placed into groups called squadrons. Most of the supply ships are in the same squadron just like the ships from Andalusia.'

Juan Carlos, again looked puzzled.

'But why is your ship not part of the Andalusia Squadron?'

Paulo, looked a little exasperated.

'No, my friend, our squadron will meet after we have picked up supplies from every port in Spain.'

Juan Carlos did not really understand, but he smiled at Paulo and continued to stare in amazement at the ships in the bay. Paulo leaned further out of the window and resumed his explanation of the ships.

'Some of the ships are too far away, but I know there is *San Francisco* with 21 cannons and *San Juan Bautista* with 31 cannons.

Paulo paused as he could see the information was impressing Juan Carlos very much, and he allowed the youngster to dwell on each ship he pointed it out before continuing.

'The nearest ships I think, are the *Santa Catalina* with 23 cannons, and one of the smallest ships is *La Trinidad* with 13 cannons. Then there is *Santa Maria de Juncal* with 20 cannons, and *San Barolome* has 27 cannons.'

Paulo edged nearer to the window and pointed towards the three ships moored along the quayside.

'The largest one is a ship called *El Espiritu Santo*, it has 32 cannons, and the next one to it is one of the Urca ships like ours, *Duquesa Santa Ana* with 32 cannons.'

Juan Carlos quizzed.

'What is an Urca?'

Paulo instantly replied.

'My ship, *Barco de Amburgo* is an Urca. It is a very heavy supply ship from the Baltic Sea that can carry a lot more supplies than the others, which are mostly galleons, but some are merchant ships being made to look like galleons or warships.'

Juan Carlos nodded, pretending to understand.

'So how many ships are in your squadron?

'We have 23 ships in our squadron, Andalusia might have larger warships, but there are only 11 of them.'

Juan Carlos looked quizzically again.

'But where is your squadron now?'

Paulo laughed at the amount of questions Juan Carlos asked, and then composed himself to explain.

'Well, my friend, our squadron is now at Cadiz, and we will meet them very soon. But we have sailed to Malaga from Amburgo, Alemania [Hamburg, Germany], which is our home, because we had to collect supplies, men and equipment for the invasion from here first.'

The boys spent some time watching the impressive display of ships with their crew ferrying equipment, and soldiers onto the vessels. The silence was disturbed only when Paulo's name came bellowing up from the dock below.

'Paulo? Where are you?'

Paulo peered over the edge of the window to see a rough looking crewman with an expression of disgust in trying to locate him. As he ran to the stairs he explained.

'I had better get back to my duties Juan Carlos, but I shall meet you tomorrow when I shall take you to see the captain.'

Although disappointed, Juan Carlos understood.

'Alright Paulo, and thank you once again for showing me everything.'

As he ran down the stairs to greet the crewman, Paulo shouted back to Juan Carlos.

'No, it is I who should be thanking you for saving my life…we meet again tomorrow my good friend Juan Carlos, goodbye.'

Juan Carlos's head was buzzing with all the information, and struggled to take it all in at once. He yawned and suddenly felt very tired, so he lay down on the soft bales and quickly drifted into a deep sleep. He was very comfortable, with warm sunshine beaming through the open window, and he lay there undisturbed throughout the night.

Chapter 5
Search for Juan Carlos

Back at the farm

Next morning at first light, before the rest of the family was out of bed, Alfredo prepared for his journey to Malaga. He returned to the bedroom and saw that Francesca was awake, so he hugged and kissed her. Alfredo went to the barn and saddled the mule, then trotted off towards the gorge, as he knew that was the route his son would have taken. Francesca stood by the open door and watched her husband go, hoping and praying he would find their son soon and return home quickly.

Although the storm had passed, the normally dry dirt tracks to the city were now wet, muddy, and full of pot-holes. Alfredo had to make several detours, due to the tracks having collapsed into the gorge, or uprooted trees had blocked his path. On one occasion he stopped to assist a neighbour to free and repair a cart that had become stuck in a deep rut. By the time he had traversed swollen rivers and streams, it was too dark to continue safely, and Alfredo had to spend the night with a cousin in one of the villages. He knocked on his cousin's door, and his cousin Manuel answered the door, a little surprised to see Alfredo.

'Que pasa Alfredo?'

Alfredo entered his home and explained to Manuel and his wife Teresa what had happened. Manuel suggested that they should go to the inn and talk to anyone who has been to the port. The village was on one of the main routes into Malaga, and many traders and merchants had passed through it on the way to the port. So that evening, Alfredo and his cousin went into a small tavern on the edge of the village to see if there was any news about the ships leaving port.

When they arrived, the tavern was full and noisy, with most of the people talking about the storm and the damaged it had done to their properties. After collecting a jug of ale, they sat down with a couple of merchants known to trade in the area. Alfredo enquired to one.

'Have you been to the port today?'

'Si Amigo, I was there this afternoon, and it looks like they are in a hurry to get away. They were supposed to leave for Cadiz today, but damage from the storm has delayed them.'

This was good news for Alfredo, as it would give him more time to find his son. The trader added.

'I cannot understand why they are in such a hurry, because with so many men on those ships, I don't think they have taken enough provisions. Perhaps they will get more at Cadiz? I don't know really, but it is a pity as we are all making lots of money from this Armada.'

The trader, who was a little drunk, staggered towards the bar for more wine, but Alfredo noticed that the other trader was relatively sober, and seemed interested in Alfredo's questions.

'You seem concerned my friend, what does it matter to you when the ships sails?'

Alfredo looked reticently at the man.

'My son has run away from home, and I think he is trying to sail with them.'

'That is not good amigo, as the ships were taking as many people as they could, no matter their age... How old is he?'

'Juan Carlos is 14 but he looks much younger. Perhaps they will not take him?'

The trader looked at Alfredo and seeing the concern on his face replied.

'Perhaps you are correct my friend, but you should get there as quickly as you can. I know what I have seen today, and as my friend said, the ships are in a hurry to leave.'

On returning to his cousin's house, Alfredo told him that he was worried he might not find Juan Carlos in time. Alfredo's cousin, Manuel, tried to console him.

'Do not concern yourself Alfredo we will find him, and I am coming with you. I think two can search better than one, and I know more people at the port than you do, so I am sure we will find him.'

Alfredo forced a smile and patted Manuel on the back.

'I hope you are right Manuel, but there is not much time, and if they sail at first light, then we might miss our chance... then Francesca will be heartbroken.'

As they entered the house, Manuel said.

'Alfredo, you go in and get some food and I will go and see my good friend and neighbour, I am sure he will help us. He has some horses we could borrow and it will make the journey easier and quicker than your old mule. He will look after your mule until you return.'

Alfredo managed a strained smile at the thought of riding a horse again, after so many years putting up with the old mule. Yet he was prepared to do anything to stop his son from leaving on the ships. Although the road into Malaga was passable, the journey would have been too dark to travel at night, and they knew there would be other dangers too, such as thieves and robbers. Instead, they decided that it would be safer and quicker to travel at dawn.

At dawn, Alfredo rose early only to be greeted by Manuel, his wife Teresa, and their daughter Carlota. Teresa had quickly prepared some food for their journey, and she gave Alfredo a reassuring hug and kissed his cheek.

'Alfredo, I know you will find Juan Carlos soon, our prayers are with you and we know how much this is hurting Francesca. When you find him, we will come and see you at your farm on Sunday.'

Alfredo returned the hug, and then gave a knowing glance to Manuel that they must be on their way. The two men collected the horses, which had already been saddled by the neighbour, and rode off towards the city. The nearer they got to the city the busier the road became, which slowed their progress. By mid-morning the sun was getting hotter, and by the time they had reached the city limits, they were only able to move at walking pace. Alfredo was becoming more and more frustrated and began to shout at people to move out of the way. He was just about to kick out at one belligerent man, when fortunately, Manuel intervened and stopped him.

'Alfredo, it is too hot… we have to stop for the horses. Let us move over there to that water trough and let the horse's drink. We can have some food and water ourselves before we carry on.'

Alfredo reluctantly agreed and led his horse to the trough, to which the horse took no encouragement to drink the warm but refreshing water. Meanwhile, the two men drank from their water bags and ate some of the bread and cheese prepared by Teresa. As they sat on the edge of the trough, Manuel wiped his sweaty brow and suggested an alternative route to the port.

'Alfredo, we can take some of the side streets towards the port. I often use them, and it should save us a little time.'

'Very good amigo, I do not think I can take much more

of these busy streets…How do people live in such crowded places?'

Manuel laughed, turning the atmosphere a little lighter.

'Ha! Ha! You are so used to living in the countryside Alfredo, you do not realise that this is a normal day in Malaga… It is always like this in the city!'

Once the horses had finished drinking, the men mounted them and headed along the side streets towards the port. However, they could only travel slowly as some of the streets were very narrow with obstacles, people and children delaying their progress.

Chapter 6
Captain Diego Mauritio

At the port of Malaga, the morning began clear, bright and very warm, but with a welcoming sea breeze. This was the best time of day to work, as the sun was only going to get hotter as the day progressed. Crews scurried about loading the last of the cargo onto their ships, and officers shouted out orders as ropes hoisted cargo into position. Many tradesmen littered each ship as they raced against time to complete final modifications, and to repair the damaged done by the storm. With no more rain expected, the giant sails were made ready to unfurl at the captain's orders.

Captain Diego Mauritio surveyed the work from the poop deck of his ship *Barca de Amburgo*, occasionally barking out orders in guttural Spanish to some imbecile of a sailor. The fleet was to leave port that day and he did not want his ship to be the last to leave.

'Que estas hacienda?' 'Oye idiota, preste atencion a lo que esta hacienda con que la carga!'

Mauritio was a stocky, swarthy man, not known for his good seamanship or patience, but he knew how to command men, and had no qualms in distributing corporal punishment when it warranted doing so. He was rejected as one of the senior squadron commanders which made him even more belligerent towards his men. Yet he was keen to impress, and he hoped that during the course of the voyage to England he might gain more respect from his superiors, which he would use to advance his career. He was going to ensure that the squadron commanders received particularly good and personal attention when fresh supplies were required for the Armada.

Today was one of those times when a supply of fresh provisions was to be taken to *Nuestra Señora del Rosario*, and the squadron commander, Don Pedro de Valdés. Captain Mauritio was going to deliver these provisions personally, and he put on his finest uniform for the occasion. Diego closely inspected each batch of produce and discarded any he thought was inferior, ensuring to slap or kick the man who brought it.

'! Idiota! go and fetch the best supplies, this rubbish will not do.'

One unfortunate recipient of a harsh backhander was noticed by Juan Carlos, who was standing on the quayside in front of the *Barca de Amburgo*, and he winced as he saw the ferocity with which the captain administered punishment. He was about to skulk out of site when Paulo shouted his name.

'Juan Carlos! Juan Carlos! Where are you going? We have to report to the captain immediately.'

Juan Carlos gritted his teeth at the thought of meeting the fierce ogre of a captain, as he did not want to be on the receiving end of one of his blows. But he had no choice as he had agreed to meet Paulo, and he couldn't let him down after all they had discussed. Juan Carlos stood rigid for a few seconds, before turning around to greet his new found friend with a forced smile, and he stuttered a nervous reply.

'Paulo, there you are… I, I thought I had missed you.'

Paulo led the visibly shaking lad up the gangplank as they made their way towards the captain. Paulo turned and gave Juan Carlos a wry smile.

'I have told the captain all about you Juan Carlos, and he is keen to meet you… I think you will be pleased.'

Juan Carlos was shocked by this news.

'Is the captain your uncle?'

Paulo laughed.

'Si, my friend… he is the captain and my uncle… so everything will be fine.'

Juan Carlos was silent, and gulped as he approached Captain Mauritio, who was pacing impatiently up and down the poop deck surveying all that was going on.

'Captain?' Paulo said. 'This my good friend Juan Carlos I told you about'

The two boys stood in front of the mighty frame of the captain, who looked even more menacing to Juan Carlos than before. With his back to the boys, Captain Mauritio stopped, turned around slowly, and faced the silent youths.

'Bien! So, this is the brave young man who saved my nephew from a nasty accident? What have you to say for yourself lad?'

Juan Carlos gulped again, but his mouth was too dry, and with no moisture to swallow he struggled to get any words out.

'Nothing sir!' He croaked 'I was only pleased to help'

'Help indeed!' bellowed Mauritio, 'I think you did a little more than that my lad. This is my brother's son and I have promised to look after him. You have saved me from a lot of embarrassment young man.'

Mauritio stepped closer and leant down to Juan Carlos so their faces were inches apart. For a second, the tension was unbearable and Juan Carlos could smell Mauritio's rancid breath.

'Tell me, young man, what will be your reward?'

Juan Carlos, who by now, was almost going to be

physically sick, wanted to get away as soon as possible, but managed to squeak a reply.

'I thought it may be possible to join you on board your ship sir, but if there is no position, then I will be on my way, thank you sir.'

Juan Carlos turned to scurry away when a large hand clasped him on the shoulder.

'Nonsense!' Exclaimed Mauritio.

'You shall become a member of my cabin crew for the whole of the journey to England and back.'

With his other hand, Mauritio grabbed Paulo and marched the two youths into his cabin. Inside the cabin, Mauritio urged the boys to sit at the captain's table whilst Mauritio poured himself a large tumbler of red wine. He placed two smaller tumblers onto the table, poured wine into them, and offered them to Juan Carlos and Paulo. Mauritio forcefully raised his glass and urged the two boys to do the same.

'To victory over the English, and a safe return home.'

Mauritio drank his wine in one mighty gulp and then waited for the two lads to do the same. Paulo, who had some previous experience in drinking alcohol, quickly swallowed his drink. But as Juan Carlos had never drunk any alcohol before, coughed and spluttered as the heady liquid irritated his dry throat.

'Cough, cough! Splutter... I am sorry sir, but I have never...'

Mauritio gave him no time to answer, then whacked Juan Carlos on his back, nearly knocking him off his feet, and gruffly interjected.

'No matter boy, you will get used to it. But now we must prepare to sail.'

Mauritio then placed a reassuring arm around Juan Carlos' shoulders, turned to his nephew and spoke.

'Paulo, show this lad the ropes, and get him settled in quickly, as there is plenty to do if we want to make the most of the day.'

Captain Mauritio then left the cabin and continued admonishing the crew to ensure his orders were properly carried out. He then left the ship to board a small boat rowed by six men and headed for the Andalusia Squadron flagship, *Nuestra Señora del Rosario*. He wanted to reassure Don Pedro de Valdés that the delivery of fresh food supplies would be personally monitored by himself, and that he was going to ensure an extra supply of excellent brandy and ibérico ham was added, which he knew was the commander's favourite. He had already done this with his own commander, Juan Gomez de Medina of the Urca Squadron when they met in Hamburg. As the morning slipped away, the fleet was finally ready to sail. The crew on board *Barca de Amburgo* busied themselves releasing rigging ropes for the giant sails, and mooring ropes to allow the huge ship to move away from the dockside. With the sails lowered, they picked up the breeze and began to billow out, allowing the ship to creep out of the harbour and into the bay.

Alfredo arrives at the port

Alfredo and Manuel reached the port just before noon, and they tethered their horses in the stable of one of Manuel's friends, then they raced through the crowds towards the harbour. As they approached the dock, they could see one of the ships being de-moored, and that others were already moving out of the harbour. The ship was called *Duguesa Santa Ana*, the Urca supply ship of the Andalusia Squadron, and its captain was hurling abuse at the crew, admonishing them for being the last ship out of the harbour. As Alfredo and Manuel approached, they kept asking the crew on board about any young boys joining the ship, to which they received either blank or angry expressions. There was still one access plank onto the ship, for those crew members who were busy untying the mooring ropes on the dock. Alfredo and Manuel ran up the plank and approached the man shouting the abuse, who they assumed was the captain.

'Señor... señor! Can you tell me if you have any young boys in your crew? I have lost my son, and he might be with you... please can you help me?'

The captain stopped shouting, and looked angrily at Alfredo.

'What are you doing on my ship? We do not have any boys with us, and I cannot waste my time with you, we have to leave NOW!'

The captain, brushed Alfredo aside and continued his shouting at the crew, but then he turned to the two men and waved an accusing finger at them.

'If you do not get off my ship, then you will become part of my crew... capiche?'

As they were leaving, one of the crew members tapped Alfredo on the shoulder and pointed towards the ship just pulling away from the jetty.

'Señor, that ship just leaving is the *Barca de Amburgo*, and it has two young boys on board. One of them looks very young, and he does not look as if he has been on any ship before... maybe he is your son, but I fear you are too late.'

Alfredo looked towards the ship, and as it was no more than 20 feet away, he could clearly see the head of Juan Carlos standing at the back of the poop deck. He shouted out his name, and fled towards the gangplank, with Manuel in close pursuit.

'Juan Carlos! Juan Carlos!'

Alfredo screamed at the top of his voice as he ran off the

ship towards the end of the harbour. But it was no use, the ship had left the harbour to form up with the rest of the fleet in the bay. For a brief second, Juan Carlos thought he heard his name being called and was about to look back at the harbour, but was distracted by the sight and noise of the giant sails as they were unfurled from the masts.

Gradually all the ships gathered together in the bay, and a trumpet signalled for them to sail, then they set off in an open formation, led by the Andalusia Squadron flagship, *Nuestra Señora del Rosario*. Everyone on board was excited and eager to join up with the main body of the Armada at Lisbon. But first, they had to go to Cadiz, where they were to form an escort for the Commander in Chief of the Armada, The Duke of Medina Sidonia, commander of the Squadron of Portugal. His flagship was called *San Martin* in Spanish, and in English as *Saint Martin*.

As the ships left Malaga, songs were sung by the crew as they set about their tasks, and men worked enthusiastically to ensure their ship looked the best when they met up with the rest of the Armada. At an average speed of four or five knots, the squadron would take approximately 30 hours to make the 132 nautical miles to reach Cadiz, which would be around dawn of the second day.

Juan Carlos could not believe that he was actually sailing on one of the largest ships he had ever seen, and he also had found a new best friend in Paulo, but unfortunately, also the daunting Captain Mauritio. It was of little importance that he was just a lowly cabin boy, as he was determined to become a sailor just like his grandfather. His imagination started to run wild as Paulo showed him his duties around the ship. It was the perfect day, the weather was warm and the sea was calm, and Juan Carlos thought that being a sailor was going to be very exciting.

Chapter 7
Onwards to Cadiz

Due to strong winds out in the Atlantic Ocean, the ships struggled to make headway to Cadiz, and crews fought hard to manoeuvre rigging and sails into position as waves constantly washed the deck. Below deck of *Barca de Amburgo*, in the captain's cabin, Paulo and Juan Carlos tried desperately to keep charts, equipment and furniture from sliding across the room. Although Captain Mauritio seemed impervious to the swaying of the ship, the boys did notice him struggle now and then as he tried to write in his log. He cursed when sudden movements made him stop writing, but then consoled himself with another swig from a brandy bottle.

As the ship rocked in troubled seas, Juan Carlos began to feel a little strange, as his stomach churned, and he felt that he might be sick. Paulo, clinging onto a chair that had slid across the cabin, noticed how much the colour had suddenly drained from his friend's face, then realising what was happening he laughed.

'Ha. Ha! Juan Carlos, this is your first time at sea... yes?'

Juan Carlos could not answer as he was too busy trying control his intermittent baulking. He clung to the wall of the cabin and then rushed out onto the deck. With one hand held tight over his mouth and the other grasping at any stable item, he rushed to the side of the ship... only to be doused by a large wave as it crashed over the side. Juan Carlos could not contain the impulses any longer, and emptied the contents of his stomach, much to the amusement of the crew and soldiers. Over the next few hours, Juan Carlos clung to the side of the ship and spewed everything out of his stomach including bile. Then as the weather eased, the fleet continued on a more even keel, and the crews were able to relax more. All except for Juan Carlos, who dare not move from his position for fear of provoking another stomach-churning vomit spasm.

He also had to endure insults and indignations from some of the soldiers, who were idling their time on-deck. One large, nasty looking soldier with scars on his face and arms, took great pleasure in 'jibing' Juan Carlos.

'Come now little man, why do you look so pale? Let me try and get some colour back into your skinny face.'

Backed up and provoked by others, the soldier grabbed Juan Carlos by the legs and held him over the side of the ship. Juan Carlos screamed in terror as he thought the man was going to drop him into the sea, and the crew laughed at the spectacle. Suddenly a sword blade from one of the crew tapped the shoulder of the big man, who looked at the blade and froze. Then a voice in a heavy French accent said.

'Monsieur, I do not think you want to do that… as the captain will not be too pleased with you… you see, this boy serves his dinner.'

Reluctantly, and feeling the sharp blade press onto his neck, the soldier released Juan Carlos onto the deck, and slowly rose to his full height before turning to face the man holding the sword. The Frenchman didn't flinch, and placed the blade under the man's chin. He was a confident, handsome man of equal height to the soldier, but of slighter build, about mid to late forties with a trimmed, black beard and shoulder-length hair. He smiled and moved the blade across the face of the soldier and added with a smirk.

'Monsieur, why do you make fun of this lad? Is it only young boys you like to play with? Does that tell us something about your manliness?'

By this time, the rest of the crew had all gathered round the two men and laughed at the sexual innuendoes of the soldier. They sensed a fight was about to take place, and urged the two men on as the tension rose, until...

'BANG!'

A pistol was fired in the air.

'Get back to your duties! The show is over,' bellowed Captain Mauritio at the top of his voice, forcing his way through the gathering.

'Save your fighting for the English... now get back to your duties or I will keelhaul those who remain.'

The two men were last to leave, as they stood glaring at each other, with the scarred soldier vowing to kill the Frenchmen for making him look a fool. Mauritio stepped between them, pushed them apart, and as the scarred soldier skulked away, Mauritio whispered to the Frenchman.

'Do not underestimate that one Frenchy... he is an evil one, that is why they call him "El Muerto" [The Dead One]. So, watch your back!'

The Frenchman gave no reply, but simply shrugged his shoulders and walked over to Juan Carlos, who was still clinging to the side of the ship. The Frenchman knelt down and placed a friendly hand on his back.

'Do not worry mon amie, you will soon find your sea legs... but you must learn to keep clear of men like that as they always pick on the weak.'

Juan Carlos eased himself round to face the man, and in a weakened voice replied.

'Thank you, sir, for saving me from that terrible man... I think he would have thrown me into the sea.'

The Frenchman laughed and stood up.

'Ha! Ha! Mon amie, he just wanted an audience, he would not have thrown you into the sea… men like that are cowards, but have no fear, because I think he wants me to suffer now instead of you… But I will take care of it.'

As he turned to leave, Juan Carlos grabbed hold of the man's wrist.

'Señor… what is your name?'

'People call me Daval… Henri Daval, but just know me as "Daval", mes amis.'

Juan Carlos looked puzzled at Daval.

'My name is Juan Carlos…But señor, your accent? It is strange…Where are you from?'

Daval laughed again, and explained the reason.

'Juan Carlos, I come from France, but have served for many countries, and at the moment I am pilot of this Spanish ship… I will help the captain to navigate our way to England because I know the sea we are going to. They can be very dangerous.'

'But is Spain not at war with France?' Juan Carlos quizzed.

'Si, mon amie, sometimes, but I work for whoever pays the most money, and England has always been France's enemy too… So here I am.'

Juan Carlos, who did not fully understand the explanation, was exhausted and stared out to sea. Daval left him to recover and strolled onto the poop deck. He was a tough mercenary soldier/sailor who was very skilled in many forms of combat, and he knew how to get out of tight situations. He could not stand men like El Muerto, who was one of 150 men on board *Barca de Amburgo* out of approximately 3000 soldiers allocated to the Urca Squadron.

Paulo went over to Juan Carlos and helped him to his feet.

'The captain has told me to take you to your bunk, Juan

Carlos. I have mixed some brandy and water for you that will make you sleep, and hopefully by the morning you will feel better.'

The two boys slowly made their way to the cabin, and after the brandy Juan Carlos drifted into a deep sleep, his mind full of thoughts of home, how safe it was there and that perhaps it was a bad idea to go to sea after all.

It was almost 07:00 hrs of the second day when Juan Carlos emerged from his bunk, he felt very thirsty and hungry, which he hoped was a sign that he might be over his sea sickness. By the time he had quenched his thirst, and eaten a small amount of bread and cheese, the fleet had followed the headland into a relatively calm Atlantic Ocean near the bay of Cadiz. The light was good, and every crew member was busy with their duties when suddenly, a shout came from the lookout in an observation position high up on the mizzen mast. A clear and booming voice echoed across the ship.

'Sail ho! Off the starboard bow,'

All those on deck immediately rushed over to that side of the ship, and anchored in the bay and moored at the harbour were several ships, all looking magnificent. Juan Carlos's eyes bulged as his ship, along with the rest of the fleet from Malaga, came around the headland into the large bay at Cadiz. As their own fleet joined them, the sight of so many ships made every crewmember gawp at the vast spectacle.

'Wow! Wow, Wow,' he said to Paulo.

'Can you see that, what a sight! This must be a truly invincible Armada, the English will stand no chance against us'

'Si, Juan Carlos they are in for one hell of a beating, I cannot wait.'

At that moment Captain Mauritio let out an ear-deafening bellow.

'Get back to your positions, you sons of bitches. Do not disgrace me when we enter the bay, or there will be 20 lashes for each man that disobeys my orders.'

The crew reluctantly skulked back to their stations, but not before each man had sneaked a final glimpse at the ships, as more and more came into view.

As the Malaga fleet slowly passed the rest of the Armada fleet, each crew greeted each other with great cheers, with banners waving and horns sounding. There was a camaraderie building, and the atmosphere was becoming electrifying. Juan Carlos sensed this, it added to the excitement of his great adventure, and he understood why his grandfather told stories with such feeling and passion. With limited space to moor, only supply ships were allowed into the harbour, whilst the rest of the fleet remained anchored in the bay. Officers and selected crewmembers were the only ones allowed ashore in rowboats. Even so, the port, harbour and streets of Cadiz throbbed with activity, and the rhythm of life was dominated by the ships. For the next 24 hours Cadiz was very busy, as it engaged in loading all kinds of naval stores, provisions and men with which to finish the compliment of the main fleet. With little time to rest or eat, each crew formed lines with which to load smaller items into the holds, whilst lifting tackle and pulleys were used to hoist the larger items aboard. Their orders were to clear the harbour as soon as possible, and to take the ships into the bay. Eventually, the only ship left moored at the harbour quayside was the Armada flagship, *San Martin*. It was a magnificent Portuguese navy galleon, with an overall length of 180 feet, and a beam of 40 feet. It had two square rigged masts and a lateen mizzen-mast, and she carried 48 heavy cannons on two enclosed gun decks, plus multiple smaller weapons. The *San Martin* was also the flagship of the Squadron of Portugal, consisting of 12 ships which were all anchored in the bay. Everyone was excited, because they were awaiting the arrival of the overall commander of the Armada, Alonso Pérez de Guzmán y de Zúñiga-Sotomayor, 7th Duke of Medina-Sidonia. He lived in a grand castle at Sanlúcar de Barramea to the north of Cadiz, and together with his senior army officer, Maestre Francisco Arias de Bobadilla, would board the *San Martin* at Cadiz before heading off to Lisbon where the majority of the Armada ships were waiting.

Chapter 8
Alfredo goes to Cadiz

Back in Malaga, Alfredo and Manuel were disappointed to have just missed Juan Carlos, and the two men walked slowly back to their horses in silence. As they passed a tavern, Manuel stopped and held Alfredo's arm.

'Alfredo, it is much too hot now, so let us have a drink in this tavern before we return to your farm.'

Alfredo's mind was in turmoil at the thought of telling Francesca that Juan Carlos was not coming home, but Manuel's suggestion would at least give him some time to think.

'Muy bien, Manuel… I don't think there is anything else we can do, and I have to think of what I can say to Francesca when I tell her that Juan Carlos has gone to England on a warship.'

They entered the tavern, took their jug of ale to the coolest spot they could find, and as they sat down, they both let out a combined gasp of despair, fatigue and heat exhaustion. For a few moments, they sat in silence, sipping ale and trying to cool their bodies and minds. Alfredo noticed the Inn was still quite busy even though all the ships had sailed. However, most of the people were traders preparing to leave the city, and as they were sitting quite close to two merchants, Alfredo could not help overhearing their conversation.

'This is a sad day my friend, because I don't think we shall see trading like that for a while.'

'I agree, I have never done so much trading, and I could have sold a lot more too. It's a pity they could not have remained in port a little longer, as I have more equipment coming from Madrid.'

'Si, my friend, and from what I have heard, I believe they are going to Cadiz to collect more supplies, and there are more ships waiting to join the fleet too. The merchants at Cadiz will be busier than here.'

'You could be right my friend, but they will struggle to supply them all in just a few days, and it could delay them. So, if I leave now, I might be able to take a carriage there and make more money... ha, ha, ha!'

The merchants laughed loudly and drank more ale.

'Ha, ha, ha! Si amigo, but it would be stupid to race across Spain in the height of summer, it would be madness.'

Alfredo suddenly stopped drinking and sat upright as an idea came to him.

'Manuel, yes! That is what I shall do.'

Manuel's eyes were closed as he felt the warmth of the room and the ale taking affect, he began to relax into a pleasant nap. Alfredo's outburst startled him, and he jolted back to consciousness, almost spilling his ale.

'Que pasa, amigo. What is it? What have you done?'

Alfredo grabbed Manuel's arm and pulled him out of the tavern. He ran to the stable followed by a bemused Manuel, and when they reached the stables, Alfredo began to saddle his horse and he turned to Manuel.

'Manuel, I have to go to Cadiz, because the traders at the inn said the ships could be delayed waiting for supplies, so I might be able to catch up with Juan Carlos before they leave Cadiz... It is a slim chance, but I have to go now.'

Manuel was still bemused and tried to make sense of this sudden strategy.

'Alfredo, even if you go by horse it will take you nearly five days to reach Cadiz, and the ships will probably have left before you get there. It will be useless... can you not see that?'

Alfredo paused for a second, trying to understand the logistics of his decision, but he was determined to go.

'I have to try, or I would not live with myself, and Francesca will never forgive me if I didn't try everything.'

Manuel could see that Alfredo had made up his mind, and was determined to go no matter how much he tried to dissuade him.

'Then I shall come with you, Alfredo.'

Alfredo stopped, turned to Manuel, and then with a big grin, he hugged his cousin.

'No cousin, you have already done enough for me. I want you to go to Francesca and tell her what has happened. She will be worried not knowing.'

Manuel then gave Alfredo what little money he had and wished him a good and safe journey. Alfredo mounted his horse and was just about to ride out of the stables when he stopped and looked back at his cousin.

'Manuel, I want to thank you amigo, for helping me, and explain to your friend that I shall return his horse soon, and pay him well for his troubles.'

'Do not worry about the horse Alfredo; just come back with Juan Carlos... Adios mi amigo.'

That afternoon Alfredo set off for Cadiz and followed the road out of Malaga heading west, but the hot sun meant that he had to take several rest-stops to water the horse and himself. He followed the safer coastal roads towards Algeciras, and then he headed northwest towards Medina-Sidonia. Alfredo rode the horse by intermittently walking, trotting, and then galloping, dependant on the surface of the track and temperature. He knew it would take him nearly five days traveling like that, and estimated he could travel 30 miles in a day. As he rode, the time and distance seemed to drag, and Alfredo had many thoughts running through his head.

He wondered if the Armada would be delayed as the trader said, if so, then there was a slim chance that he might get to Cadiz before they sailed. But once he got to Cadiz, there would be many more ships to search, and it would take too much time.

Suddenly he remembered something one of the sailors had told him at Malaga…

'The name of the ship? What was the name of the ship the crewman said Juan Carlos was on?'

Alfredo wracked his brain in an effort to remember the ship's name, but the problem was that when the sailor spoke to him, the day was hot, they were rushing, and he only heard the name for the briefest of moments. He kept repeating fragments of the name to himself.

'It was Barca… something? But what … what was the name?'

Alfredo cursed himself for not remembering, but he was sure that he would recall it by the time he reached Cadiz. He continued for the rest of the first day following the old coast road built by the Romans, until he reached Arroyo de las Represas, a river outlet that flowed into the Mediterranean Sea, which was fed by cool mountain streams from the hills above Marbella. Alfredo secured the horse near to good grazing and with easy access to the water. He ate bread and cheese from the sack of food Manuel's wife had prepared, and drank from his leather water sack, before sleeping in the open air under a warm starlit sky.

The next day as he journeyed through the long hot summer day, Alfredo realised that travelling like that was too exhausting for the horse, and himself. So, he decided that as the summer daylight hours were now getting longer, he was going to travel in the early hours of the day, rest during the middle of the day, then continue as far as possible through the night. That way he would be able to make better time and could be in Cadiz earlier. By the end of the third day of travelling, Alfredo had reached one of the oldest cities in Spain, Medina-Sidonia, an elevated city within sight of Cadiz. As he rode towards the main plaza, Alfredo noticed that the streets and taverns were very busy, as if a festival was taking place. As it was almost midnight, he decided not to travel any further, and stabled his horse at a coaching inn. As he was hungry and thirsty, he entered the inn for a little food and wine, and although it was late, the inn was very busy. People were eating, drinking and dancing to music played by a trio of musicians. Alfredo approached one of the serving girls.

'Why is everybody celebrating señorita?'

The girl was very pretty, but sweating profusely as she rushed around the inn trying to deliver jugs of wine and ale to many people. She looked Alfredo up and down quickly, and realised that he must be a stranger to the town.

'Why señor the Duke of our city Medina-Sidonia, has ordered the people to celebrate the departure of Spain's glorious Armada.'

She did not dwell in conversation as she was being pulled by many hands trying to get their ale and wine. Alfredo sat in the corner of the tavern and tried to speak to an old man who was clapping and stamping his feet in time to the music.

'Señor! Señor! Can you tell me if the ships have left Cadiz yet?'

Alfredo had to raise his voice to make himself heard above the music, but eventually the man heard him.

'Ah! Si! Si! The ships are to leave tomorrow, I think? But they are waiting for the Duke… he has not yet arrived at the port… no one knows why? So, we party until the Armada sails.'

The old man took a large slurp of wine out of his jug and started laughing.

'Ha, ha, ha señor, you must drink with us… the ships have brought much wealth to the region and the Duke has paid the people to celebrate their departure… Ha! Ha! We have been celebrating for two days now, and still the ships have not gone… We are having a wonderful time.'

Alfredo had heard the Duke mentioned a few times and asked the old man.

'Sir… I am not from these parts, so can you tell me who the Duke is, and why is he important?'

The old man looked bemused at the question, and although he was quite drunk, he gave a legible reply.

'Amigo, he is the commander of the Armada, Alonso Pérez de Guzmán… 7th Duke of Medina-Sidonia. He lives in a big castle near here, and the fleet cannot sail without him. The King has decreed it… and I used to work at the castle…'

The old man continued to regale his stories of working at the castle, but Alfredo had heard enough.

Alfredo thanked the man for his information, although he did not hear him for the noise in the inn.

'Muchas gracias, señor. I would really like to join your celebrations, but I have urgent business to attend to in the morning… muchas gracias.'

After making his excuses to leave, Alfredo took some food and wine back to the stables. He slept there until it was light, and before the town had awoken, he was on his way to the port. He didn't really understand the explanation of the Duke, or why the Armada was late in sailing, but he was pleased to have the opportunity to find Juan Carlos before the Armada set off for England.

Chapter 9
Spain – Port of Cadiz

As he left the city of Medina-Sidonia, with the sun shining in a bright blue sky, he could clearly see the port of Cadiz from the elevated location of the city. It still looked a long way to travel, and to save as much time as possible, he rode his horse in a series of trots and gallops for most of the way. He reached the port around midday, and stopped at one of the street water troughs for the horse to cool down and drink. Alfredo also drank some water and soaked a cloth to place around his neck, and as the streets were too busy for the horse to travel any further, he looked around for a coaching inn. After stabling the horse, he set off on foot in search of the port, and he passed through bustling streets full of people, market traders, food stalls and entertainers. The whole area was on tenterhooks waiting for the final farewell celebrations and ceremonies, which could not take place without the Duke. It gave him time to search the harbour for Juan Carlos, and he hurriedly weaved through the crowds towards the ships.

As he approached the harbour, Alfredo's heart sank, as there was only one ship moored at the quayside. At the same time, soldiers had begun to section off the harbour in readiness for the Duke's arrival. He spoke to one man whom he thought looked like a seaman heading to the ship.

'Señor! Señor! Can you tell me the name of this ship?

The man was indeed a crewman from the ship and replied.

'Si, si señor... she is *San Martin*, flagship of the Duke of Medina-Sidonia.'

Alfredo was disappointed but continued.

'Can you tell me if there is another ship here called 'Barca... something?'

The crewman laughed, and pointed over to the ships in the bay.

'Si señor... you must mean *Barca de Amburgo*... she is over there in the bay, and we are all going to sail to Lisbon as soon as the Duke arrives, which will be very soon now.'

Alfredo was convinced that was the name of the ship his son was on, but there was no way of knowing if Juan Carlos would still be on that ship... Alfredo wanted to look around the harbour just in case his son was there, but getting past the guards was going to be difficult.

He tried several times to make his way towards the harbour wall in an effort to catch sight of his son, but each time he was forced back by soldiers who were only letting through troops and crew associated with the *San Martin*. Reluctantly Alfredo went back to the coaching inn, as he was hot, tired and in need of food and water. The coaching inn was a very large two storey timber building with several rooms. It was a very busy establishment which, like everywhere in the city, was enjoying the farewell celebrations. There were also a few military personnel taking advantage of the Duke's delay, trying to make the most of their shoretime for what could be months at sea.

Eventually, Alfredo was served a jug of wine some hot stew, and a large chunk of bread, and sat at a small table next to an open staircase leading to the bedrooms. As he ate, Alfredo watched the antics of people celebrating too much, and the inn was a cacophony of noise. The inn was also used by prostitutes, who plied their trade in some of the first-floor rooms. Alfredo watched one drunken soldier being particularly belligerent towards a pretty, buxom woman in her early twenties, as he brutally forced her up the stairs. But the noise of the inn prevented her cries being heard, and he forcefully bundled her into one of the rooms. Alfredo became concerned, and he cautiously went up the stairs. He stood outside the door and pressed his ear to it, and on hearing the girl's screams of terror he forced open the door.

The soldier, an arquebusier, who wore a flat plumed cap with a narrow brim, heavy cloth tunic and embroidered breeches, was ripping at her clothes.

The girl was panicking and afraid of being badly hurt, but the soldier was too strong and held her down on the bed. Alfredo reacted instinctively and grabbed a large metal water jug from the dressing table next to the door and slammed it over the soldier's head. The soldier crashed to the floor unconscious.

Alfredo stood rooted to the spot, shocked at what he had just done.

'Forgive me señorita, but I could see that he was hurting you, and I had to do something.'

The girl staggered off the bed, her clothes were ripped, and she attempted to place strips of torn clothing over her naked breasts. Wiping tears from her eyes she thanked Alfredo.

'Gracias! Gracias señor… You have saved me from a terrible beating from that drunken pig.'

She kicked the unconscious soldier, and Alfredo took a cotton sheet off the bed and wrapped it around her, he then sat with her on the edge of the bed until she had calmed down. She laid her head against his chest, and he placed a comforting arm around her shoulders. Alfredo wondered what to do with the soldier, he was also concerned with his own actions, as he was generally a law-abiding citizen. Yet the incident provided a solution to his problem, and he decided to borrow the soldier's uniform so that he could gain easier access to the harbour.

It only took the girl a few moments to regain her composure, and she began to admire her handsome hero, and she stroked Alfredo's thigh and started to squirm erotically against him.

'Señor... my name is Isabella... is there any way I can repay you?'

Alfredo began to squirm too... but nervously, and stopped the girl's hand from wandering over his body, he stood up and quickly replied.

'Si Isabella, you can help me get the uniform off this soldier, as I would like to borrow it.'

Isabella blew out her cheeks in disappointment, and pondered for a second at the strange request, then began to help Alfredo remove the uniform. After a few minutes, the soldier was lying semi-naked in a cupboard, his hands and feet were tied, and his mouth gagged. As Isabella was making herself a little more presentable, Alfredo quickly removed his clothes and then dressed into the uniform. It was a little loose for him as the soldier was much stockier, but as he placed the cap on his head, Alfredo approached the girl.

'Isabella, do you think you can keep this man here for a few hours? I have to look for my son who is on one of those ships, he has run away from home to join them, but he is too young. This uniform will help me move around the harbour to search for him.'

Isabella lifted the heavy water jug from the floor and patted it.

'That will be my pleasure señor, you can be certain that this pig will not be going anywhere today.'

Isabella moved closer to Alfredo, raised herself onto her toes and kissed him on the lips. Alfredo was taken by surprise and reluctantly pulled away.

'Señor, you know where to find me if ever you want anything… I mean anything señor.'

Alfredo became a little embarrassed, grabbed the soldier's sword from the floor and opened the door, but before he left the room he paused and looked at the girl.

'Thank you, Isabella, you have helped me more than you know… perhaps I will come back and see you sometime… Oh! my name is Alfredo by the way.'

Isabella smiled and blew a kiss to Alfredo.

'Do not make it too long Alfredo… As it is I who owe a debt to you, and I want to repay you soon.'

Alfredo left the inn and headed towards the harbour, and as he was feeling a little more confident in the uniform, he was able to blend in with other soldiers. By the time he reached the harbour, horns started to blow to signal the arrival of the Duke. The crowds gathered in the streets leading up to the harbour, but were forced to one side to allow the Duke to pass. Moments later a horse-drawn carriage arrived and The Duke of Medina-Sidonia alighted from it in front of the *San Martin*. Alonso Pérez de Guzmán was 38 years old when he was given the position of overall commander of the Armada, and many thought he was too young and inexperienced. He was of average height and build, with black hair and a trimmed goatee beard and moustache. He looked resplendent in his thick doublet and breeches, long black leather boots, with a large ruff around his neck, along with an opulent chain of office that gleamed on his chest. He also wore a large brimmed black hat, and a heavily decorated sword of office, draped neatly around his waist. As the crowd surged forward, Alfredo was grabbed by an officer from one of the arquebusier units.

'You there, get into line and form a security cordon for the Duke... and do not let this rabble get near him.'

Alfredo found himself linking arms with other arque-busiers, and was beginning to think his idea was becoming a disaster, but he had no choice, except to stand there until the Duke had boarded the ship. With crowds surging towards the quayside, it took over an hour for the Duke to acknowledge all the praise being bestowed on him by fellow dignitaries, local politicians and councillors.

The crew of the *San Martin* was becoming more and more impatient to sail, not to mention other commanders waiting on their ships in the bay. Eventually, with the speeches over, the Duke went on board his ship and it immediately prepared to leave Cadiz. Alfredo, along with the other soldiers in the cordon were able to relax when the order came to stand down. He started to walk away from the ship in an attempt to mingle with the crowds as they gathered along the harbour, but his path was blocked by the same officer who made him part of the security cordon. The officer bellowed and pointed to the *San Martin*.

'Where do you think you are going man... the ship is that way?'

Alfredo looked very uncomfortable as he realised the officer thought he was an actual soldier.

'No! No! You do not understand... this is not my uniform I, I...'

But the officer interrupted him, just as other soldiers from the coaching inn came staggering onto the harbour. Gesticulating to them, the officer bellowed again.

'Take this man and get on board that ship all of you, or I will have you flogged'

Two of the soldiers stood either side of Alfredo, grabbed his arms and forced him onto the ship. A few minutes later the *San Martin* was heading out of port to the sound of trumpets from the ships waiting in the bay. As the *San Martin* passed the other ships to lead the squadron, the Duke absorbed the accolade of their crews from the poop deck of his flagship, and began waving his hat in acknowledgement.

As the ships sailed out of Cadiz, Alfredo crouched into a corner of the lower deck and wondered how he managed to get himself into such a pickle. Meanwhile, Juan Carlos was marvelling at the spectacle of so many fine ships leaving Cadiz in such splendid formation. As they looked out to sea, both Juan Carlos and Alfredo could not help thinking about their family, about life on the farm, and they simultaneously wondered if they would ever see them again.

Chapter 10
Onwards to Lisbon

Although the sea was moderate and the summer sunshine warm, the roar of the wind, rattling of sail against the masts, and crashing of waves over the ship's bow prevented the crew from singing their usual ditties as they went about their tasks. It would take about three days to reach Lisbon, and so during the voyage, crew and soldiers quickly settled into their daily routines. Soldiers were kept busy cleaning weapons, training, and inspecting supplies, whilst the ship's crew worked with ropes and sails to get the most out of the wind. Other crew members were given the task of swabbing the decks and cleaning out the hold where the animals were kept. Also on board were barbers, who often doubled as lay doctors, and some were trained to bleed the sick members of the crew, which was associated with many deaths. Diets consisting of broths, chicken and white biscuits were provided to assist in the recovery of health, and frequently they were more therapeutic than the work of the barber/physician. Many illnesses were the results of overuse of alcohol products or from infected accidents or battle wounds.

Crewmen mostly worked barefoot which made climbing ropes and rigging easier, and they wore loose fitting shirts that did not constrict movement. The material was usually of a light canvas-like material, sown into a bag-like garment with holes for the head and arms. Because mariners had to repair sails during a voyage, they became accomplished sewers, which enabled them to make their own clothes, and even embellish shirts with embroidery. Those that wore hats usually opted for anything with a flat appearance, except for officers who tended to wear tricorn, or three-cornered hats. Trousers varied, consisting of a loose-fitting garment gartered at the knees, often called "Venetian Breeches" or "Venetian-hosen" which were also popular amongst landsmen at the time.

As the squadron sailed towards Lisbon, Captain Mauritio and Daval discussed the voyage in the chart room on board *Barca de Amburgo*. Meanwhile in the captain's cabin next to the chart room, Paulo and Juan Carlos were busy cleaning and preparing the captain's cabin to ensure he had fresh fruit, water, brandy and wine at all times. However, as the door was open Juan Carlos could not help overhear their conversation.

'Daval, for now we only have to follow the squadron into Lisbon, but when we head for England, I want you to help me plot the course and speed... I do not want any surprises. Especially if we get split up by storms... or even worse... the English... Ha! Ha! Ha!'

'Certainly captain, I think this should be quite an easy voyage... With so many ships on the same course it would be very difficult to stray off course. But I shall keep a close eye on our speed and distance.'

From out the corner of his eye Mauritio noticed Juan Carlos listening to their discussion, turning sharply he startled him.

'What are you doing boy? Have you not got other duties to do?'

Juan Carlos flushed with embarrassment and just stood looking at the floor, and began to tremble with fear.

'Sorry señor… I… I did not mean to disturb you, señor.'

Mauritio stood in front of the boy to admonish him.

'Call me "Captain" … you are part of the crew now boy, so you must call me "Captain or Sir" … understand?'

Juan Carlos stood trembling.

'Si, sir… I… I mean captain… sir.'

Daval thought that Mauritio was going to swipe out at the lad, and quick-wittedly interjected.

'Captain… You should let him assist me… It would be quite useful to have someone to keep regular checks on the sea depth and speed, as there are many places to run aground as we get nearer England.'

Mauritio paused, looked at Juan Carlos menacingly for a second, then realised that Daval could be right.

'Very well Daval… I will place him under your wing, but be sure he does not become lazy… I cannot tolerate lazy people.'

'Certainly captain… I shall train him very hard… have no fear.'

Before Mauritio could change his mind, Daval took Juan Carlos to his quarters which he shared with the ship's physician. Once inside, Daval closed the door and grinned at Juan Carlos.

'So, Juan Carlos, it looks like the captain is not the ogre you thought he was, or he would not have allowed you to help me.'

Juan Carlos did not realise, or appreciate what had happened, as he was still shaking, but was pleased to have the chance to work with Daval.

'I thought for a moment I was going to get a beating… but this is almost like a reward for me… So maybe he is not such a bad man after all?'

Daval smiled, patted Juan Carlos on the back, and laughed.

'Ha! Ha! My friend… he is not a monster, but you still have to be very careful with him as his mood can change very quickly.'

Daval then took out a large wooden box from under his hammock, and opened it to reveal several naval instruments. Before he explained their meaning, Daval asked one important question.

'Juan Carlos… can you read and write?'

Juan Carlos looked quizzically at Daval, and at the same time was amazed at the array of equipment and tools he had in the box.

'A little señor… My grandpapa was teaching me, and he understood your charts and told me a lot about them… But I will learn quickly señor.'

Daval however, was not too convinced.

'I think we will take this nice and slow, as it is a long sea voyage, and we will have plenty of time for you to learn.'

As the instruments and tools were laid out onto the floor, Daval briefly explained their purpose.

'This sandglass measures time at sea as it takes 30 minutes for all the sand to fall through from the top to the bottom, so we can work out the speed we are moving at, and this is a compass which gives direction of travel as it always points to the north.'

Not allowing Juan Carlos time to dwell on each item, Daval continued.

'Then there is the telescope for sighting land and enemies, and at night the navigator uses an astrolabe… But I will explain that when it is dark.'

Juan Carlos recognised some of the items and names, from the things his grandfather had told him, and now he could see and touch them he really wanted to know more.

Daval was pleased to see how keen Juan Carlos was, and decided to give him a demonstration, so he stowed all the equipment away except for two items. Then they went onto the deck of the ship where Daval explained their task.

'I think the best way for you to learn Juan Carlos, is to see how each instrument is used. You see… we write down all the information from these instruments, of the ship's speed and direction, so we can plot the time and route to our destination. To find out the ship's speed, a log line, which is a weight attached to the end a line, is thrown from her stern and allowed to drop to the seabed.'

Juan Carlos watched eagerly as Daval prepared to throw the log line over the stern of the ship, and as he did so he continued the lesson.

'The line, which has equally spaced knots tied in it, is allowed to reel out as the ship moves forward. Then using the sandglass, we count the number of knots that are reeled out in one minute. Multiplying this by 60 gives us the speed in knots per hour.'

After several attempts to satisfy Juan Carlos's curiosity, of the method of multiplication and principal of time, it was decided that the ship was traveling at 5 knots per hour. By the end of the lesson Juan Carlos was pleased to have learned so much from Daval, and spent the rest of the day trying to memorise each movement until his head began to buzz. Over the next few days Juan Carlos and Paulo spent lots of time learning about the different instruments, and Daval would test them to see who had remembered the most.

Chapter 11
Portugal – Lisbon I

Early morning of the third day, the Spanish ships from Cadiz arrived safely at Lisbon. Similar to their arrival at Cadiz, all the crew and soldiers were amazed at the number of ships waiting in the large bay, with some ships spilling out and moored off the Atlantic coastline. Even the officers were awed at the sight, and joined in the cheers and excitement from the crew of every ship they passed.

It had taken most of the day to anchor or moor all the ships into their allotted positions, allowing their captains to go ashore for senior staff meetings. All the crews were given strict orders to remain on board ship and to ensure that maintenance works were completed in readiness for the next part of the voyage. Paulo and Juan Carlos worked hard to complete their duties of cleaning the captain's quarters, together with the chart room, private cellar and surgeon's quarters. This included polishing Mauritio's battle sword, pistols, and preparing all his uniforms. Everything had to be perfect, as they realised that their captain was a stickler for tradition and attention to detail. They knew he was quick to admonish the boys when things were not neatly stowed or in the right place. Apart from Mauritio's unpredictability, they were well looked after, and had better sleeping quarters than most of the crew, which was a small storage room next to the master cabin. However, they were often kept awake at night with Mauritio's loud snoring, interrupted periodically when the ship caught a nasty wave which shook him out of it. Paulo reminded Juan Carlos that Mauritio was his uncle after all.

'He promised my father that he would look after me during the voyage. As my father is a wealthy merchant, he told my uncle that he would receive his pick of the rich cargo routes after the invasion was over.'

As the day wore on, it was well past noon before Captain Mauritio eventually returned to the ship. Juan Carlos happened to be on deck when Mauritio swung his bulky frame over the side of the ship, using a square rigging net thrown down to him in the small rowboat. When he landed on deck, his face was thunderous, and did not say a word. No one dared to look at him, as Juan Carlos was sure that person would have been turned to stone in an instant. Juan Carlos quickly hid behind one of the deck cannons until Mauritio had disappeared to his cabin. He was pleased that he and Paulo had spent the morning cleaning everything, and that sloppiness would be the last thing they could be targeted for. Later that afternoon, Juan Carlos had just started to relax again in the pleasant sunshine on deck, practicing his navigation techniques, when he heard a mighty yell from Mauritio

'Paulo… Juan Carlos!… where the hell are you?'

Juan Carlos's face turned pale as he stumbled his way towards the yelling voice, trying to think of what they had done wrong to make Mauritio shout out their names so loudly.

By the time Juan Carlos had reached the captain's cabin, Paulo was already there, standing in the usual admonished position with head bowed and hands clasped behind his back. Juan Carlos gulped and sheepishly entered the cabin to join him in the same position.

'There you are!' Mauritio bellowed.

'Did you not see me come aboard? And why are you not working in my cabin? The place is a mess!'

It wasn't a mess because the cabin was spotless and had never looked so clean, and it gleamed in some places. Mauritio, though simply wanted to vent his anger on someone... anyone.

'But uncle?' Paulo stuttered

'Don't uncle me you insolate dog; I am captain on this ship... Do you understand?'

Mauritio pushed his face close to Paulo until their noses almost touched.

'Yes, my captain,'

Paulo replied sheepishly, and he could feel the heat emanating from his uncle's face, along with the dry rancid smell of stale wine on his breath. He stepped back to clear a space between them. Mauritio just glared at him, then turned to Juan Carlos, who feared he would take the rest of his anger out on him. Instead, Mauritio stopped in his tracks, and headed for his liquor cabinet where he poured himself a large brandy. As he drank the brandy, in one gulp, he let out a great bellow of air as if a safety valve had been released.

'Why am I surrounded by imbeciles?' he bellowed.

The boys froze and feared that Mauritio would begin to beat them, and they dare not move. But nothing happened, and they seemed invisible and oblivious to Mauritio as he paced up and down his cabin, drinking glass after glass of brandy and cursing in guttural Spanish to no one in particular.

'Those fools on board that flagship do not realise that without captains like me, and without my valuable food supplies they would not make it to England at all... their ships and armies would be useless.'

Mauritio continued to pace up and down and added.

'How dare they refuse to acknowledge me? How dare they treat me like a lowly rating... I am their equal... a captain... yes, a captain, and yet they didn't even see me... Who does Sidonia think he is? He hardly knows a ship's bow from her stern... the ... the man's a... a... Jondido Tonto!'

Mauritio was angry because he had been discharged from the main meeting that morning, unlike a similar meeting at Cadiz, where all captains were present. However, at the Lisbon meeting only fleet commanders were asked to remain for the final part of the meeting, which was to include important war strategies. As Mauritio's fleet commander was Juan Gómez de Medina from the Urca Squadron flagship El Gran Grifón, Mauritio was asked to leave.

The boys suddenly realised that it was his visit to the Armada meeting that made him angry, and not any misdemeanour they had caused, and that they were merely an excuse to vent his anger. A quick glance at each other reassured the boys that it was the right time to leave the captain's cabin, especially as he was getting redder and redder in the face.

'He might even explode'

Giggled Paulo to Juan Carlos as they shuffled out of the cabin. The two boys slipped away completely unnoticed by Mauritio who was busy pouring yet another glass of brandy. The ranting and cursing could be heard throughout the ship for several minutes, even though Paulo had closed the cabin door. All the ship's crew looked worried, and feared the outcome of the protracted rant by their captain. Minutes later though, the ranting ceased, as Mauritio eventually succumbed to the alcohol and slumped onto his bed into a brandy induced sleep. The ship's crew spent the rest of that day going about their work as quietly as possible, just in case the captain awoke in an even nastier mood.

Juan Carlos and Paulo also kept away from the cabin and busied themselves in the ship's galley, helping the cook to prepare the captains favourite meal. They hoped that it would put him in a more favourable mood when he eventually awoke, and without too much of a hangover. The boys had become the best of friends and talked constantly about their new adventure. 'Have you seen an actual battle Paulo?' Paulo pondered a little before answering. 'Not really... I have watched the ship firing the cannons when we were out at sea, which was very loud, and I had to cover my ears, but I have never seen anyone get killed yet.'

Juan Carlos was amazed.

'Wow! I can't wait to see that, and I want to see our ship fighting in a real battle.'

'Yeah... me too,' Paulo quickly replied.

At that moment, the cook interrupted them. 'Clear off you boys because you are getting in my way, I will let you know when the captain's meal is ready. Now shoo!'

The two boys went back onto the deck to admire the ships and to see which ship had the most cannons. Then they continued to practice their navigational skills as they wanted to impress Daval more than Captain Mauritio.

Chapter 12
Portugal – Lisbon II

May 27: The only ships to be moored at Lisbon harbour dock were the Urca supply ships stowing the last of the provisions from the port. Of course, their flagship, *El Gran Grifon*, selected the best position on the dock which conveniently made it easier for the fleet commander, Juan Gómez de Medina to attend meetings and visit influential people in the city. Indeed, all the fleet commanders took the opportunity to enjoy the comforts of city life before the arduous voyage to England. However, the other flagships, including the Armada's overall commander, the Duke of Medina-Sidonia's ship *San Martin*, were moored in the middle of the harbour and not in the dock due to lack of room, as 26 supply ships took up a lot of space. This did not go down too well with the ship's crew, as they hoped to get some final shore time too. One of which was Juan Carlos's father, Alfredo, who was still pretending to be one of the soldiers. He hoped he would be able to meet up with his son and try to convince him to go home with him. Yet the ban on shore leave prevented Alfredo from going anywhere, and the *San Martin* was too far away from the *Barca de Amburgo* to be able to make contact with his son. Of course, Juan Carlos was oblivious to his father's presence, and concentrated only on his duties to Captain Mauritio, his friend Paulo, and his new mentor Henri Daval.

The day was really hot and those left on board ship worked in as much shade as they could, and by late afternoon hardly anyone was on deck. Those who remained on deck stripped off their clothes and took turns to throw buckets of cool sea water onto each other. Later that evening the air was still hot, and the clear sky showed no sign of fading as the crews finally completed their duties for the day. As they ate their food in huddled groups all over the ship, Alfredo overheard some of the soldiers planning to swim ashore when the light faded. He purposely edged closer to them in an effort to get involved in their plan. One man said.

'If we bribe the lookout then we can swim ashore for a couple of hours... No one will miss us.'

Out of the six men discussing the plan, four mumbled in hushed agreement.

'Aye... Si.'

Yet the other two disagreed.

'No ... we cannot swim that far... it is too dangerous for us.'

At that moment Alfredo stepped up, much to the surprise of the others, and they immediately grabbed him, pinned him against the side of the ship and one man threatened him with a knife. He was a dark haired, mean looking man with a heavy growth of beard hiding broken and crooked brown teeth.

'Are you spying on us señor? Because if you are... we'll cut out your tongue to stop you telling anyone.'

Alfredo was shocked at first, but managed to make himself heard.

'Listen... I want to go ashore as well, but it is too far to swim. So why don't we create a diversion at one end of the ship so one of the small boats can be lowered at the other end?'

The six men looked at each other for a moment, and then the man holding the knife to Alfredo's throat replied.

'Maybe you're right… But how can we trust you?'

Alfredo gulped, but managed to keep his nerve.

'I will create the diversion so you can get the boat in the water, then I will slip over the side to join you.'

The man lowered the knife from Alfredo's throat, and the six men huddled in a corner to discuss his plan.

'I don't trust him,' one man said.

Another added 'But I have heard he is looking for his son, so he has good reason to go ashore.'

The man with the knife, listened to their arguments, and interjected.

'I think it could work, but one of us will stay with him when he creates the diversion… just in case he is a spy.'

As the group all nodded and grunted in agreement, they turned to Alfredo, then knifeman told him.

'Very well my friend… the idea is good… we will use the boat, and I will help you with the diversion. We will do it as soon as it gets dark.'

Alfredo and the others agreed and then split up so as not to cause too much interest from others.

Knifeman grabbed Alfredo's arm, to give him a final caution.

'I will be watching you very closely, and if you make a mistake then…'

He drew the knife in an arc inches from Alfredo's throat as a warning.

Alfredo gulped again, but as he was determined to go ashore, he faced the man and replied.

'Just make sure your men are ready… I will not make any mistakes.'

Darkness finally descended on the Lisbon harbour, so Alfredo and the others gathered on deck eager to get ashore, but they kept quiet and well hidden in the shadows away from the main poop deck light and other fire torches. The ship's lookout had already been bribed and was told about the diversion. Alfredo and knifeman made their way to one end of the ship where many of the crew, including some officers, were resting in the cool evening breeze.

Alfredo had gathered some tar soiled rags and feigned falling next to one of the flaming deck torches. As the rags caught fire, he threw them onto some crates that had been stowed on deck all day in full sun, and they were tinder dry. The sudden burst of flames lit the whole deck, causing immediate panic. Officers shouted orders to get the water buckets, and men scurried about trying to extinguish the flames. In the ensuing mayhem, at the other end of the ship, the other plotters had prepared to lower one of the small rowboats into the water. Alfredo and knifeman slipped over the side of the ship and swam to the waiting boat, unseen by anyone. As they rowed towards the shore, they watched the chaos on the ship as the flames appeared to take hold, but by the time they had reached the shore they were extinguished. The plotters laughed as the tension eased from their faces.

'That was a good plan'

One of the men said to Alfredo, patting him on the back.

'Si señor... you are a clever man, and we are pleased to have you with us.'

Knifeman grunted his displeasure at being proved wrong about Alfredo.

'No matter men... what we need now ... is a drink!'

'Aye' another said. 'And I want a woman before we sail...'

They all agreed in unison, and laughed as they made their way off the cobbled shore towards the lights of the city.

As they secured the boat, Alfredo grabbed the arm of knifeman, who turned in surprise at the movement.

'I shall not be coming with you as I have other plans for tonight. Just be sure to wait for me for the return.'

Knifemen laughed and pulled away from Alfredo's grip,

and then he lowered the tone of his voice to a menacing growl.

'We shall wait... as we have to get back on ship before light, but I have not finished with you my friend, I could use a man with such cunning.'

The two men scowled at each other for a second, but nodded in agreement, then went their separate ways.

Because they had come ashore well away from prying eyes and city torch lights, it took the men several minutes to reach the port. The boat was secured and hidden, then Alfredo veered towards the dock, whilst the others headed into the city centre. The inns were full of traders, merchants, and men enjoying the bonanza of wealth that the Armada offered. It was easy for knifeman and his men to blend in, and they intended to make the most of their stolen night of freedom. Alfredo however, was intent only in finding Juan Carlos who he now knew was on board *Barca de Amburgo*. He carefully made his way to the dock, keeping close to buildings and hiding in their shadows. Although the dock was quiet, there were still guards patrolling up and down keeping watch for those disobeyed the order to stay on board ship. It took Alfredo several minutes to locate the *Barca de Amburgo*, and once he found it, getting onboard and finding his son without raising suspicion, was going to be difficult.

Over the next hour, Alfredo waited and watched the movement of two of the guards allocated to his end of the dock, and noticed how they repeated their route. At the same time, he monitored the deck crew on board the ship, who similarly repeated their watch. It was a warm evening, and each patrol took the opportunity of pausing for a sip from a flagon of carefully hidden wine and chatted. When the time was right, Alfredo made his move and quickly ran across the dock, up the gangplank of the ship and hid behind some barrels. He watched carefully to ensure he was not too conspicuous, as the decks were strewn with dozing sailors, and soldiers enjoying the warm evening following a hearty meal. They knew the food would not be as fresh once the ship was at sea, and most took the opportunity to eat well. Those not sleeping, were playing cards and dice games to while away the evening before bed. Most of course would sleep on deck, on canvas sheets or makeshift hammocks. They took little notice of anyone coming on board, and admired those that did disobey the order to stay on the ship.

Meanwhile, Juan Carlos was in Mauritio's cabin helping Paulo to clear away the table after the captain's meal. The stern windows were open, as was the cabin door, allowing a welcome breeze to pass through the cabin. Mauritio slumped at his desk with a large glass of brandy, muttering to himself about lack of respect from his fellow officers.

'Buffoons! imbeciles! I will show them all soon that I am worthy of their respect.'

As he slurped from the glass, Paulo whispered to Juan Carlos.

'Come, let us clear the table quickly and eat the captain's leftovers, as the chicken smells really good.'

'Si! I shall also remove the bread and wine, as I am sure he has no further use of it.' Juan Carlos replied with a wink.

Quickly and quietly they cleared the table and closed the cabin door, before making their way to their own quarters. The boys placed the food onto their own tin plates, poured the wine into tin cups, and then Juan Carlos gathered the captain's good crockery and utensils.

'I shall take these down to the galley now, as we don't want the captain to catch us eating his food from his best dishes… I shall not be long Paulo… don't eat all the food my friend.'

Juan Carlos emerged onto the deck, and paused to throw

some chicken bones over the side. Alfredo saw him and tried to attract his attention without disturbing the slumbering crew, or alert the watchmen. But Juan Carlos did not hear him and so he made his way towards the galley, which annoyed Alfredo as he was so close to his son. In a spurt of desperation, he tried to jump over the sleeping bodies, and accidentally kicked one man in the stomach. The man let out a deafening cry of pain.

'Ooohhh! Que pasa? What are you doing? Look where you are going... Idiota!'

The noise alerted the ship's watchmen, and at the same time, the dock patrol was alongside the ship in the process of being relieved by fresh men, and they were accompanied by the officer in charge. They boarded the ship to confront those causing the disturbance.

'What's the problem here?' The officer barked, who coincidentally was the same officer who had tangled with Alfredo in Cadiz. For a split second Alfredo and the officer's eyes met, and Alfredo's expression sank pitifully.

'You again!' the officer yelled.

'Why are you always causing trouble... and what are you doing on this ship... it's not your ship? you should be on *San Martin*.'

Alfredo tried to splutter some concocted explanation.

'I can explain sir. I... I... '

'Enough! Take him to the harbour jail.'

Alfredo tried to plead with the man, but it was of little use.

'NO! I don't want to know what your excuses are... You will face severe punishment for insubordination and breaking the order.' The guards grabbed Alfredo by the arms, and they began to march him off the ship, just as Juan Carlos and Paulo emerged on deck to see what all the commotion was. It was then that Juan Carlos saw his father for the first time.

'PAPA… PAPA!'

Juan Carlos started to run towards the gangplank, when suddenly a large hand grabbed him, and the man wrapped his strong arms around him as he struggled frantically to reach his father.

'Let me go! Let me go! I must go to him.'

The man was Daval.

'No… no… Juan Carlos you must remain here, because they will take anyone who causes trouble, and the punishment can be severe… You are too young for such treatment.'

As Alfredo was dragged towards the port jailhouse, he looked back towards the ship and his eyes met with Juan Carlos's. Their gazes locked for a few seconds and thoughts of strong family ties came welling up over Juan Carlos, who collapsed in floods of tears into Daval's arms.

That night, as he lay weeping on his bed, Juan Carlos tried to understand why his father was there. Why had he travelled so far to be near him? How did he manage to get on the ship? He could only assume that he came to fetch him home. Mixed emotions began to tear him apart as he missed his family very much, but at the same time he was enjoying his adventure, and the new friends he had made. He also feared for his father, because of what Daval had told him, yet he felt useless to help him.

The dock jailhouse was an old stone-built building annexed to the side of the port offices with one heavy wooden door. Inside, a dividing wall separated a small room with an old desk and single chair, from two cells with floor to ceiling iron bars and no windows. Both cells were full of men from the Armada, who had been caught breaking the curfew, and the air inside was hot and sticky, with a heavy smell of stale ale and sweaty men. A guard unlocked one of the cells and Alfredo was thrown unceremoniously into it. With him in the cell were two of the men he came ashore with, one of whom was 'knifeman'. They were both drunk, dishevelled and had taken a severe beating before being dumped at the jailhouse by the shore patrol. They did not speak to each other as the noise from snoring, groaning bodies prevented any legible conversation. Instead, they just glared at each other, and then Alfredo sat in the corner of the cell to reminisce on the events of the night.

Chapter 13
Portugal – Lisbon III

May 28: Early next morning as the sun shone in a clear blue sky, Alfredo and the other prisoners were taken in shackles to the harbour, where they were confronted by senior naval and military officers in the harbour master's office. The harbour dock was a hive of activity as the Armada began making final preparations to sail out of Lisbon, and an official departure ceremony with the city's dignitaries awaited the Armada chief of staff. However, before the public were allowed onto the dock to cheer the ships off, the prisoners had to be dealt with and removed from sight.

Looking bemused dishevelled and feeling the worse for a night in the cells, the prisoners lined up outside the office. One by one they were pushed into the office to be confronted by the harbour master and a senior officer from the Armada. They were quickly charged with disobeying the order to stay on board ship, and were sentenced to be whipped 25 times each, and given hard manual tasks until the Armada reached the English Channel. After sentencing, the men were taken to their respective ships, which for most, was the supply ships docked at the port. Punishment was to be administered when the ships were well out to sea. Alfredo and the other prisoners from the *San Martin* were held back in the office, as their ship was still anchored in the middle of the bay.

At the dock, with all supplies loaded, the Urca Squadron made its way into the bay of the harbour, allowing the *San Martin* to come into the dock. This enabled the Duke of Medina-Sidonia to board easier, as he had spent the night in the city enjoying some last-minute hospitality. It also enabled him to acknowledge the farewell celebrations the city had prepared. Once the *San Martin* had moored up, the crowds were allowed to gather around a bunting festooned podium mounted on the dock, made ready for the official launch of the Armada. At the same time Alfredo and the other prisoners were ushered quietly onboard ship, and dumped into the hold until the ship had sailed. As the morning wore on, the harbour became very busy, and was buzzing with cheering crowds, bands playing and flags waving.

Eventually, officials and guests of honour mounted the podium, and the Duke of Medina-Sidonia acknowledged good luck speeches, and gave positive announcements of victory. Finally, with all the pomp and ceremony completed, Sidonia boarded his flagship, and the crew scurried around frantically trying to make a speedy departure on the ebbing tide.

So, on 28th May 1588, the mighty fleet of Spain weighed anchor and sailed down the Tagus to the open sea. From the deck of the *San Martin*, the Duke of Medina-Sidonia ordered the signal gun to be fired. The *San Martin* led the way, followed by the Squadron of galleons of Portugal, which received a special cheer from the Lisbon crowd. Trumpets sounded from several ships, including the Squadron of Castile under the command of Don Diego Flores de Valdez on board the *San Cristobal*, who was appointed by King Philip II to be the mentor of the Duke of Medina-Sidonia. Then the Squadron of Andalucía set sail under the command of Don Pedro de Valdez on board *Nuestra Señora del Rosario*, a brave and experienced admiral with the best knowledge of the English Channel. Bringing up the rear was the Urca Squadron of supply ships under Don Juan Lopez de Medina, and his flagship *El Gran Grifon*, along with the embittered Captain Mauritio on board *Barca de Amburgo*.

It took several minutes for the fleet to sail out of the Lisbon harbour into the Atlantic Ocean. From coastal cliffs and hilltops, crowds gathered to watch the colourful banners and ship's flags wave a heroic goodbye, as the impressive sight of the Armada left the port. They could hear drums banging, and horns blaring out across the bay in a triumphant display of strength. Ship after ship unfurled their giant sails, released from their tethers by the skilled hands of hundreds of experienced sailors. The rest of the crew scurried about the decks securing ropes and equipment, as captains barked out their orders from lofted positions on the poop deck of each ship. Soldiers fired a salvo of gunfire into the air, with plumes of dark smoke blown away by a gentle sea breeze. It took a long time for all the ships to sail out of the bay and into the open sea. A few minutes later, as the Armada sailed from view, Lisbon became a quiet and desolate place, leaving many to wonder how many would return.

As soon as the *San Martin* was well out to sea and under full sail, the prisoners were brought on deck for their punishment. Alfredo and the others were strapped to the mizzen mast one at a time and given their full quota of lashes. Alfredo winced as each lash tore into his flesh, the gathered crew and soldiers groaned in sympathy for their shipmate's agony. When the final lash was delivered, Alfredo was cut down and dragged back to the hold by two crewmen. The strength had gone from his body as he slumped to the floor in searing, pulsating pain. His only consolation was that

Juan Carlos had finally seen him, and that maybe, just maybe they might meet up again. Later that day, orders were given by King Philip II that it had to be instilled into every crew member that the Armada was sanctioned by the Catholic Church. There were two hundred priests and friars sailing with the Armada led by chief priest Alarco, and it was compulsory for each sailor and soldier to confess, to receive communication and a card of absolution. In the evenings, the ships-boys were to assemble at the mainmast of each ship to sing Ave Maria. This was to be carried out every evening with unfailing regularity, unless the weather made it impossible.

It wasn't long before the weather started to play a significant role in the journey towards the English Channel, skies darkened and a storm with strong head winds caused the ships to struggle in maintaining their speed and direction. This was made all the more difficult, as distressed ships had to work really hard to prevent themselves crashing into each other as they sailed north. By the time the ships had reached south of Cape Finisterre, the crews were exhausted, broken ropes caused damage to rigging and sail spars. Worse, was the rumour of hundreds suffering from dysentery, brought on by half-putrid food and drink, stowed in poorly made or green barrels from untreated wood. Water, salt meat and biscuits had been contaminated and lay rotting in the barrels. Spanish sailors, as with all sailors throughout history, took these signs as omens, and although some thought the journey to be a mission sanctioned by God, others saw the run of bad luck telling a different story, and rumours of an ill-fated mission began to spread.

On board *Barca de Amburgo*, the noise from the wind, crashing waves, rattling ropes and canvas created a din of nightmare proportions. Although the whole ship appeared to be in abject chaos, everyone could still hear the booming voice of Mauritio as he yelled his orders across the ship. His officers scurried about like rats trying to complete them, and often slipped on wet decks or took action against flying booms and cargo.

'He is inhumane,' one crew member muttered to others.

'We should make to port!' Another exclaimed

Daval used his experience of having spent many years at sea to help the crew keep a steady course. Juan Carlos and Paulo assisted where they could, and although their slight frames did not have the strength of men, they learned valuable lessons during those tortuous heavy seas. Struggling with a rigging rope, the ship suddenly lunged into the trough of a large wave, causing Juan Carlos and Paulo to instinctively cling on to the rope before they were swept overboard. Daval appeared from nowhere and grabbed the rope, securing it to a deck rail. Paulo's relieved expression spoke volumes.

'I… I… thought we were going to be swept into the sea señor… Thank you for saving us.'

Daval laughed and winked at him.

'I have been watching you both and I wanted you to learn how dangerous the sea can be… let this be an important lesson.'

With the storm still raging and Daval distracted by the boys, El Muerte seized the opportunity to attack him. He took a heavy grappling net to the deck above Daval, and hurled it onto him. The weight caused Daval to lose his footing, and as he became entangled in the net, he was knocked off balance. Juan Carlos and Paulo watched in horror as Daval slid across the wet deck, and the lurching ship caused him to be thrown over the side. Frantically the boys rushed over to side of the ship afraid that their friend was lost. As they clung onto the side rail, Juan Carlos noticed a tangled bundle that was somehow stuck to the side of the ship.

Waves lashed at the bundle as it was tossed from side to side, held only by a single rope from the net. Any moment the waves could lift the bundle from its anchor and drag it down to the murky depths.

At that moment Paulo pointed to an arm reaching out of the bundle.

'Look! Juan Carlos… There! I can see Daval's arm… he is still alive.'

Juan Carlos looked around the ship to see what he could use to help his friend, and peering through the constant sea spray he noticed a grappling hook stowed securely to the deck. He painstakingly made his way across the wet deck as the heavy spray and violent winds hampered each step, and he eventually untied the hook.

'Quickly! Juan Carlos' Paulo screamed. 'I think the sea will take him.'

Juan Carlos secured the hook rope to the deck and threw the hook at the bundle, just as it was being lifted off its anchor by the powerful waves. Fortunately, the hook grabbed the net, but the bundle was thrown further down the ship until the rope was taught, causing the bundle to bounce against the ship, then it disappeared under the waves.

'It's too late Juan Carlos, we did not save him.'

'No! you are wrong Paulo… look!'

They boys peered over the side of the ship to see the bundle being dunked into the sea, and then out again as the ship lurched in the storm.

Suddenly Daval's arm emerged again out of the net, but this time he was holding his knife. Slowly he was able to cut his way out of the net and as he emerged out, he grabbed the hook rope. The boys watched intensely as he made his way out of the bundle and up the side of the ship. Paulo quickly fetched one of the crew to help Daval to safety, battered and exhausted Daval slumped onto the deck. Other

crew members arrived and they took Daval to his cabin to recover on his bunk. Mauritio ordered the two boys to take care of the ship's navigator, which pleased the boys as they did not like being on deck during the storm.

Chapter 14
Port in a Storm

By the time the fleet approached Cape Finisterre, the storm had subsided, and the Armada got a favourable breeze, much to the relief of the crew. During the light, early evening, with everyone feeling much better, the Armada sailed gracefully around Cape Finisterre and into the safe port of La Coruña, a Spanish Galician city at the southern end of the Bay of Biscay. The commanders decided to allow those ships who needed it to take on board much needed supplies and carry out any repairs, whilst others would remain in the bay. The Urca supply ships were instructed into port first to check all supplies and replenish where necessary. The *San Martin* would remain in the bay, although the Duke would be taken by rowboat into port, as would the rest of his senior staff.

As the ships settled down for the night, Juan Carlos went to the hold where the mules were stowed, and he stroked and fed them. The smells reminded him of his farm and of his family, and he found peace and solace tending the animals. A little later, Daval appeared, looking none the worse from his exploits. Juan Carlos was very pleased to see him, and hugged him.

'Don't worry mes amis, I am ok thanks to you and your quick thinking.'

As they both stroked the mules, Daval continued.

'Accidents can happen at any time when at sea mes amis, and you should always keep your eyes and brain sharp.'

Juan Carlos nodded in agreement, happy that he was able to save his new friend. Daval sighed a little and spoke softly to Juan Carlos.

'I would have told you about your father earlier if it was not for the storm mes amis. Although, I only know that he is held prisoner on board *San Martin* and that he is reasonably well.'

Daval did not explain about the lashes his father would have received for disobeying an order. Juan Carlos sighed, and was relieved to know where his father was, but also concerned that he had followed him. He knew that it meant his father had come to take him away from his adventure. He looked quizzically at Daval.

'Do you think he will be released to take me home?'

Daval gripped Juan Carlos's shoulder, shook it, and answered reassuringly. 'I doubt it my friend… I think he will have to serve the Duke now as a punishment. I doubt that he will be able to leave the ship until we reach England.'

Juan Carlos looked puzzled not knowing if that would be good or bad for his father. Daval noticed his concern and added.

'But if you both make it safely to England, maybe you can talk to him … it will be a difficult time for you both as you do not know the dangers of war. I will watch over you, but you must listen to me at all times mes amis.'

Juan Carlos was pleased he had found such a good friend in Daval, and he was keen to learn as much as he could from him. Later that night Juan Carlos lay in his bunk thinking of the days to come. He was both excited and terrified, as he realised that his adventure was becoming a reality.

The next day Daval sought out el Muerto, and eventually

found him skulking in one the holds, and so confronted him. Although he did not see the face of the man who threw the netting over him. He was convinced it was him, and that it was no accident. El Muerto, surrounded by his fellow henchmen, noticed Daval approaching and stood up to his full height. Daval stood in front of him and the two men eyeballed each other for a few moments.

'I know it was you who threw that net on me… you coward!'

El Muerto laughed.

'Stupid Frenchman, you know how accidents happen onboard ship during a storm'

He looked menacingly into Daval's eyes and sneered.

'Maybe you will not be so lucky… next time'

As the two men squared up to each other with the atmosphere turning black, a crew member called to them.

'All hands on deck!'

The Captain had ordered every able-bodied man to check the ship's supplies and replenish the barrels with fresh water and food.

A new day brought back the excitement of war. Spanish rumours were rife that the Queen of England only had 30 ships, and when they met the Armada, they would be doomed. When the ships closed into each other, the superior weaponry and height advantage of the larger Spanish war ships would wreak havoc on the smaller enemy ships. Also, Spanish ships are all musket proof above, and small arms fire would clear the English decks as they towered above them. Delighted at the thought of an easy victory, the Armada's crew and soldiers busied themselves all day cleaning and preparing for the voyage across the Bay of Biscay towards the English Channel. No shore-leave was allowed and everyone had to be sober of thought, mind and deed. Night watchmen were set along the harbour and on each vessel to ensure against rebellious behaviour. All patrols were doubled, and severe punishment was threatened no matter what rank, and this of course did not go down well with many of men. But after a hot and busy day, and with the stores of La Corunna depleted, much to the wealth of the local businessmen, the harbour stilled to a quiet evening.

Onboard *San Martin*, Alfredo slowly regained his strength, but felt resigned to being taken to England as part of the invasion force. Although he would look for an opportunity to see his son again, for now, he had to wait. Meanwhile, on board *Barca de Amburgo*, Daval decided to teach the boys more navigation techniques to distract them. He explained that to prevent a ship running aground, a lead weight was used to measure the depth of water. Attached to a marked line, it was thrown overboard, and sticky tallow on the base of the lead weight would pick up mud from the sea bed. From the type of mud picked up on its base, a skilled navigator could tell how close the ship was to shore. The pilot used several instruments and techniques to help him, but it was the captain who decided on the ship's course. The captain then issued orders to the helmsman who operated the wheel to steer the ship, and the boatswain led the crew to adjust the rudder and sails to maintain her course.

Chapter 15
Onward to England

With fresh provisions and a good heart, the huge fleet eventually left La Corunna Harbour on July 12. They set sail across the Bay of Biscay, following traditional sea routes towards the English Channel. The weather was set fair for a good crossing and everyone settled into a steady routine. Ship's crews maintained a regular 24-hour rota system to ensure each ship sailed safely in formation. Soldiers were allocated specific duties to keep them focussed. Officers for the military arranged for regular weapons inspections, including checking that the gunpowder was kept dry and stowed safely. Everyone was given laundry duties and teams were given a rota to clean each deck of the ship. The hold where mules, horses and other animals were stowed was the worst job. Also, each ship was given a military surgeon to assist with the ship's surgeon when the time came, and some soldiers were being trained as medics. With so many men onboard a controlled system of feeding them was put into place. The galley was located midships and low in the hold, due to the weight of the fire bricks that were used to protect the wooden hull. The bricks were contained in fireboxes for stability, with a layer of sand, brick, slate or stone slabs. An iron funnel went up through to the weather deck to remove the smoke. Extra fireboxes were added due to the large number of crew and soldiers aboard. A large copper cauldron was suspended over each firebox to allow for movement of the ship. The ship's cook and military cooks worked together to keep meals separate, and were generally eaten around shift changes. The meals consisted mostly of wheat biscuits, beans, pulses, and rough red wine, with salted beef or fish, depending on supplies, and the day of the week. With so many men crammed in together, conditions became smelly and unhygienic. Rats were a serious problem, attacking food supplies and any animals on board. Other vermin such as cockroaches, mice, scorpions, and fleas added to the discomfort. So, it was important that each ship was thoroughly cleaned, including pumping the dirty water out of the bilges on a daily basis.

One morning, Juan Carlos noticed Mauritio cleaning his pistols in his cabin, and as everything was on course, the captain had some time to relax. He enjoyed looking his best and every officer worth his salt owned a fire pair of pistols. Mauritio saw Juan Carlos, and rather than scold him for being "nosy", beckoned him to sit by his side.

'What do you think of these fine pistols boy?'

Mauritio waved them in front of Juan Carlos and pretended to fire them.

'Sir, they are truly awesome and they shine so much in the light.' Mauritio smiled, knowing that they were magnificent.

'Si, amigo, I always keep them clean and ready for use… because you never know when they will be needed.'

He let Juan Carlos hold one of them.

'Wow sir, it feels good to hold, and very comfortable… can… can I fire it?'

Mauritio laughed very loud, and a little taken aback as to the impertinence of the boy. 'Ha! Ha! Ha! Well lad, I don't see why not? Let's go out on deck.'

Mauritio took the pistols and picked up a small leather satchel that he kept them in, as it also contained the powder and shot. When they got outside, they went to the stern of the ship, to a section that did not overlook other ships, as he did not want to shoot anyone by accident. Then he carefully showed Juan Carlos how to load and prime one of the pistols, which were a pair of single-shot, muzzle-loading handguns, employing a flintlock ignition system. Mauritio repeated the method several times until Juan Carlos understood. Then he carefully showed him how to load the gunpowder, which he kept dry in a small animal horn container. The small round iron ball and padding was fitted and rammed into the nozzle. Upon priming the flintlock section of the pistol, Mauritio took aim into the water and fired.

Bang!

Juan Carlos was shocked with how loud it was. 'Wow! Captain, that is amazing.'

Mauritio prepared the next pistol, and carefully instructed Juan Carlos what to do.

'Keep your arm straight and rigid, look down the length of the barrel then point to a target.'

A piece of cloth was thrown into the sea, and Juan Carlos was asked to shoot at it. After carefully aiming the pistol, he fired and the shot entered the water just a few inches away from the cloth. However, the recoil knocked Juan Carlos backwards a little, and he was amazed at the power of the weapon.

'Perfect! My boy, that was a good shot for your first time.'

After several more rounds were fired, Mauritio returned to his cabin, and Juan Carlos watched him reclean and reload the pistols, before stowing them safely away into the leather satchel then placing it into one of the cupboards.

'Now boy, get back to your duties because I have a lot of work to do.'

Juan Carlos was pleased with how kind and understanding Mauritio was, and left the cabin with a big smile on his face.

The Armada had to be careful sailing too close to land as there were many reefs and hidden dangers, and detailed instructions were issued to all captains and commanders to be watchful. With favourable winds, they eventually reached the north side of the Bay of Biscay. Then the fleet headed west off the island of Ushant on the northwest corner of France. With so many ships in the fleet, it was too dangerous to sail east of Ushant, as there were too many smaller islands and many rocky reefs warning of danger. Onboard *San Martin*, Alfredo was kept busy swabbing the decks, along with other prisoners and a few experienced sailors. He questioned the sailors on the Armada's chances of success, as he worried about the dangers of war, and for the safety of his son.

'Do you think the English navy will be difficult to defeat?'

One sailor stopped his work and pointed at the other ships in the fleet.

'Look and see my friend, you will never see so many magnificent ships in one place, and there is not a navy in the world good enough to defeat us.'

Alfredo was impressed by the magnificence of the fleet, but was not reassured.

'But there will be lots of fighting before they are defeated, and we may suffer much damage… with many dead.'

The reply was not what Alfredo wanted to hear.

'Of course, but that is war… you should be pleased that you are on this ship, because it is the greatest war ship in the whole of Spain… We will be fine, but I think the smaller ships could suffer.'

As night fell the fleet slowed, and a flurry of activity amongst the crew gave an air of anticipation for everyone.

Commanders on board the *San Martin* gathered in the map room and reviewed all the maps, charts and orders that had been issued. Through the night, a series of predetermined signals were sent from ship to ship using lanterns. Eventually, with everything prepared, the fleet waited for dawn. During this time, thousands of men were consoled by priests and blessed for a favourable day ahead. Hymns were sung and communion taken by the priests, with private prayers given. Later in their bunks, men contemplated their own fate ahead, with many making notes for loved ones, and confiding in others to ensure their wishes were met. Daval used this time to advise the boys what could possibly lay ahead.

'My friends, the next few days could be very dangerous for everyone.'

He paused to ensure both boys were listening closely.

'This is not going to be easy mes amis, and the enemy will be firing cannons at us.'

The boys stared with open mouths at every word.

'You two must stay with the ship's surgeon at all times, because he could be very busy attending to the wounded, should we be fired upon.'

The boys remained silent.

'He will need as much help as possible and there could be a lot of blood. You must listen to him and try to keep calm.'

Juan Carlos interjected anxiously.

'But where will you be?'

'I will be busy on deck with the captain, trying to maintain our course and organising the crew. The soldiers also have a surgeon working on deck and they might need your help too.'

Daval smiled reassuringly.

'But we could be alright, as we will be in the centre of the fleet and protected by the bigger warships... We might not be involved in the battles at all, but you have to be ready mes amis.'

Both boys were anxious, but also a little excited at the thought of what lay ahead. Daval told them to eat and drink a little before going to sleep. But there was too much to think about, and neither boy wanted to, or could, sleep that night.

Dawn came quickly, and Juan Carlos could feel the ship rock into action as sails were unfurled, causing the ship to pick up speed as the wind billowed them out. Loud voices echoed throughout the ship, as crew members climbed rigging and lashed ropes. Juan Carlos went on deck and looked over the side. He could see the vast array of ships manoeuvring into position. Paulo joined him, just as a large wave swept across the deck as their ship turned into position, washing their feet and tunics. They reacted instinctively, and clung on to the nearest rope or rigging, bringing their senses to the full. Daval appeared.

'Get to the surgeon's room and see if he wants anything doing.'

Then he quickly disappeared, and the boys made their way inside.

The ship's surgeon, was a stocky, balding man in his forties, and his face conveyed the years of trauma that only a surgeon could have experienced.

'Ah!' he said. 'You must be my assistants.'

He laughed loudly as he prepared his equipment, and stowed everything that was not going to be needed. Pointing to a cupboard in the corner of the room he gestured to the boys.

'Inside are several buckets, and I want you to keep them clean and full of fresh sea water at all times.'

As the boys fetched the buckets the surgeon continued.

'I hope we don't need them, but you must do everything I say, and don't ever question me.'

He paused... waited for the boys to acknowledge him, then continued.

'Daval tells me that you two are good and quick workers, so I hope he is right... we could be busy and there are some things you should know.'

As he laid out his equipment onto a table, he explained how the surgeon room worked. First, he padded his hands on the central heavy table which was anchored to the floor.

'This is my operating table, and when I tell you to, you must wash it down with sea water, and don't worry about the mess or what you see on it.'

The boys pulled grimacing faces as they imagined what they would see. Then the surgeon pointed to his instruments, which were very gruesome to say the least, and all had traces of dark, dried blood on them.

'These are my surgical instruments, and you never touch them unless I say so... capiche?!' His voice rising loudly at the end in an attempt to drive home his point.

In unison the boys echoed the sentiment.

'No sir... of course sir.'

The surgeon continued to prepare his operating room, including a canvas bag with straps, in which he kept several smaller items. This he placed over his head so it was easily accessible at his side. The two boys filled the buckets and watched everyone on board prepare for action.

Chapter 16
Enemy Sighted

Daybreak on July 21 the massive Spanish fleet formed a great half-moon over several miles as it sailed into the English Channel. With Captain De Leyva on board *La Rata Santa María Encoronada*, a converted Genoese merchantman in the Levant squadron holding one point, and Captain Don Juan Martinez de Recalde on board *El Gran Grin* the vice-flagship from the Biscay Squadron holding the other. The *San Martin* was to take up centre position so it could relay signals and messages to the fleet. The valuable supply ships took their positions in the bowl of the crescent for maximum protection. Each captain had to be very watchful of their course, and care was needed not to encroach adjacent ships. They did not want to damage their own ship, or anger the Commander in Chief.

Yet the English were well aware of the Spanish threat, and the day before, on July 20, the English fleet positioned its ships off the south English coastline, with the Armada upwind to the west. That night, in order to execute their attack, the English tacked upwind of the Armada, thus gaining a significant wind and tide advantage. At daybreak on July 21 the English fleet engaged the Armada off Plymouth near the Eddystone rocks. Attacking the Armada from the rear, the English used their lighter, and faster ships to outmanoeuvre the Spanish. The English knew that the Spanish had the advantage in close-quarter fighting, so they kept their ships beyond grappling range and bombarded the Spanish ships from a distance between one hundred and two hundred yards. Firing four-pound to 60-pound iron cannonballs, the English could inflict more damage than the majority of the smaller Spanish cannons, that were not as powerful. However, the big Spanish galleons also had larger cannons, but it was difficult for them to manoeuvre into position, sailing in such a tight formation. However, the rocky seas affected the English lighter and smaller ships, so it was difficult for their gunners to be accurate. Nevertheless, casualties were inevitable, and on board *Barca de Amburgo*, Juan Carlos and Paulo watched from the side of the ship as the events unfolded. They could hear the loud bangs of the cannons firing, and see the smoke as it billowed and drifted from each ship as they fired their cannons in reply. Soldiers and crew members, not busy sailing the ship also watched. They felt safe within the protection of the large crescent formation of the Armada.

All of that suddenly changed when two stray cannonballs came hurtling onto their ship. They smashed into the rigging and deck of the ship, causing large sections of splintered wood to be scattered in all directions. Some of the pieces speared those men closest to the impact, throwing them backwards in agony. Blood washed over the deck as the men shrieked in agony. Captain Mauritio immediately took command of the situation and shouted out orders from the poop deck.

'Get those men to the surgeon, and make good the rigging. Then clear the deck quickly… we must keep our course.'

Mauritio called down to the helmsman steering the ship on the quarterdeck.

'Helmsman… keep her steady and watch your line.'

'Aye-aye Captain.' Came the quick reply.

The surgeon, on hearing the commotion, came out of his quarters and assessed the situation. He summoned the boys.

'Get over here you two, and bring the buckets quickly.'

Shocked, open-mouthed and rooted to the spot, the two boys did nothing. They could not believe what had happened, and the sight of such gruesome injuries and blood would remain in their minds for a long time.

'NOW!'

Yelled the surgeon, and he whacked the boy's heads with the palm of his hand. Staggeringly, the boys reacted and fetched the buckets as was asked. A reassuring voice came from behind them.

'Try to keep calm mes amiss, and remember what I told you. It is important to be alert at all times.'

The boys had no time to talk, and could only 'nod' in agreement at Daval's words.

The injured men were laid on the deck, where the military surgeon and experienced crewmembers used their skills to stem the blood as they waited their turn for the surgeon's table. The boys had to pass the injured several times, as they carried bucket after bucket of fresh seawater for the surgeon. Blood was everywhere, and some of the injuries were terrible. Time was of the essence and the surgeon acted swiftly to remove the splinters, repair damaged internal organs, and stitch up the wounds before moving on to the next man. Those that were unconscious were fortunate not to feel the pain, but others screamed in agony, that was heard throughout the ship. Two crewmen helped him to dress the wounds and take the injured to their quarters. All the while, the boys delivered fresh water so the surgeon could wash down his bloodied operating table and floor. With eight men wounded, some of them seriously, it was going to be a busy time for the boys. It was several hours before the last man was treated, friars and priests were called to help and comfort all, and thankfully, there was no more stray cannon fire to their ship. The rest of the crew acted quickly too and soon the damage was assessed so repairs could be carried out. Sailors quickly cut down the damaged rigging and replaced it with new. Damaged floor timbers were removed and replaced with fresh beams from the hold, and then sealed.

Although the distance was too great to be effective, the English kept pouring shot after shot into the Spanish fleet throughout the day. It caused plenty of chaos and confusion, and two ships were badly damaged when they collided trying to hold formation against enemy fire. *San Salvador* from the Squadron of Guipuzcoa lost control of its steering when cannonballs smashed into the deck, killing the helmsman and destroying the wheel. Out of control, the ship veered into the rear of *Nuestra Señora del Rosario*, which was the flagship of Don Pedro de Valdés of the Andalucía Squadron. It damaged the steering system and caused the huge vessel to be swept away by the tide and winds. Unable to sail, and under enemy cannon fire, the men and crew removed all their heavy clothing and equipment, then abandoned ship. The swell of the waves caused some to crash against the hull knocking them unconscious, others drowned as many could not swim. Most of the men, including Don Pedro de Valdés, were rescued by the nearest ships as ropes and nets were cast into the sea for them. Using rowboats, survivors still onboard ship was taken off, along with any other stores of food and powder. They also managed to locate the treasure chest, which was saved and taken on board the nearest ship.

Meanwhile, the rest of the fleet could only watch from a distance, and onboard *San Martin*, the Duke of

Medina-Sidonia and Maestre Francisco Arias de Bobadilla, the senior army office, watched through field glasses to assess the damage.

One of the ships at the centre of the fleet had her upper deck badly damaged, although still able to sail, 200 of her men were blown into the waves below. Those onboard *Gran Grifon* were signalled to get the rowboats out to save as many as possible from the chilling waters. The *San Martin* signalled for the rest of the fleet to cut their sails in order to assist where possible, which allowed the commanders time to review their attack options. At one point the Duke of Medina-Sidonia decided to head for the protective shores of the Isles of Wight. The English would have had to move closer to prevent it, and therefore give the Spaniards a chance to fight close up. Sidonia could then use the galle-asses and their oarsmen to get closer to the English ships. After repeated attempts to close-grapple had failed, the commanders decided to abort that plan. There was also a danger of sudden high winds moving the ships onto rocks around the Isle of Wight, and so the decision was made to head for the coast of France, and to maintain the crescent formation. The English however, preferred to stick to their plan of using the Spanish great galleons as long-range targets. For days the cat and mouse battle raged with both sides fighting against the wind and currents of the English Channel, but the Armada sailed on.

Chapter 17
France – Calais

On July 27, the Armada put into the French port of Calais, where Sidonia wanted to use the haven to carry out repairs to damaged ships and men. The French Governor of Calais, Giraud de Mauleon was a sympathetic Catholic, the 76-year-old also lost his leg during fighting, to recover Calais from the English in 1558. He allowed the Spanish to anchor offshore by the guns of the town fort, to assist with the wounded, carry out repairs and to buy fresh food, and water. Sidonia was also expecting to meet up with Alessandro Farnese, the Duke of Parma, who was coming from Holland with extra soldiers and siege artillery to complete the invasion. The Armada warships would blockade the English Channel, allowing the rest of the fleet to swiftly invade England with as many soldiers as possible. On arrival, Sidonia found that the troops had been delayed by the Dutch Navy who blockaded the coast, stopping Parma sailing his barges along to Calais. Instead, Parma had to find an alternative route overland and was not expected to arrive for another week or so.

All through the next day, which was Sunday and with little time for mass, the crews were kept busy cleaning, mending, knotting and patching up. One of the ships, *San Pedro Mayor* [St Peter the Great] from the Urca Squadron, became one of two hospital ships. Badly injured men were taken from each ship and billeted there, or taken ashore to other medical centres. Onboard *San Martin*, men were being prepared for transport to the hospital ship, and Alfredo, was chosen as a stretcher bearer. He thought that this was a perfect opportunity for him to try and find his son, and one he could not resist. Along with others, Alfredo carried the casualties from the ship's hold onto the deck and secured them in the rowboats. The boats were then lowered into the water, and a small crew took them to shore, and the hospital ship moored on the harbour jetty. With so much activity in the port there was little time for armed escorts for the stretcher bearers. Once he had dropped off the casualties from the *San Martin*, Alfredo remained diligent at the port, watching for injured men to arrive from *Barca de Amburgo*. He kept asking all the stretcher bearers as they arrived.

'¿Eres de *Barca de Amburgo*?'

Time and again he repeated the question.

'Are you from *Barca de Amburgo*?'

He didn't have long to wait, and he quickly assisted their stretcher bearers by directing them onto the hospital ship. In the confusion, he easily mingled with them, and boarded one of the rowboats heading back to *Barca de Amburgo*. On board ship, and keeping a low profile, Alfredo slipped away from the returning men and quickly entered one of the holds. Juan Carlos and Paulo were too busy attending to Captain Mauritio when Alfredo came aboard ship. It was a very busy day, and all captains were summoned to a meeting at the town hall, so Mauritio had to look his best.

'Clean those buttons again boy!'

He shouted angrily at Juan Carlos.

'I have to look my best to meet the Duke of Medina-Sidonia.'

He postured exaggeratingly.

'Aye-aye Captain'

Juan Carlos replied obediently with a stifled sigh, then continued polishing the buttons as hard as he could. He and Paulo were relieved when Captain Mauritio eventually left the ship for the meeting, although he did look resplendent in his uniform.

The Renaissance period at that time was considered a "jewelled age" and it was expected that the Armada maintained the highest of standards when they invaded. The proud officers and noblemen aboard had every intention of looking their best when entering London as victors, and there was a lot of fine jewellery on show. There was also an immense hoard of treasure on the Armada, with thousands of gold and silver coins. The meeting was important to regroup the Armada, and to ensure all commanders and captains understood their duties, and were ready to sail as soon as the Duke of Parma arrived. As the meeting continued into late afternoon, those onboard ship either continued with the replenishment of supplies, carried out repairs, or used the time to get some much-needed rest. For many it was a chance to re-live the events of the past few days, and to remember their lost and injured comrades. A lull had descended on the fleet, and many began to question the validity of the mission. Sailors are notoriously superstitious, and bad omens and signs of ill-luck kept happening, and now the Spanish fleet had to wait for Parma to arrive, which was another bad sign. Also, they were anchored in the strong tidal currents of the narrow seas close to Calais – and positioned very close together, a sudden storm could cause serious damage.

Alfredo found himself in the hold where the mules were kept, and the familiar smells reminded him of home that he missed so much. He realised that it was time to look for his son, so they could slip off the ship and return home.

He decided to travel through France back to Spain as soon as it was dark. Alfredo used his anonymity as an ordinary Spanish soldier to wander through the ship. Slowly he made his way to the ship's cabins and waited on deck to see if Juan Carlos would appear. The deck was busy with men working, resting, or cleaning. Others were enjoying what food they could scrounge from the galley. Juan Carlos appeared with a bowl of fruit and bread for the officers on deck. Upon his return to the galley, Alfredo put his hand over his mouth and dragged him to one side. Juan Carlos struggled at first, but then saw that it was his father.

'Papa… what? How? Where did you come from?'

Alfredo put his finger to his lips.

'Shhhh quiet Juan Carlos, there is no time to talk… we must leave the ship now and go home.'

Juan Carlos was delighted to see his was father alive and safe, but he was not sure that he wanted to return home just yet.

'Papa… I cannot leave, I… I have my duties… and my friends are here.'

Alfredo did not want to argue with his son, but he was not going to leave him either.

'Juan Carlos, it is too dangerous now, and you must have seen some terrible things already… Trust me when I tell you that it is only going to get worse, it is safer and better to return home, so we are going now.'

He looked deeply into Juan Carlos' eyes.

'Son… I am not leaving without you… your mother misses you very much.'

Juan Carlos looked distraught but reluctantly agreed.

'If we must papa, but I will have to say goodbye to my friends.'

Alfredo understood this and looking over towards the setting sun, he replied.

'It will be dark in one hour, and then we will leave. I will be with the mules until you are ready to go my son.'

Juan Carlos left his father and returned to the galley. He did not want his father to get another beating and he reluctantly realised that it would also be safer for his father to go with him. Alfredo returned to the hold and waited, not sure if he had convinced his son to leave with him.

In the chart room Daval was talking to Paulo.

'I am surprised that your father has allowed you to come on this voyage Paulo. Did he not realise how dangerous it could be?'

Paulo was engrossed in the charts, trying to locate and memorise the different countries.

'My uncle told my father that we would only come here, to Calais, then he would leave me here until he had finished with the Armada. Tomorrow he is taking me to stay with someone he knows, then when he returns, we will go home to Hamburg … Look Daval… on the chart, here they are?'

Paulo pointed to Calais and then Hamburg on the chart, he was pleased to have found them. He continued trying to impress Daval with his skills.

'And here is England… it is very close to France Daval.'

Daval tried to reassure himself that Captain Mauritio had made the correct decision to bring his nephew on such a dangerous mission, but deep down, he knew it was wrong of his uncle.

Chapter 18
Fireships

August 7: As darkness fell, Alfredo waited impatiently in the hold by the steps leading to the deck. He was keen to get away as quickly and quietly as possible, he muttered to himself.

'Come on Juan Carlos... where are you?'

At that moment, banging on the side of the ship signalled the return of Captain Mauritio, and he climbed back aboard with a small crew of men and officers. The meeting was finally over and all ships were ordered to be ready to sail as soon as the troops had arrived. Alfredo was angered that something like this would happen, and crept further into the hold to wait for his son, still determined to leave the ship. Meanwhile Juan Carlos rushed into the chart room to see Daval and Paulo.

'Daval, my father has escaped and he is hiding on our ship, he is wants to take me home now... I don't want to go, but I have no choice and I have collected my things ... he is waiting for me in the hold.'

Daval of course was surprised but agreed.

'Si, mes amis you have to do it... he is your father and he has suffered greatly to find you.'

'But I want to stay with you and Paulo.'

Daval put a reassuring hand onto Juan Carlos' shoulder.

'I understand mes amis, but this is the best thing to do for you, your father and your family… please mes amis… go quickly.'

Juan Carlos then hugged Daval, and Paulo.

'I shall miss you both and I will never forget you.'

Paulo replied tearfully.

'I will miss you too mi amigo.'

Just as they were about to part… A loud and terrifying yell was heard by all across the harbour.

"Fireships!!!"

Once the Spanish ships were anchored at Calais, the English prepared eight unmanned ships loaded with barrels of tar, gunpowder and other flammable materials. They were taken across the Channel under cover of darkness, where a small crew steered the ships as close as possible. The fireships were set alight and sent in to cause maximum damage and confusion, and the crew abandoned them. Frantically, the Spanish tried to escape the blazing fireships, and they either raised their anchors or simply cut the ropes to escape. The Spanish fleet tried to unfurl their sails quickly, in order to get the momentum needed to sail out of the harbour and to safety. Exploding barrels of gunpowder added to the chaos, and blazing fireships lit up the harbour and sea walls. Leaping flames spread to some of the Spanish ships, and crews rushed to extinguish them with sea water.

'All hands on deck!'

Shouted Mauritio, as crew and soldiers grabbed as many buckets as they could to wet the decks and rigging, as they had to prevent any fires spreading to their ship. He was standing on the poop deck above the cabins, and he noticed Alfredo trying to enter the cabins to look for Juan Carlos.

'That man there!'

He bellowed, and Alfredo looked up. Mauritio pointed an angry finger at him.

'You there! Help with the anchor quickly.'

Alfredo could do no more than to follow his order, and he headed towards the bow of the ship to assist others with the anchor. Juan Carlos, Paulo and Daval appeared on deck. Mauritio bellowed again, still pointing and waving.

'Get to the buckets and slew the decks with water… Daval, assist the helmsman to keep us clear.'

Soldiers and crew rushed around in chaotic bewilderment to keep their ship clear of the exploding fireships.

Juan Carlos eventually found his father and tried to apologise for the delay, Alfredo was not pleased.

'Idiotica mi hijo… now we have lost the best chance to escape… next time you have to be ready.'

Juan Carlos left him to collect more sea water, but he knew how much he had upset his father.

Although none of the fleet were badly damaged by the fireships, it was enough to cause panic, and several ships collided. Many tried to leave the harbour, breaking their crescent shape and then sailing straight into a volley of fire from the awaiting English fleet. For many hours the English used their advantage of speed and wind to engage the Spanish. No longer in their protective crescent formation, the Armada fleet became more vulnerable to close-quarter fighting. But the English were very wary of fighting like this and for the main part, kept their distance. Yet the more experienced, quick-loading gunners, allowed the English to cause greater damage to both men and ship. All the time the winds were picking up as a heavy storm threatened.

The crews of those ships anchored outside of the harbour were frantically trying to pull up anchor, to set sail away from the escaping ships. The last thing they wanted was to be involved in collisions with their own fleet. At the same time, gun crews were preparing their cannons to retaliate against the enemy. Although they managed to fire several rounds at the enemy, none hit their target, as the English kept their distance and used their own longer-range cannons to cause as much damage as possible. As the night wore on, visibility became poor with smoke from fires and cannons obscuring targets and other ships. It was very difficult to manoeuvre safely, and the enemy added to the confusion by their continued bombardment. Eventually, all the ships from the fleet made it out of Calais harbour and into the open sea, albeit that many suffered some form of damage from the fireships, collision or enemy fire. It was going to be a long night for each captain and commander to regain control of the crescent format, which proved valuable for the safety of the Armada.

Chapter 19
Battle of Gravelines

The battle continued during the night and throughout the next day, where strong wind and currents caused the ships to drift towards the east of Calais, into the region of Gravelines off the coast of France. In rough seas, the battle lasted for more than eight hours, with great damage being done to the Spanish fleet. With the Armada scattered and dishevelled, the English piled shot after shot into the fleet. At close-range, some of the 60-pound cannonballs crashed through the five-foot-thick beams of the larger ships, causing physical mayhem to many troops sheltering inside. In complete disarray, the Spanish were unable to return fire due to a lack of trained gunners, and tried to out manoeuvre the enemy. Four Armada ships were sunk or left stranded at or near Gravelines; *Santa Maria Rata y Coronada* from the Levant Squadron; *San Lorenzo*, flagship of Don Hugo de Moncada from the Squadron of galleasses of Naples; *San Juan* and *La Maria Juan* from the Squadron of Biscay. Over a thousand men were killed and 800 men wounded. Surgeons, trained crewmen and soldiers worked frantically to save lives and to assist the wounded, and it was a bloodbath of terror for many. Similar chaos was happening onboard *Barca de Amburgo*, where many men were killed or wounded, as round after round of cannon fire crossed the fleet. Mostly stray shot hit their ship, but still caused damage to rigging, masts, hull and of course men.

Mauritio was steadfast on the poop deck trying to instil some kind of control and order during the barrage, and was constantly shouting his orders with his arms waving all around his body. It reassured the crew that all was not lost, and eventually their own gunners were able to return fire, often shouting and cheering when they hit back at the enemy. Mauritio, acting like a conductor in an orchestra, continued steadfastly.

'Clear the deck of that debris, and get the wounded below... put those fires out, and replace the rigging... quickly... quickly.'

Daval was experienced in battle conditions and took it upon himself to organise small groups of soldiers to clear the decks, and help the wounded. He also kept Alfredo, Juan Carlos and Paulo close by to assist him and to keep them safe as possible. Alfredo was not a seaman, but he knew how to work fast with his hands, and he worked well with the damaged rigging and ropes.

'You are a skilled man Alfredo.'

Alfredo grinned and nodded his head. Juan Carlos and Paulo kept filling the buckets for the surgeon, or assisting the crew with damaged rigging. Their arms and bodies were aching, but they had become a little more hardened to the horrors of blood and debris. Their sea-legs were getting stronger as they managed to balance against the stormy waves, causing the swaying ship to lurch constantly. Waves washed over the decks helping to clear the blood and debris, the smell of burning tar, timber and rope filled the air along with fumes of acrid gunpowder. Clouds of blinding smoke was everywhere and blocked out the sun time and again.

At the peak of the battle, El Muerto, who was organising gunpower and cannon shot for the ship, saw Daval in the thick of the chaos. He decided that another casualty of war would be understandable, and he carefully crept up behind him. As the ship lunged from yet another giant wave, El Muerto pushed Daval towards the side of the ship. Daval reacted instinctively and grabbed the nearest anchor point, but El Muerto had the advantage and was much too strong for him. Alfredo, alerted by Juan Carlos, grabbed a piece of wooden debris and smashed it onto El Muerto's back, knocking him off balance. It allowed Daval to fall onto the deck safely, but it took him a few seconds to recover. El Muerto got up instantly and drew a knife from his belt, and attacked Alfredo, who fought desperately, as he tried to fend off the knife, but he was struggling. Daval quickly regained his senses and was about to tackle the villain, when "bang!" a shot rang out of the chaos, and El Muerto slumped to the deck… dead. Daval and Alfredo looked at each other in astonishment as neither of them had a gun. Alfredo turned towards the cabin door, and saw Juan Carlos holding a pistol, with smoke emitting from the nozzle. 'Juan Carlos… you … you killed him!'

Juan Carlos knew that El Muerto did not like Daval, and he wasn't going to let him hurt his friend or his father.

'I… I… I had to papa. He was going to kill you and Daval … I had to do something.'

Alfredo hugged his son closely. 'You did the right thing my son… you saved me… I am very proud of you.'

Daval came over to them and took the pistol from Juan Carlos. 'Mes amis, where did you get the pistol?'

Juan Carlos, who was still in shock with what he had done, tried to explain. 'I… I know Captain Mauritio had pistols, and I know where he stows them. I … I had to do something.'

Daval and Alfredo looked at each other, then looked up at the sky to praise God for his timely intervention. They took El Muerto's body over to the area where other corpse lay, and covered him with a section of sail cloth that had been torn down in battle. Alfredo took Juan Carlos to his bunk to help him come to terms with what had happened, and he sat and hugged him waiting for him to recover. Captain Mauritio was at the stern of the ship trying to control a fire, and did not witness the event, but they were not sure if others saw what happened.

Later in the day, with clouds of heavy smoke acting like a thick fog, the English suddenly ceased firing, broke away from the battle, leaving the Spanish galleons to drift on alone. The wind had shifted, and in the teeth of a strong current that threatened to drive the rest onto the rocks, it was imperative that the fleet regained control. During the battle, the English suffered almost no damage at Gravelines, and although the Spanish lost men and ships, they still had the majority of their ships and men. They were still intact and effectively undefeated, bloodied but unbowed, even though the English commander thought he had "plucked the feathers" of the great Armada eagle. The Spanish commanders, were apprehensive about how long their fleet could remain battleworthy, but the majority of the officers and men were willing to continue the fight. All was not lost, and with Parma's soldiers they could still force their way across the Channel to continue the invasion.

Throughout the day, the Spanish fleet took stock of their losses, and began to regroup as best they could. An emergency meeting with senior commanders was held on board the *Sam Martin*. By evening, The Duke of Medina-Sidonia and Maestre Francisco Arias de Bobadilla, decided to abandon the quest of ending heresy in England, and to make their way up the North Sea. They would round the north passage of Scotland and steer west of Ireland, then head back to Spain. The signals were given, and the fleet headed for the North Sea to the east of England. Many of the soldiers and crews were angry and furious at this order as they wanted revenge for their dead comrades, and they voiced their opinions loudly.

'We are still too strong for the enemy, so why leave like this?'

'Spain is shamed and disgraced'

'We are sorely defeated'

'To fly like this, with many of our ships unharmed is a travesty'.

'The corpse of Santa Cruz, would have led us better than Sidonia'

'Why did Philip give his navy to such a fool?'

By this time the weather was getting worse, and heavy storms forced the Armada eastwards, making it virtually impossible to maintain the crescent formation. However, as the English had stopped harassing them for some reason, the fleet tried to regroup as best they could. Spread over many miles, the fleet struggled to maintain headway, let alone formation, and all the while they kept watching for the enemy coming out at them from ports along the east coast. Those nearest *San Martin* relayed messages to others who were lagging behind, and they were told that it was imperative that the fleet remained in close quarter.

Chapter 20
The North Sea

The Armada commanders discussed the option of going west and back along the English Channel, but it was thought to be too risky, as progress would be slow due to bad weather and strong westerly winds. Also, lack of speed would make them easy targets for the enemy who could pick them off at will. For the moment, they had to persevere through the present storm to reach the North Sea. The commanders decided to keep the fleet together as much as possible for security, and to assist each other with repairs. It was imperative that each ship was as made as seaworthy as possible.

So, men and crew were kept busy replacing timber, rigging and sail, to prepare the ships for severe weather, and it was thought that many of the ships were not suitable for such journeys. Some were riddled through with shot-holes, and floundered as they went along, while others were kept afloat by superhuman toil and effort.

As the seas became heavier, the winds shrieked about the masts and sails, causing timbers to groan and creak, and what sails they could use, flapped against their rigging and masts. The noise was deafening, and no matter how much the officers barked out their orders, no one could hear in such a tumult. Now and then huge waves broke on board, and a great rush of seawater came across the main deck, pouring through damaged timbers into the decks below, soaking the crew and supplies. Although crews worked frantically to carry out repairs, every wave caused men and materials to be scattered across the deck, and for many inexperienced men, it was a living nightmare.

At this point, the ships really began to struggle, and it was the weather, not the enemy that was starting to take its toll on the Armada. *São Mateus* and *São Filipe*, part of the 12-strong Portuguese Squadron, lost their battle with the elements as they ran aground between Nieuport and Ostend in Belgium. The disharmony remained strong amongst the men, and many reiterated their thoughts.

'Now we have lost more ships and men to the weather.'

'It would have been better to continue with the invasion… the English only had a few ships.'

'With Parma's men, we could've invaded England quickly.'

'Somebody should do something about this travesty.'

Senior officers tried to quell the disturbances and break up the disruptive instigators. Mostly, the weather and sheer exhaustion kept everybody else too busy to argue about the decision.

The bad weather continued for many days, and knot by knot the fleet slowly made their way northwards. By now the crews were exhausted from working on the great ships in heavy seas, having to trim the sails and rigging to suit the conditions. Many men had to stand firm in the spindrift of the storm to work the ropes, whilst others spent muscle splitting hours toiling at the bilge pumps.

They had no suitable clothes on board for working and living in such harsh conditions. They left Spain with the idea that in the Invincible Armada, they would have simply had a grand and victorious journey to England.

On board *Barca de Amburgo*, as on many ships, priests gave last rites to those casualties close to death, and then performed burial rituals to those who had already lost their lives. The corpses were wrapped in sail cloth then weighted, before ceremonially cast over the side of the ship. Captain Mauritio and his officers, along with Paulo and Juan Carlos attended the ceremonies, standing as firm as they could against the swell of the cold, unforgiving seas. Whilst working with the crew, Daval and Alfredo talked.

'I think that your son has learned a valuable lesson Alfredo?'

Looking pensive, Alfredo replied.

'I too have never been to war, but I realise how dangerous it is, and how easily lives can be lost. I think he will be pleased to go home now... With the grace of God that is.'

Alfredo stared at the ceremony taking place, and the storm seemed to ease slightly as the corpses were cast overboard.

'I have you to thank Daval, for looking out for my son... I don't think he would have got this far without you.'

Daval gave a Gaelic shrug of his shoulders.

'I have seen many things mes amis, and fought many battles where only my wits have saved me. I know that Juan Carlos is a good lad and it was his quick reactions that saved my life... Don't worry mes amis, I will try to look out for you both until you can return to Spain.'

Later, when Alfredo found himself alone with his son, they talked.

'I really don't know why you left home without letting your family know Juan Carlos... You have caused a lot of worry, and many people have been looking for you. It was by chance that I found out that you were on this ship.'

Juan Carlos looked sheepish and sad at the thought of upsetting his mother.

'When I think about it now papa, I know that I should have

said something, but there didn't seem enough time as the ships were leaving, and I know you would not let me go. Then when I met Paulo... everything seemed more exciting than ever.'

Alfredo tried to understand, and did not want his son to worry anymore.

'Well now that I have found you again... I am not going to let you out of my sight, and as soon as an opportunity comes along to return home... then we must take it.'

Juan Carlos had learned many things during his time at sea, and his father could see that his son was becoming a young man. Yet the position they were in was not a good one, and Alfredo wondered if either of them would make it home alive. Alfredo attempted to cheer his son a little by asking about Paulo.

'So, how come Paulo is on this ship? Are his parents worried about him too?'

Juan Carlos did not know everything about his friend, but he explained as much as he could.

'Captain Mauritio is his uncle, and he was only taking Paulo to Calais... so he was never going to be involved in the invasion of England. After the invasion he was to be taken back to his home in Germany... Hamburg I think.'

Although Alfredo thought that the reason for Paulo being there was strange, he nevertheless, accepted it. For the rest of the day Alfredo and his son continued to reaffirm their bond.

Onboard *San Martin*, Sidonia held another meeting to discuss their situation, and after several heated exchanges, a decision was made for the fleet.

'Because of the extended route we are now facing, and that food supplies taken in at Corunna have turned out to be far shorter than expected, the order will be signalled to reduce all food rations forthwith.'

Following disgruntled mumbles and groans, the commanders eventually all agreed.

'Half a pound of bread, half a pint of wine, and a pint of water, will be the daily ration now till we get back to Spain, or have the luck to meet with friends upon the coast of Scotland and Ireland.'

The meeting ended, and signals were sent out immediately to the other ships. In daylight using semaphore, consisting of a pair of handheld flags, rods, disks or paddles, they conveyed information via signals that was encoded into messages. Guards were to be stationed at each store location to deter looters, and any man caught would be severely punished. A few days later, a patache, which was a light, two-masted sailing ship used for coastal surveillance, appeared with a mutilated corpse swinging from her yard-arm. It ran down the side of *Barca de Amburgo* as she passed. A herald called to the ship to ask what it was about, and a voice boomed back. It was the corpse of Don Cristobal de Avila, who had disobeyed the sailing orders. The Duke had given positive command that all vessels were to follow his, and if any captain disobeyed, they would be hanged. The smaller ship was trying to sail into the nearest port to carry out repairs, but it was stopped and severe punishment handed out as a warning to others. Everyone on the deck of *Barca de Amburgo* stared at the lifeless body, and many thought it to be yet another bad omen.

Another man, Captain Francisco de Cuellar, from the *San Pedro* of the Castille Squadron, was also accused of possible desertion, and for sailing too far in front of *San Martin*. However, he was transferred to another ship, *La Lavia* from the Levant Squadron, where Captain Martin de Aranda, who was also the Judge Advocate gave him a stay of execution, but he had to remain on board *La Lavia* as his punishment.

Worse was to come, as slowly the fight against the storm began to scatter the fleet over several miles, and most of those onboard ship was entering unknown and perilous waters. Ships were blown offcourse to Germany, others drove on towards the islands of Holland and Zealand into the enemies' hands, others went to Shetland, and Scotland, where they were lost and burned. The majority of the fleet continued north towards Scotland, but a few held northwest, hoping to make Iceland and the Nordic fishing posts, regardless of the Duke of Medina-Sidonia's orders. Some ships had lost the use of one or more of their bilge pumps and had to reduce the ballast to gain buoyancy, which included the livestock. Mules and horses could be seen thrown overboard along with bulky non-food stock. Juan Carlos was distraught when he saw one ship running along next to them doing the same.

'No… no… what are they doing papa? Why are they throwing the animals overboard? I don't understand… it is too cruel.'

He sobbed into the arms of his father, who tried to comfort him.

'Son, it is either the mules or men that will lose their lives today. The storm has forced the captains to make very hard decisions to survive this terrible journey.'

Daval interjected to explain the reason.

'The ship is too low in the water and there is a danger that the storm will sink their ship… maybe their pumps are not working… it is the captain who must decide for each ship mes amis.'

Juan Carlos was beginning to realise just how terrible war can be, and his initial dreams of adventure was quickly fading. The strain was also beginning to have a psychological effect on some of the crew, with many hallucinating and seeing strange things. Many thought that curious seals swimming off the east coast, were actually people, or mythical beasts.

Chapter 21
Shipwreck I

After several days of arduous sailing conditions, the fleet eventually made their way out of English waters, into Scottish waters. Scotland was considered by many countries to be an ally of King Philip of Spain, as it would provide many advantages where both countries could benefit. It offered Philip both a convenient base from which to attack England, and also provide a potential successor to the heretic Queen Elizabeth. Spain considered her sister Mary, Philip's wife, to be Queen of Scotland and of England too. Although she seemed likely to die in captivity, her son was free, and the obvious heir to the dual crown. Clearly it would be worth the while of mighty Spain to pursue the friendship of insignificant Scotland, and to this end Spain was prepared to spend money, and provide a skilful military resource from both navy and army.

The Duke of Medina-Sidonia sent orders to sail to the north of Scotland, then go westwards to gain the Atlantic Ocean. He wanted the fleet to sail between the Shetland Islands and Orkney Islands, which was considered to be the safer passage. However, as the ships of the scattered Armada approached the northeast corner of Scotland, the skies darkened yet again. Soldiers and crewmen worked side by side to maintain an even keel as they approached the passage towards the Atlantic Ocean. As the storm grew stronger, its high winds and violent currents tried to push many ships towards the reefs of the two islands. For many ships within the fleet, skilful Spanish sailors proved their worth, and passed through the straits without incident. Unfortunately for one ship, it was not enough, and their luck ran out.

September 1: The crew fought hard against the storm, and everyone aboard *Barca de Amburgo*, used every sinew of strength and skill to sail the ship into clear water. On approaching the southeast headland of the Fair Isles, a small island directly between Shetland and Orkney Islands, the ship sailed too close, and the rudder was badly damaged on the rocks. Unable to steer herself out of trouble, the ship veered out of control, where wind and waves pushed her closer to the island. No matter how much Mauritio bellowed out his orders, there was nothing the crew could do, and the ship drifted closer and closer to the jagged rocks. Men could be seen heading for the rowboats in a desperate attempt to abandon ship, and hopefully survive the storm and the dangers of the reefs, whilst others simply jumped overboard and tried to swim to safety. Suddenly, the ship smashed against the rocks with immense force and came to a grinding halt. The rocks ripped open the hull on the starboard side, and the sea gushed in with unstoppable power. Below deck, men and animals were thrown to their deaths, and the ship began to sink lower into the water. On deck, the sudden impact meant that crew and soldiers were also thrown off the ship and onto the rocks, killing them instantly. High winds also broke sections of the masts, which came crashing down onto those men who survived.

When the ship first lost its rudder control, Daval told Alfredo, Juan Carlos and Paulo to secure themselves inside the captain's cabin. He quickly spoke to Alfredo.

'Mes amis, this is very serious and you do not have the

experience for what will happen. You must stay in the cabin for as long as you can, and secure yourselves with rope.'

As Daval was about to leave them, Alfredo grabbed his arm.

'Daval... thank you my friend... but what about you? What will you do?'

Daval shrugged his shoulders, but did not reply, then quickly went on deck. He made his way to the helmsman and attempted to secure the ship's wheel, although it was of no use. When the impact occurred, both Daval and Marcos the helmsman managed to cling onto the wheel which saved them from being thrown overboard.

For what seemed an eternal length of time, there was no sign of life, and the wind, rain and stormy seas continued to smash into the ship. Inside the captain's cabin, debris was scattered everywhere, and one of the broken masts had speared through the roof. A hand suddenly twitched back to life, as Alfredo gradually regained consciousness, and took in his surroundings. He had roped himself, Juan Carlos and Paulo to the large centre table, which was anchored to the floor of the cabin. When he was able to focus, Alfredo checked the boys for signs of life. As he touched his son, Juan Carlos opened his eyes, and as they were both so pleased to see each other, that they hugged for a few seconds.

'Are you hurt son?'

'No... no, I don't think so papa.'

As they untied the securing ropes, they looked at Paulo who was still unconscious, and they noticed that his leg was trapped against the table by part of the mast. Blood was oozing out of a nasty gash in his leg, and Alfredo tried to lift the obstacle off him, but it was too heavy. As he and Juan Carlos attempted to free Paulo, Daval appeared at the open door of the cabin, he was supporting Marcos, and both men looked dishevelled and bruised but otherwise unhurt, he asked.

'Is everyone alright?'

Daval quickly assessed the situation and noticed how quickly the ship was breaking up as it lay on the rocks.

'We must leave the ship now my friends, there is no time to lose.'

Alfredo was frantically trying to release Paulo, and called out.

'Daval… the boy is unconscious and trapped, we must free him before we can leave.'

Marcos picked up a large section of the broken mast.

'Here, use this to release the mast, then you can pull him out.'

Daval and Alfredo took the heavy piece of timber and used it as a lever to free the boy. Juan Carlos helped Marcos to pull the boy away, then Alfredo quickly wrapped a piece of cloth around the wound to stem the flow of blood from his leg. They grabbed whatever items they thought could be useful from the cabin, and with no time to spare, the group grappled their way out of the cabin, across the deck to the side of the ship. Daval and Marcos looked for the best option to escape, while Alfredo and Juan Carlos carried Paulo.

'There! Mes amis… look, one of the small boats is still intact.'

Daval pointed to the stern of the ship, and hanging over the edge was a single rowboat swinging from its securing ropes as it was tossed by the storm. Someone had tried to launch it but the mechanism had become trapped.

'Marcos, you and I will cut the boat free, then come back for the others, but we have to be quick… the ship could be gone soon,'

'Aye Daval, I hope the oars are still in the boat, otherwise it will be useless, and we will be smashed onto the rocks without them.'

Swiftly, Marcos and Daval attached a rope to the boat, and cut it from its harness, then they positioned it in the water where they could board it. Fortunately, two oars were still secured inside the boat and Marcos quickly untied them. When Daval returned to the others, three men appeared, two crewman and one of the soldiers. They were all badly bruised with many cuts to their bodies, and the soldier also had a broken arm. Everyone made their way to the side of the ship where the rowboat was waiting, and they climbed over the side and scrambled into the boat, as the waves, wind and rain hampered every step of the way. Once they were all aboard the boat, Marcos and Daval used all their skill and strength to row clear of the wreckage and head for the shore. The others huddled down as low as they could into the boat, so as not be swept overboard. Alfredo clung onto both his son and Paulo, who was alive, but unconscious. The skies were very dark, and the rain pounded into their faces, but gradually they battled through the ferocious waves. For what seemed an eternity, the little boat was buffeted by the wind and waves as it made its way to shore. As it hit the shallows, the able-bodied men jumped out into the cold water and dragged it clear of the water and onto the beach. When they were safe, the men collapsed exhausted onto the shore, and everyone remained motionless, too tired to move any further.

When daybreak came, the storm had eased, and the rowboat lay beached onto a small, shingle beach on the Fair Isle. Unconscious, Daval, Alfredo, Marcos and the crewman lay on the cold shingle with cold sea water lapping at their legs, whilst the others lay in the same state in the boat. They had given every ounce of strength they had left to survive, and only willpower was keeping them alive now. Daval was the first to regain consciousness, and he slowly tried to drag himself onto his feet. Suddenly, a large hand grabbed his shoulder and helped him up. It was the ship's surgeon who, along with approximately 100 men, had managed to survive the shipwreck.

'Ah! Frenchman … it is you… are you alright?'

Daval began slowly to comprehend his situation.

'Oui… oui, yes I am fine… but what of the others?'

As the surgeon helped him to his feet he answered.

'Your friends are ok and there are about 100 or more survivors… some of us abandoned ship into the boats before the ship crashed on to the rocks, and others tried to swim, but I am afraid that many… many died in the shipwreck.'

Daval looked over at the other survivors.

'What of the captain?'

The surgeon looked at him, and woefully shook his head.

'Unfortunately… he did not make it.'

Daval understood just how dangerous a shipwreck can be, and he tried to be positive and reassuring as he helped Alfredo and Marcos to their feet.

'Come my friends… we are alive, we must help the others and get to shelter quickly.'

When they made their way over to the little boat, the other men had regained consciousness and the surgeon was trying to secure the soldier's broken arm. Juan Carlos was awake and saw the surgeon.

'Sir… you have to help Paulo… he has a cut on his leg, it is still bleeding and he has not yet woken up… please help him.'

The surgeon finished putting a splint on the soldier's arm, then went over to Paulo. Alfredo raised Paulo's leg so the surgeon could get a better look at the wound.

'Mmm this is a nasty cut, and it must be closed to stop the bleeding.'

He reached into his shoulder bag that he always carried around his neck, and produced a needle and thread.

'Get me some water to clean away the dried blood, then I will close it.'

Immediately, everyone looked around for something that would hold the water, then one of the soldiers handed over his leather water bottle.

'Here use this… I grabbed it before we left the ship… it has fresh water in it.'

The surgeon washed the wound of dried blood so he could clearly see the cut, and his deft hand slowly placed neat stitches to close up the wound. Then he took a length of cloth out of his bag and wrapped up the wound.

'Hopefully he will recover, but there is always a danger of disease getting into the wound, but I will observe him closely.'

Alfredo carried Paulo over to some sheltered rocks, where the other survivors were trying to keep warm in front of several small fires. Using dry grasses and timber from one of the badly damaged boats, they used a flint to start the fires. They knew that the bitingly cold wind and water of the North Sea could quickly lead to death, so it was important to keep warm. One of the other boats was dragged closer to the biggest fire and tipped onto its side, so the injured could use the lea of the boat to shelter from the wind.

When everyone had dried out a little, they looked at their surroundings. The men realised that they were in a small bay, with cliffs leading up to a grassy headland. When they had fully dried out, Daval, Marcos and Alfredo along with ten of the other survivors, left the surgeon to treat the wounded whilst they looked for a route to climb the cliffs. They eventually found a narrow, but passable route, before slowly making their way up. At the top of the headland the wind was stronger, but it was a fairly clear day with a good horizon. They all pointed to the wreck of *Barca de Amburgo*, as it was slowly being eaten away by the waves crashing relentlessly into the ship's carcass. They strained their eyes for more survivors, but could not see any sign of life. Marcos looked further out to sea.

'Look… look out there on the horizon… a ship!'

Everyone focussed their eyes, and eventually they could all pick out the outline of a sailing ship. Daval reacted quickly.

'Find as much dry wood and material as you can and we will build a signal fire… hopefully they will see it.'

They searched in all the sheltered rocky crevices for drift-wood, straw, and dried grasses, then quickly built a large pile, and those with flints managed to light a fire. With more and more wood added, the bonfire was soon ablaze, and by adding wet grasses, smoke began billowing upwards by the strong winds. The wind took the smoke towards the ship, and everyone watched to see if it would turn its course towards them. They waited for what seemed an eternity, then Marcos shouts.

'Look! it's turning… I think it has seen us.'

When they were convinced that the ship had seen them, and that it was sailing towards them, the men climbed back down to the others. Alfredo immediately went over to Juan Carlos to see how Paulo was doing.

'Papa, he is awake… but he is not talking.'

Alfredo took one look at Paulo and could see that the boy was very pale and weak. He did not think that he would survive, but nevertheless he reassured his son.

'Don't worry Juan Carlos, I am sure he will be fine… we have seen another ship and it is heading this way. We have to get ready to row out towards them, because the ship cannot get too close to those reefs.'

Juan Carlos managed a smile and nodded in agreement, but he was still very worried about his friend. Alfredo carried Paulo to their beached boat, which was still intact, then he placed the two boys at the rear of the boat and tried to make Paulo as comfortable as possible. The other men inspected their boats and found that only three were seaworthy, and so they discussed their options. It was decided to use the boats to ferry back and forth to the ship, with the strongest men rowing, and the wounded to go in the first boats. They quickly prepared themselves and pushed the boats into the sea. The boats were rowed in single-file out of the bay, trying to keep clear of the rocks all around them. Daval, three men, the surgeon and Marcos were in the leading boat, along with Alfredo and the two boys. Injured men were in the other boats with four strong rowers to each boat. The rest waited on shore, and everyone hoped and prayed for a safe transfer onto the ship. Fortunately, the weather was good, and the sea-swell was slight, then after a few tense moments, they cleared the last of the obstacles into the open sea. Ahead of them, the ship was anchored in a safe location well away from the reefs. It was *La Trinidad Valencera*, part of the Levant Squadron out of Sicily, a Venetian merchantman that had been converted for the Armada. Square rigging and ropes were cast over the side of the ship for those strong enough to climb onto the ship. Daval and Marcos secured ropes to the rowboat so it could be winched up with the wounded. When they were clear, the men in the other boats did the same, and all able-bodied men clambered up the rigging onto the ship. On informing the captain that there were more survivors waiting to come on board, the crew of the ship lowered their own boats and headed to shore. By using all the rowboats, everyone was soon safely on board *La Trinidad Valencera*, and warm blankets were placed over the injured.

Captain Armando Abad greeted them onto his ship, he was a tall, thickset man, with straight, swept back black hair and a well-trimmed beard. Marcos told him what had happened.

'Captain, we lost our steering, and the ship was blown onto the rocks by the storm, there was nothing we could do.'

Daval added gratefully.

'We are very pleased to see you captain, but unfortunately many men… including Captain Mauritio have perished in the wreck.'

Captain Abad replied.

'Si señor, we saw your ship hit the reef last night, but we had to keep clear until this morning. We hoped there might be survivors, and we were pleased to see your signal.'

They all looked out towards the wreck, and were sad to see a fine ship meet such a terrible end. There was a thoughtful pause, then Abad continued…

'We have to proceed quickly through the straits to the Atlantic while the weather is good. As soon as your men are stowed aboard, we will get under way… For now, see to your wounded, then get yourself below for some food and dry clothes. We will talk later.'

As they separated, Captain Abad grabbed Daval's arm.

'Tell me my friend, you are not Spanish, and what was your role on the ship?'

'Si, captain, I am from France, but I have served many countries over the years. I was the navigator on board our ship… I know the waters around England. I can also speak English as well as good Spanish.'

Abad thought for a moment then replied.

'Ah… I see… Very useful… my navigator was killed at Calais, so it is good that you are aboard, you can help me set a course when you have rested … You and your friends can use the navigator's cabin and chart room, it will be cramped, but better than the hold'

Daval touched his forelock in acknowledgement.

'Thank you very much captain.'

Captain Abad went onto the poop deck to instruct his officers that they were to set sail for the Atlantic. His ship had also suffered damage from the storm and battle with the enemy, they also had many casualties, and men were recovering all around the ship. A little while later, all able-bodied seamen from the wreck were given their duties, and the badly injured men were taken into the hold to be cared for along with others. With everyone at their stations and a routed charted, *La Trinidad Valencera* continued on her way.

Chapter 22
Atlantic Ocean

The storm had caused the fleet to scatter, with many ships sailing for safer waters off Norway and Iceland. It was left to individual commanders to set their own course, and Captain Abad had decided to follow his last orders and continue around Britain.

With good daylight and a strong wind, the ship made steady progress through the strait and into the Atlantic Ocean. Captain Abad, with Daval's assistance, set a course that followed the north coastline of Scotland. Everyone kept lookout along the coastline for other Armada ships, as they too may have been wrecked and in need of rescue. Yet with calm seas, there was an easing of tension in the air, and many were pleased to be clear of the North Sea and England. The crew soon settled into familiar routines, and with extra crew available from the wreck, their work was much easier. Sightings of inquisitive whales kept men entertained for hours as they busied themselves with a routine of daily chores. However, the weather was much colder in the North Atlantic Ocean, and those crewmen gifted in sewing, manufactured capes out of old or damaged sails to keep the biting wind from their bodies. During the day, Daval, Captain Abad and his fellow officers inspected the state of the ship, and spoke about their next objectives.

'Daval, with so many men onboard ship we do not have enough supplies to make it to Spain… We will have to go into one of the ports soon.'

'Yes Captain, I understand. I will look at the charts, then report back to you.'

Daval headed to the chart room, whilst Abad continued the inspection with his officers. There was a sense of lethargy amongst the men, and it was decided to create various tasks to keep them occupied and healthy. Military officers organised exercises and competitions to keep their minds and bodies active. Sailors organised fishing lines, providing fresh food to supplement their meagre rations, and Juan Carlos was particularly pleased with that. A little later, Daval advised the captain that Thurso, on the north mainland of Scotland, would be the best port to use. With the captain in agreement, the ship sailed south, passing the islands of Orkney on their port side. After a few days, their ship approached the north mainland of Scotland, and not knowing what sort of reception they would meet, the captain ordered the officers in command to prepare their soldiers. He also made ready the ship's 48 cannons, as he did not want any surprises. By late afternoon the ship approached Thurso and slowly entered the bay.

Thurso was a fishing port with direct links to the Orkney Islands, it was nestled in a large bay, providing good shelter from the Atlantic Ocean. The inhabitants were mostly unaware of the Armada, and Spain's battle with the English, although there had been several sightings of fighting ships from its fishermen. Slowly the ship sailed into port and moored up along the harbour wall, and the giant ship towered above all the smaller fishing vessels. Armed and ready, Captain Abad and a small group of men prepared to leave the ship. Daval was with them to hopefully interpret and to tell them that it was a peaceful visit. The town of course, had no means to defend itself, should the Spanish attack, so it made an effort to be neutral, and a welcoming committee made their way to greet them. Daval approached the town's appointed leader and spokesman, then introduced the captain.

'Good day gentlemen, may I introduce Captain Armando Abad as the representative of his imperial majesty, King Philip of Spain.'

The townsmen were mightily impressed with the introduction, and welcomed them with open arms, and then one man stepped forward.

'Welcome… welcome to our humble port, I am the appointed Mayor of Thurso. We are pleased, and honoured to greet you to our small community, and we would like to help you in any way that we can. Pray tell us the nature of your visit.'

By this time a small crowd had gathered, curious to see the magnificent ship and its strange inhabitants. The crew also watched the proceedings from their elevated advantage points along the deck. Juan Carlos stood with his father and looked at the people with their strange clothes, which appeared to be much warmer than their own clothes.

Daval, on conversing with Captain Abad, continued.

'We would like to purchase some supplies for our ship, for which we will pay you handsomely for your kindness, then we will be on our way.'

A bag of silver coins was offered as a gesture of goodwill and intent, then Daval and Captain Abad waited whilst the townsmen discussed the request. The Mayor accepted the offer then replied.

'But of course, and we will provide you with as much as we can spare. Let me know what supplies you require and it shall be prepared for you… In the meantime, can we offer you some refreshments.'

Although Captain Abad did not understand the language, he could tell from the man's body language that all was well, and he acknowledge with a respectful bow. The Mayor led the way to a nearby inn, and Abad, Daval and the ship's senior officers followed the entourage. A prepared list was given to the spokesman, and the townsfolk scurried away to provide as much as possible.

Instructions were given to the innkeeper to prepare a feast for the strangers, and flagons of ale was brought to quench their thirst. As they sat around a large, round wooden table, a conversation began to which Daval translated. The Mayor queried...

'Can you please explain why our fishermen have seen so many ships pass by these waters recently?'

Before Daval could provide an answer, he went on...

'There have also been many rumours of a major conflict taking place in the south between Spain and England... is there any truth in this?'

Daval conversed with Abad, then replied.

'My Lord Mayor, it is true that there have been some issues with England concerning religious issues against the Pope, but we believe that Spain has no such issues with Scotland.'

Abad tapped Daval on the arm to add more information.

'Many of our fleet experienced extremely bad storms, and it was decided that the safest passage was in Scotland's waters. Unfortunately, our supplies have not lasted as well as we would have liked, and so we have come to you to purchase fresh supplies so that we can complete our journey.'

As the Mayor conversed with his fellow dignitaries, Daval continued.

'As soon as the supplies are on board ship, we will sail at the next tide.'

Following what appeared to be a few disgruntled comments between the townsfolk, the Mayor replied.

'We understand, and as you say… Scotland has no such religious issues with Spain. So please, gentlemen, let us enjoy a meal together as two friendly nations, and then we will wish you a safe and speedy passageway back to Spain.'

Ale was drunk and cooked fish was served with fresh vegetables and warm bread. For two hours the meeting continued under very diplomatic circumstances with neither party wanting to disrespect or antagonise the other.

Back on board *La Trinidad Valencera*, instructions were given for everyman to remain on board ship, and guards were posted at the main access off the ship. However, a dozen men were made available to bring on board the supplies when they arrived, and they waited impatiently on the harbour wall. With fresh medical supplies running low, and Paulo not responding very well to treatment, the surgeon asked the senior deck officer to be allowed to see the town's physician. After heated discussions, the officer finally agreed, so the surgeon and Alfredo carried Paulo on a stretcher, whilst Juan Carlos walked by their side. As soon as they reached the solid ground of the harbour, Alfredo and Juan Carlos felt very strange as they walked.

'What is happening papa? I… my legs feel strange.'

Alfredo laughed as he explained to his son.

'Juan Carlos… your legs have been on a moving ship for too long and now on firm ground you feel strange. It happened to me on the island when I first walked up the cliffs. Don't worry, it will pass.'

They were guided to the town's physician who was a kindly, older gentleman who could speak a little Spanish following many years as a ship's surgeon. The ship's surgeon explained the nature of their visit, and gave the physician a small bag of silver coins. They placed Paulo onto a bed, and the physician examined him closely. The physician's wife was there to remove the bandages and tried to comfort

Paulo, who kept slipping in and out of consciousness. She spoke concerningly.

'The poor wee laddie, he is in an awful state.'

The physician prodded and poked at the wound and could tell immediately that it was serious.

'I'm afraid that if we don't cut his leg off, then this laddie will not live much longer.'

The surgeon agreed immediately, and turned to speak to Alfredo.

'It is as I feared my friend, his leg is diseased, and we have to cut it off or he will die.'

Juan Carlos overheard this and ran out of the room crying. The surgeon continued...

'I don't think he will survive the journey back to Spain, it is a very dangerous journey and a test for even a healthy man... I think he stands a better chance of survival by staying here.'

Alfredo took in the information and thought for a while.

'Si... I understand, and now that his uncle, Captain Mauritio is dead, then the boy's father must be informed. When I return to Spain, I will try to find him... I think he is a merchantman, so he should be able to come for him.'

The two men spoke to the physician as best they could, and it was agreed that Paulo would be better off staying in Thurso.

'Until he is stronger, my wife and I will take care of the boy. There are many good folks in this town, and we will find him a good home.'

While his wife stayed to comfort Paulo, the physician arranged for all the medical supplies to be taken to the ship. Juan Carlos returned to the room and remained with Paulo until it was time to leave, and the physician's wife tried to comfort him too. On returning to the ship, they were greeted by many people from the town who had brought all the supplies that they had requested together with many other items. The womenfolk had rallied round when they saw how cold the crew looked and brought hundreds of items. Warm, heavy knitted sweaters and hats were donated, along with blankets, waterproof coats, boots and gloves. All the gifts were gratefully accepted, and on makeshift fires built along the harbour, and with tables quickly placed, the whole crew were treated to a meal of cooked fresh fish, shell food and vegetables, washed down with flagons of ale. It was a good morale booster for the men, so Captain Abad decided that the ship should remain in port until the next day.

The festivities went on into the evening with music, dancing and singing sea shanties by both crew and townsfolk. Although the language was difficult for long conversations, everyone understood each other. Daval was at the centre of a large group of towns folk as they were keen to learn more about the events in England.

'We have heard that Spain had sent a very large fleet of ships to invade England, but they were defeated… is that true?'

'We have heard that the Queen will be executed along with all the members of the protestant church… is that true?'

Daval tried to be as diplomatic as he could.

'Unfortunately, the very bad weather bad forced the ships of Spain to alter their course, and so there was no time for any invasion or executions… All we are trying to do is get back to Spain safely.'

Others interjected.

'Are you aware that the Queen of England has ordered all Spanish sailors and soldiers to be captured and killed… whenever they are found?'

Another added.

'Yes… I too have heard about that, and you should know that there are many Lairds in Scotland that wish to please the Queen of England, and they have been sending out troops to capture and kill anyone from Spain.'

With that information, Daval quickly left the conversation and reported back to Captain Abad. Upon hearing of the potential danger, the captain made a decision.

'Alright… thank you for telling me. We must get everyone aboard the ship, and post guards through the night. At first light we will sail.'

A flurry of activity occurred, as men responded quickly to the order. The harbour party was cleared, and with everyone on board, Captain Abad and Daval spoke to the Mayor.

'Thank you very much for your generous assistance with our supplies, and for the kind reception you and your people have given us. But we must prepare the ship for departure as soon as it is light.'

The Mayor seemed a little perplexed as to why the celebrations had ended so quickly.

'But you are welcome to stay a little longer if you wish? The town has been pleased to meet you, and we would really like to learn more about your country.'

Captain Abad hinted to Daval that they must get back to the ship, and so he translated his best wished to the Mayor.

'Thank you for your hospitality, but we have a long journey and so we must get ready to sail.'

They left the Mayor and his entourage standing on the harbour, as they boarded the ship. With everyone on board, the crew began to raise the walkway from the harbour.

'Wait! Wait! I have to fetch my son.'

Alfredo ran quickly to collect Juan Carlos from the physicians, but he was reluctant to leave his friend. The physician and his father tried for several minutes to persuade Juan Carlos to leave.

'I will find Paulo's father and he will send a ship for him… don't worry Juan Carlos, because Paulo is in good hands here with the physician.'

Eventually, Juan Carlos agreed to return to the ship, and he left with his father for the harbour, as soon as they boarded, the walkway was dragged aboard and secured. The ship moved away from the harbour and into the bay to wait for dawn, and armed guards were positioned throughout the ship in case they were attacked.

Chapter 23
Scotland

September 10: Having left Thurso safely behind, *La Trinidad Valencera* continued on a clear and safe passage heading for the northwest corner of Scotland, and the Cape of Wrath. Progress was slow due to a strong westerly wind, and the ship had to tack against the wind to make any momentum. Everyone on board was kept busy trying to respond to Captain Abad's orders, by adjusting the sails to get the most out of the wind. He insisted on a keeping a tight ship and wanted everything to be in good order before they reached Ireland. He knew from experience that the weather in that region could be very dangerous, and he wanted both ship and crew to be ready. However, food rationing was better proportioned, and spirits were beginning to return to the crew following their stopover. Even the wounded seemed to be recovering better, and everyone hoped for a good and safe return passage to Spain. For many it felt good to be sailing home, and to get away from the strange and dangerous seas around Britain.

Whilst working on navigational charts in the cabin, Daval and Alfredo spoke quietly.

'Mes amis, you have come a long way to find your son, and you have seen many things… so, do you wish you had stayed on your farm?'

Alfredo smiled a little.

'Yes, I wish I could've stayed on my farm because I enjoy working with nature, but I had no choice. I did not think of myself at all, and I only wanted my son to be safe… I could not return home to tell my wife that I could not find him.'

Alfredo in turn, asked Daval about his life.

'Tell me my friend, why is a Frenchman fighting for Spain?'

Daval laughed.

'Ah! It is a long story, but for me, I found myself working on many ships because I enjoy sailing to different countries, I have enjoyed the comradeship, and I have seen many beautiful places.'

Alfredo tried to imagine and understand.

'But surely it is a dangerous life too?'

'Of course, it is, and I did enjoy that side of it in the beginning, but now? I think that I am running out of luck, so maybe it is time to find a quieter life.'

'Well, my friend… you can always come and work on the farm with me and Juan Carlos.'

They both laughed out loud at the thought.

'Maybe, but I think that is too quiet for me mes amis, but I would like to visit your farm one day.'

'So, what will you do when we return to Spain?'

'Ah! I will return to France, I have a brother in Bordeaux, and he has a beautiful vineyard… and then? I don't know really… we will wait and see.'

Captain Abad came to see Daval, and Alfredo left them to discuss the proposed route around Ireland.

'Daval, we have to be careful going to the west of Ireland because it is prone to sudden storms and fierce westerly winds. The coastline is riddled with dangerous rocks and reefs.'

'Yes captain, I understand… I have sailed these waters before… I agree that they are very dangerous.'

Abad, looked out of the cabin door, peered at the skies, and rubbed his chin.

'Mmmmm! It all depends on the weather for a safe voyage, but we will prepare the ship for the worst, and pray to God for better… I have an uneasy feeling in my stomach.'

Suddenly, one of the crewmen yelled out from the lookout post perched high on one the masts.

'Ship ahoy!'

'Ship ahoy! On the port bow.'

Excitement spread across the ship, and those on deck-watch trained their field glasses towards the call's direction. Another ship appeared, coming out of one of the many inlets along the north Scottish coastline, and it looked to be in good condition under full sail. *Napolitana* was one of the sturdy Urca supply ships from the Squadron of Galleasses of Naples. Like *La Trinidad Valencera*, it had gone ashore to carry out repairs and replenish supplies. Its lookouts signalled to *La Trinidad Valencera* in recognition, and heaved-to so they could come along side. Heralds spoke to one another, and it became clear that both ships were in good order after repairs and purchasing supplies, and they were very pleased to be sailing back to Spain with another ship. Captain Pepe Luis Perez of *Napolitana* was a big strong man, in his mid-forties, clean shaven and handsome. Using semaphore, he and Captain Abad, decided on the best route to take, and plotted their course accordingly. Keeping a safe distance between the ships, they sailed close to the coast of Scotland following key marker points along the way.

Meanwhile, inside the cabin that they shared with Daval, Alfredo and Juan Carlos ate a small meal as they sat on a single bunk together. The wooden cabin creaked as the ship moved, and a single oil lamp rocked back and forth on the ceiling hook. Juan Carlos had opened a box containing the ship's navigational instruments, and talked about Paulo.

'Son, I know you are upset about leaving him behind, but with his injuries... it would have been foolish to take this journey... I am afraid he would have died.'

'Si, papa... I understand... but we have become good friends and I did not want to leave him there alone.'

'I could not let you stay Juan Carlos... think of your mother... what could I have told her?'

'I know papa... ... it... it's just...'

He could not finish his answer, and instead tried to distract himself by looking at the ship's instruments.'

Alfredo noticed how skilful his son had become in putting together some of the items.

'Wow! Juan Carlos, you seem to know what you are doing... who has been teaching you?'

Juan Carlos could not help but smile at the thought of his father being pleased with him.

'Oh! Daval showed me and Paulo how to use some of these things... we really enjoyed it.'

On thinking of Paulo again, Juan Carlos became solemn, and to distract him, his father showed interest in the equipment.

'Tell me ... what is this thing for?'

Alfredo picked up the compass rose in an effort to distract his son from thinking of Paulo. It worked, and Juan Carlos became keen to explain.

'It is called a compass that helps the navigator know where north is, I think it uses something called a magnet, which always points to the north. Although we haven't really tested it properly.'

For the next few hours, Alfredo and his son enjoyed each other's company looking at all the instruments, and Juan Carlos told his father everything that Daval had shown him. Alfredo was pleased to have his son close to him, and prayed that they would make it back home to the farm and their family.

September 14: As the ships reached the Western Hebrides, strong winds began to stir up the sea into giant waves, causing each ship to rock unpredictably. Earlier, each crew had made ready their ship by securing all supplies above and below deck, and were now trying to trim the sails in an effort to keep their ship under control. The waves built up higher peaks and deeper troughs, causing the ships to rise and fall violently, sending heavy spray onto the beleaguered crew. Below deck, soldiers crammed themselves into the holds, each one trying to find a secure anchor point with which to combat the erratic, swaying motion of the ship. By the time they had reached the Isles of Lewis and Harris, heavy rain was falling, making the decks slippery and dangerous. Although the ships tried to maintain a similar course, each crashing wave against the hull caused another adjustment for the helmsman to make. It wasn't long before the ships began to drift apart, just as the main body of the Armada did when first it entered the North Sea. For what seemed like hours, the ships battled against the wind and the waves in an attempt to maintain their course. Upon reaching the Isle of North Uist, the skies darkened as storm clouds gathered, blocking what little daylight there was, and bringing nightfall earlier than was due.

September 15: Although the storm had not fully reached its peak, the weary crews fought night and day against strong westerly winds trying to keep their ship under control. Sailing past the Isle of Barra as night fell, both Captain Abad and Daval realised that they were heading into open sea before reaching the north coast of Ireland.

'Are we going to try and ride out the storm captain?'

Clinging onto the rail of the poop deck with the poop lantern highlighting their anguished faces. Abad thought long and hard as to what his decision should be.

'We have lost sight of *Napolitana* and I am not sure what the captain will do.'

Daval tried to reason with Abad.

'There is a chance that they will head for a safe haven at one of the islands to the east of us. The charts showed large bays to the lea of the storm which could be the safer option to wait out the worst of the weather… Maybe we should go there too?'

Captain Abad considered the options.

'No Daval, I think we should cross the open water and head for Ireland, there are safe inlets there too. Then we will ride out the storm until it is safe to go on. I think it is better to be on the open sea at the moment.'

'Aye-aye captain.'

Although Daval agreed, he was not sure if it was the best option as the other islands were much closer.

Meanwhile, the captain of *Napolitana* had decided the opposite, and made for the Isle of Islay. His ship was having problems with its bilge pumps, which needed to be repaired due to the amount of sea water coming aboard. As it approached the island, a light could be seen from another ship. *La Trinidad de Scala*, a converted Genoese merchant-man from the Squadron of Levant. It had taken shelter from the bad weather earlier in the day. The crew went ashore for fresh water from streams, and bartered for fresh meat from farmers in the area. Like many of the Armada ships, it was separated from the main fleet due to bad weather. Its rigging was damaged, and most of its crew had fallen ill due to a lack of fresh food or disease. The ship's lookout warned the captain of *Napolitana*'s approach, and he realised that it was yet another wayward ship of the Armada. In turn, the

Napolitana made a course to sail towards the other ship, and quickly realised that it was in a more sheltered location out of the storm. So, it dropped anchor nearby and the crew furled the sails, before making their way to the relative shelter of the ship's hold. All both ships could do now… was wait for the storm to abate.

Chapter 24
Shipwreck II

September 16: As *La Trinidad Valencera* headed south towards the northern coast of Ireland, the storm became even more violent. The sky was black and the sea began to whirl and foam as the storm gathered its terrifying momentum, creating great swirling, powerful waves that threw the ship around with ease. The great poop lantern had been left unlit in order that its glare had no chance to dazzle and mislead the straining eyes of the drenched watchers on deck. As they kept lookout for dangerous reefs, the crew strove to pierce the gloom, and strove in vain… before a blue flash of lightning showed them swift glimpses of the dreadful path ahead. They were powerless to control the seething waves along which their devoted ship was being driven, and *La Trinidad Valencera* headed unerringly towards the snarling rocks off the coast of Ireland. They could only assume that the same fate had happened to *Napolitana*.

Marcos and the ship's helmsman doubled up at the wheel, in a combined effort to guide the ship away from danger, but it was of no use as the waves were too large and powerful. The ship was now at the mercy of the storm, and as if by an unseen hand, it was being thrown onto the rocks. Priests prayed for a favourable intervention which would save lives, some men took comfort from being with the priest, whilst others prepared themselves for the worst. Alfredo and Juan Carlos anchored themselves in their cabin, as did everyman aboard ship.

'Sailing in these waters is too dangerous for any man Juan Carlos, and I pray we survive yet another wreckage… We must be ready to act quickly, so gather only what you can carry and we will stay together… no matter what happens tonight.'

'Si papa… I thought fighting the enemy was very bad, but being in these storms is very frightening.'

Alfredo clutched his son into his arms, as they waited for their fate. Everyone onboard was not sure where the ship would end up, and those from the last wreckage could only imagine a fate as bad, if not worse than that. Everyone clung on for dear life as the ship bounced over the waves with increasing speed, closer and closer to the shore, then a call came out for those on deck.

'Make ready the boats… prepare to abandon ship.'

Captain Abad made a judgement call to abandon ship as close to land as possible, and he sent his officers into the holds to prepare the men. The officers yelled the order for all to hear.

'Head for the boats as quick as you can… leave everything, and save yourselves.'

A flurry of activity saw man after man scramble out of the holds and onto the deck. The ship's crew were trying to untie the boats from their anchorage, but the heavy rain, spray and winds threw the men all around the deck. Some had to cling onto the rigging and rails to stop themselves from being washed overboard, and yet one or two were thrown over the side and into the cold Atlantic waters.

With seconds to spare the boats were hauled into the sea with men jumping, falling or clambering into them. Desperately they tried to use the oars to prevent the boats from being capsized. Alfredo and Juan Carlos tried to board one of the boats, but Juan Carlos was too small to get passed any of the men, as they were much too big and panicking to get off the ship. Alfredo decided to search for Daval to see what he could do, and they found him trying to control the ship's wheel with Marcos. Captain Abad was with them trying to give advice about the ship's course, but there was no visibility through the giant waves as they washed relentlessly over the bow. With a mighty crash and crunching of timber, that splintered as if it was made of matchsticks, the ship came to a juddering halt on the rocks in Kinnagoe Bay, Glenagivney, Donegal, Ireland. Those still on deck were thrown forward by the sudden impact and landed in a crumpled heap across the deck, but apart from a few cuts and bruises, everyone seemed to be alright. Somehow the ship found the only bay with fewer rocks, and the ship remained upright. Although badly damaged below the hull, it remained intact, and ran aground just a few hundred yards from a soft, sandy beach. Yet, it was slowly being dragged into deeper water by the storm, which was still raging.

By the time everyone on board had gathered their senses, Captain Abad had assessed the situation, and barked out his orders.

'Quickly men, gather up the wounded and make for the shore.'

He then grabbed the arm of one of the officers in charge of the soldiers, and had to shout to make himself heard against the din of the storm.

'Gather as many men as you can and arm them, we have to treat these shores as hostile, and so we have to be prepared.'

The officer understood immediately and began to organise those men still on the ship. They gathered weapons, gunpowder and shot from the nearest hold, and passed them over the side into the men standing in shallow water. Although the depth of the water was neck deep, the men were able to wade to shore with equipment and injured. Gradually, the row boats had also managed to make their way to shore, and everyone was very grateful to be alive as they dragged themselves and the boats onto the beach.

Daval and Marcos approached Abad.

'Captain, we have had a look at the ship, and we don't have much time before it sinks into deeper water.'

Abad made his own assessment.

'I understand, but there is something we must do… come with me.'

The three men followed Abad to his cabin, and inside a heavily locked storage cupboard, he brought out a foot-long chest. Placing it onto the table, he opened it.

'This is the treasure chest that each ship was been given to pay for the invasion. For crew, soldiers, materials, food… or anything else the Armada needed to establish itself in England.'

He sighed a little before continuing…

'But now we might have to use it to survive or bribe our way off this land… Also, I don't want the enemy to profit from finding it.'

Daval and Marcos had never seen so much gold and silver before, all held in linen bags. They managed to restrain showing their excitement enough to help the captain stow them into three leather satchels, together with a pistol in each bag.

'It belongs to the King, so you must keep this a secret, or there will be many men trying to steal it… it could be our only way back to Spain.'

Each man carried a satchel and went back on deck, where the storm continued to batter the ship. The hull was slowly being ripped apart by the movement of the waves, tide and strong winds. The noise of splintering wood echoed through the ship, which was sad for the captain to hear. Eventually, all men made it to shore, taking what shelter there was from the nearby cliffs. The ship remained visible, but was being relentlessly pounded by ferocious waves as the night wore on.

September 17: By dawn, the storm had eased but the heavy rain remained, and the men huddled together for warmth, sheltering wherever they could. Although soaked to the skin, most of the men wore the waterproof clothing supplied by the people of Thurso, whilst others wore makeshift capes. Small fires were lit against the cliff face, but were kept small so as not to attract attention to their location, yet it allowed clothing, powder and food supplies to be kept dry. Some of the men had salvaged a little food and water before they left the ship, and it was being issued to those who needed it. Surgeons worked their way through the men checking for any major injuries, and helping others where they could. The rowboats were assessed for damage, and prepared for launching back into the sea, as soon as a ship was sighted. There was nothing to do but wait, and everyone watched the ship in silence as it slowly disintegrated, slipping deeper into the water.

Daval and Marcos approached the captain who was talking with other officers, trying to form a defensive position. Daval handed the two satchels full of treasure to the captain for safe keeping, and three armed guards were placed around them.

'Captain, this is a similar situation to the last time, and we should go to the headland to look for other ships... Hopefully *Napolitana* has survived the storm and could be looking for us.'

'Si, Daval... take some men up to the headland and let

us pray that they find us. I am not sure what the Irish will make of us when we are sighted.'

'Aye-aye captain, we will take weapons with us in case we meet any resistance.'

Daval, Alfredo and Juan Carlos, together with 20 armed men, set off to find a path up to the headland, whilst Abad and his officers discussed tactics for protecting themselves and getting off the land as safely as possible. When they reached the furthest point on the headland looking out towards the ocean, the men gathered as much dry grasses, twigs and wood as they could to set up a signal fire. Some men searched the horizon for any signs of a sail, whilst others looked inland for signs of danger from the inhabitants. They waited, hoped and prayed that they would see something soon, but they didn't want to light the fire too soon, in case the enemy sighted it too.

When word of the Armadas' fate reached Dublin, Queen Elizabeth issued instructions to her government minister, Lord Fitzwilliam. He was to issue a proclamation from Dublin Castle which was to reveal, by its severity, the alarm felt by the English, and that it was expected of Ireland to facilitate in the capturing of all enemy men, equipment and vessels.

The instruction read:

"We authorise you to make enquiry by all good means, both by oaths and otherwise, to take all hulls of ships, stores, treasures etc, into your hands; and to apprehend and execute all Spaniards found there, of what quality soever. Torture may be used in prosecuting this enquiry."

Almost immediately, soldiers on horseback were dispatched to patrol the coastline in search of ships and possible survivors.

At Islay

Although the storm had ceased, the incessant rain remained, with light winds causing uncomfortable working conditions. Crew and soldiers emerged onto the deck from each ship, to inspect the damage and to get some fresh air away from the stinking holds. Captain Adelardo Garcia of *La Trinidad de Scala* was one of the older men of the Armada, but with many years' experience, he was short, stocky with thick grey hair and beard. He used one of the rowboats to join with Captain Perez of *Napolitana*, and when he had climbed aboard, he was informed that Captain Perez was in the chart room.

'Well captain, we both managed to escape the worst of the storm. Do you have much damage to report?'

Captain Perez looked up from the chart he was studying.

'No… no señor. We had a little issue with the bilge pumps, but they are working again… The main issue now is to try and locate *La Trinidad Valencera*, which is the ship I was sailing with when the storm hit us.'

'I see… and do you think it has survived the storm?'

'I hope so because I think Captain Abad is a fine sailor, and knows these waters very well… I am sure they are looking for us too. We both agreed that it would be best to sail together.'

Captain Perez, completed his study of the chart and suggested a course.

'We should set sail for Ireland immediately, and hope we meet up with them. Follow my course captain, and watch out for other ships from the fleet… until last night, I did not know about your situation, so maybe there are others.'

'Certainly captain, we will follow your lead… let us hope we get as many ships and men back to Spain as safely as possible.'

Perez acknowledged.

'Aye-aye to that captain.'

As soon as Captain Garcia reached *La Trinidad de Scala*, the ships prepared to leave the safety of Islay, and set course for Ireland. By the time they had sailed into the Atlantic Ocean, it had gone from a raging torrent to passable swell within a few hours. Although heading into a strong westerly breeze, the ships took full advantage of the calmer weather as they tacked across to Ireland.

When they reached the waters off the north coast of Ireland, more lookouts were posted in search for ships, wrecked or otherwise.

Chapter 25
Ireland – Kinnagoe Bay

Lookouts posted by Abad's soldiers were positioned at the highest point along the cliff to look for any signs of a potential threat from the military. Although Ireland had a positive Catholic inhabitant, the Protestant Queen was in ministerial command, and therefore posted the biggest threat to their safety. As they trained their field glasses across the countryside, one man saw something.

'Sir… men approaching on horseback from the south.'

The officer took the field glasses to get a better look at the distant movement.

'Ah, yes. I see them, and they are headed this way. Go and warn Captain Abad.'

One of the soldiers quickly made his way back down to the beach, to where Captain Abad was inspecting the condition of the men.

'Captain, soldiers on horseback have been seen heading this way.'

Abad, was angry that they had been discovered so quickly, and could only assume that the wreck of his ship was seen by locals and reported to the nearest authority. He looked for someone to run to Daval, and pointed to one of his men.

'You there, run to the headland point and alert our men

up there that we have been seen, also... Find out if they have sighted any ships from the fleet.'

Abad was hoping to make their getaway as soon as possible, so they did not have to incur any further conflicts that could lead to the loss of his men.

Within minutes, the Irish soldiers arrived at the bay. There were about 40 heavily armed men, and from their vantage point on top of the cliffs, they immediately saw the shipwreck in the bay and the survivors.

They opened fire at Abad's watch party as they made their way back down to the beach, and one man fell in the first salvo. The soldiers on the beach took cover behind rocks then returned fire. For the next few minutes, the gun battle continued, with loss of lives from each side. Daval and his team was on the western side of the bay, which stood out further into the Atlantic Ocean. Upon hearing gunfire, he left Alfredo and Juan Carlos to keep watch for the ships, then led the others towards the gunfire. The runner sent by Abad caught up with them, and panting hard he informed.

'The... the... there are soldiers attacking us... and the captain wants to know if you have seen any ships.'

Daval went a little closer to see if he could create a crossfire to deter the attackers, upon his return, he told his men of the plan.

'Follow my lead and keep low, we have to get as close as possible... and do not fire until I tell you.'

They all nodded in agreement and followed Daval in single file. An undulating countryside, together with ample bushes and reeds, gave Daval and his men a little cover as he approached the Irish soldiers, and his men took position with a good view of the enemy. The Irish soldiers were shooting down at Abad, and therefore left their flank exposed, Daval took full advantage and opened fire.

At least five Irish soldiers fell immediately with two

more badly wounded. Their officer, alarmed at the ambush, reacted by taking his troops back towards the horses. Daval's men kept firing, and although they killed one more soldier, the others got away.

'Damn! That means they will be back with more men.'

When they were convinced that the soldiers had gone, Daval led his men down towards Abad.

'What's the damages captain?'

Abad, pleased to see Daval, replied.

'Four men killed and three wounded… Did you kill all of the enemy?'

'No captain… they managed to flee, and I know they will be back with more troops.'

Abad continued.

'And what of the ships? Any sightings?'

'No captain… not yet… But I have left Alfredo and his son up there to keep watch.'

Two hours later, Alfredo appeared at the top of the headland and shouted as loud as he could.

'Ship ahoy! Ship ahoy!'

Everyone looked up and could see him pointing out into the ocean. From the beach, Captain Abad could just make out two sailing ships on the horizon, and he reacted immediately to give order to his officers.

'Get the injured to the boats and take as many men as you can in each boat. The rest of the men can wade out as far as possible and take cover behind the rocks in the sea… it is our only chance.'

On the headland, Alfredo lit the signal fire, whilst Juan Carlos fetched wet grass for smoke. Alfredo paused, and looked inland, as he saw the Irish soldiers returning in force, and the signal fire was not yet big enough. They had to stay to ensure the ships saw their signal, and so he called down to the men on the beach.

'Soldiers! Soldiers are coming.'

Daval heard the call and looked across to the other side of the bay, where he could see movement on the clifftop. He turned to Abad.

'Captain… the soldiers have returned. Head for the ships.'

Abad and his officers reacted immediately and set up a rear guard to defend themselves whilst the men got into the boats. Daval assessed the situation for Alfredo and Juan Carlos.

'Captain… Alfredo will not make it to the beach… I will go to help them find another escape route.'

'But Daval, you will be killed before you reach them.'

'I have to try captain… I think there is enough cover for one man not to be seen.'

Grabbing a couple of pistols, Daval set off up the cliffs in an attempt to reach Alfredo. He used the bushes and shrubs as cover, but the Irish soldiers were getting ready to fire.

Back on the headland, Alfredo and Juan Carlos could see what was happening, but could do nothing about it.

'I wish I had taken a firearm Juan Carlos… we are completely defenceless.'

'Papa, we are not… I have my bag… look!'

Juan Carlos opened the sack bag he always carried with him, as it contained what little belongings he could salvaged. Yet he also had the small leather satchel where Mauritio kept his pistols.

'Look papa… I took this bag when we left our ship… I am sorry, but I really like the pistol…there were two, but one must have fallen out in the shipwreck.'

Alfredo grabbed Juan Carlos and kissed him on the head.

'Well done son… you did the right thing, here let me load it.'

The Irish soldiers were too busy firing at the men on the

beach to notice the signal fire, so Alfredo and his son kept watch in some bushes. As they waited, Alfredo finished loading the pistol and began to look closely at the leather satchel.

'What else did Mauritio keep in here, I wonder.'

Alfredo searched the bag and discovered a small pocket in the side of the bag that was very difficult to see, as it had been held closed by a few very neat stitches. He was amazed when he broke the stitches with his knife and looked inside.

'Wow… Juan Carlos… did you know about this pocket?'

Juan Carlos looked into the bag.

'No papa, I have only tried to keep the pistol clean… because it is so pretty and feels good to hold.'

Alfredo opened a linen pouch containing several gold and silver coins, and there were also several coloured stones.

'Juan Carlos… there is a lot of money here. He carefully replaced the pouch and place the satchel around his own neck using the straps.

Out at sea, *Napolitana* and *La Trinidad de Scala* had seen the wreck and the signal fire, and anchored as close as they could to the shore. Using their field glasses, the captains assessed that there were many survivors stranded on the beach, so they sent out as many rowboats as they could. They also saw that they were being attacked by soldiers, and the ships came about broadsides to line up their cannons. Yet they could not be sure that their aim was accurate enough to distinguish between their own men and the enemy. Captain Perez, on board *Napolitana*, signalled to Captain Garcia to elevate the pitch of the cannons to fire over the heads of everyone, and hopefully it will create a diversion for their men on the beach.

On the beach, the Irish soldiers were firing volley after volley at the stranded men, and although Abad was returning fire, they were taking too many casualties. Suddenly, the ship's cannons boomed, and their shots whistled overhead, landing about 20 metres over the clifftops. This caused panic in the ranks of the enemy, and they ceased fire, as their officers tried to assess their situation. Meanwhile, the lull allowed Abad to get his men into the boats and row out towards the ships, though there were still many men stranded on the beach, and he urged them on.

'Hurry men, get moving before they regroup and fire again.'

The ships cannons continued to fire volley after volley to create a valuable respite for the stranded men, allowing many to escape, but they were not sure how long they could fool them.

Daval also used the disruption to sneak past the soldiers in his effort to reach Alfredo. Then a shot rang out from one of the soldiers, and Daval slumped to the ground.

'Daval! Papa… papa… we must help him.'

Juan Carlos was about to jump out of the bushes and run over to his friend, who was only a few yards away. Alfredo stopped him.

'No Juan Carlos… there is nothing we can do for him… we will be captured if we try.'

Almost instantly, two soldiers ran to Daval and grabbed him, but Daval had only been grazed on the head by the shot and had quickly regained consciousness. He tried to fight the soldiers, but they were too strong and they wanted him alive. Alfredo took careful aim with the pistol and fired, and one the men dropped to the ground. Reactively, Daval grabbed the other soldier and stabbed him with his knife, and then ran over to Alfredo where they hid for a few moments. The remainder of the Irish soldiers did not see or hear Daval's altercation, as the noise from the cannons masked their gunfire. However, it did not take the Irish soldiers long to realise that the cannon fire was only a distraction, and they resumed their attack on the men on the beach. Yet the distraction was enough for Abad to get most of the men off the beach and into the waiting boats, although they had to leave many wounded or dying in their haste to escape.

As soon as it was safe, Daval, Alfredo and Juan Carlos fled from the headland and headed west, keeping the contour of the cliffs in sight. They ran until they were sure the soldiers were not following them, and eventually they paused for breath in a sheltered spot away from the stiff westerly breeze. A small brook trickled down the hillside nearby, falling into a larger stream that wound its way to the sea. Alfredo attended Daval's headwound, and cleaned the wound with the water. He managed to stop the bleeding, but Daval's head was pounding.

'We should rest here Daval… drink some water and I will go up the hill to see where we are. Juan Carlos, stay with Daval.'

Both Daval and Juan Carlos were pleased to rest and they collapsed onto the soft grass by the stream. Alfredo took the pistol and climbed the hill, keeping as low as he could so as not to be seen. From his vantage point on the hilltop, he could see nothing but open grassland, shrubs, trees, and a few farmers crofts scattered around the countryside, and there were no major settlements, towns or cities within sight.

'Good.'

He thought, as it meant they could move more quickly without being seen. Then he slowly returned to the others, drank some of the cool water and laydown on the grass.

'It looks clear Daval with no major buildings to be seen… If we stick to the coast, then I think we can make good time to the next bay, and then look for a ship.'

Daval, having rested a little replied.

'Si mes amis, but there will be soldiers everywhere, and

we must be careful. We cannot be sure that they are not looking for us, and when they find the soldiers we have killed… maybe they will try to track us down.'

In silence, Daval and Alfredo thought about the predicament they were in.

Back at Kinnagoe Bay

Captain Abad and his men eventually reached the ships, and crewmen helped them on board. The rowboats were then raised and safely stowed into position, and those boats from the stricken *La Trinidad Valencera* were cast adrift. Captain Abad found himself on board *Napolitana* where Captain Perez greeted him.

'Come to my quarters captain, and my crew will see to your men.'

Abad gratefully accepted and the two men went to the captain's cabin to discuss the events. Warm clothing was given to him while a mug of hot mulled wine was ordered from the galley.

'Please captain, take your time and get out of those wet clothes. We will then discuss everything.'

Pleased to be inside familiar surroundings again, Abad changed into the warm clothes and sat with Perez at a round table in the centre of the cabin.

'I am afraid we lost about a dozen men today, and I think about 20 others were taken prisoner… I don't know what will become of them.'

Perez rubbed his chin and thought for a moment.

I don't think it will be good, because Ireland is controlled by Elizabeth… I fear they will be shot or hanged captain.'

Dismayed, Abad drank the warm, comforting wine, and added.

'I hope that is the last casualty we suffer on this unbelievable journey. I think everyone just wants to get home now.'

'True captain, I agree, but these waters are some of the most treacherous seas I have ever met… I don't think it has finished with us just yet.'

Abad suddenly remembered Daval.

'Captain one of my best men and his colleagues are still on land, and I hope they have not been captured. He was trying to get his friends to safety when the soldiers arrived… We must stay in the area for a while and keep a sharp eye open for them, because I know he will try to return to us… he is a good man.'

'I understand captain, but it is a longshot… nevertheless, we will set a watch to lookout for them. We will remain in the area for two days, but if the bad weather returns, then we must set sail immediately for sheltered waters.'

Chapter 26
Ireland – Buncrana

September 18: Having fallen asleep at the foot of the hill, Daval awoke. Shaking his head and rubbing his eyes, he was unsure of where he was and if he was injured, and only when he touched his headwound, he remembered what had happened. He got to his knees and peered through the bushes, and in the distance, close to the cliff edge he could see horsemen. He placed his hands over the mouths of Alfredo and Juan Carlos, who were still sleeping. As they woke up, Daval put a finger to his lips.

'Shhh! Be very quiet mes amiss... there are soldiers over by the cliffs, and I think they are looking for us. We must leave now... follow me.'

The group kept low and made their way around the hill to the south. Using bushes, reeds and anything else for cover, they slowly made distance between themselves and the soldiers. Heading inland, in an effort to keep clear of the soldiers, the group found themselves at a small village where stone crofts surrounded a small church. Daval spoke with Alfredo.

'This looks like a Catholic church mes amis, so I will try to find the priest who could help us.'

'I will come with you Daval.'

'No... no Alfredo... I am French and not Spanish so they

will not suspect me. I will fool them into thinking I am a pilgrim trying to get back to France.'

Reluctantly, Alfredo agreed, and he and Juan Carlos, remained hidden in the bushes until his return. Just as Daval was about to leave, Alfredo gave him some silver coins from the leather satchel.

'Daval, take these coins… it may be of help.'

Daval was at first amazed, and then wondered where and how he had so much money. He was about to question Alfredo further, but Alfredo interjected.

'Never mind my friend… I will explain later.'

Daval scanned the area to ensure it was clear, then warily approached the church, and opened the main door. Inside, a priest wearing a heavy woollen ryasa, or cassock, was kneeling in front of the altar. As he entered the church, Daval's footsteps echoed off the stone floor and the priest flinched his head slightly at the sound. The priest calmly genuflected, stood up, then turned to face him and spoke in a local Gaelic language. Daval replied in English.

'I apologise for intruding upon your prayer father.'

The priest, a man of medium height and medium build with grey swept back hair, was a little surprised at both the manner of this person and the unfamiliar accent, and he answered in clear English.

'Ah! My son… you are not from these parts, and clearly, from your accent, you are not English either.'

'You are correct father, I am just a simple Frenchman trying to make my way home, but I am a little lost and would appreciate if you could direct me to the nearest sea port.'

The priest was initially wary of the stranger, but as he appeared to be an educated man and not a vagabond, he directed Daval accordingly.

'Follow the track south and it will take you to the port of

Buncrana, which is a small fishing village. They might be able to assist you further.'

The priest was beginning to suspect that the stranger had more to explain than he was suggesting.

'But... for some reason, I think you need to be there sooner my son, as it is a two day walk from here... I have heard rumours of Spanish ships being found along the coast, and there have been many soldiers looking for their crew.'

Daval was trying to think quickly and was not sure how much to reveal. He took out the silver coins and offered them to the priest.

'Father... it is true... I and my friends were on one of the ships that ran aground, but we are not part of the Spanish navy... we... are just trying to get home... Please take this money as a token of our gratitude for helping us.'

The priest looked at the silver coins, and assessed if the man had an innocent and honest nature, or was indeed part of an invasion army. Satisfied with the former, he beckoned Daval to follow him.

'Come with me my son.'

The priest took him to the rear of the church, where a tethered mule was lazily eating hay, and next to the mule was a small cart.

'Go and fetch your friends and I will take you to the port myself... no one will stop us.'

Daval beamed with gratitude and ran off to collect Alfredo and Juan Carlos. By the time they had returned, the mule was harnessed to the cart and several sacks were placed in the back for them to hide under, but when the priest saw Juan Carlos, he was shocked.

'Oh my... he is just a boy! Why is he here? Was he on the ship?'

Daval did not have time to explain everything.

'It is a very long story father... we thank you for your help, but we really need to get going.'

A few minutes later the cart set off for the port of Buncrana, and Daval, Alfredo and Juan Carlos hid under the sacks, praying that they would not be discovered.

The journey itself was uneventful, but by the time they reached the Catholic church on the outskirts of Buncrana, there was a lot of activity, and troops were everywhere. The priest drove the cart to the back of the local church and warily spoke with Daval.

'My son there are many soldiers looking for you and I fear it is not safe for you here.'

Daval spoke quickly with Alfredo then turned to the priest.

'Father we have no choice and we must get to the harbour where we might be able to secure passage on a boat.'

He hesitated to reveal much more information but continued.

'There are Spanish ships off the coast waiting for us, and if we can sail, or row out to them we will be safe.'

The priest thought for a moment, then looked at Juan Carlos.

'Stay where you are and I will take the cart down to the harbour, you may be able to secure a boat with my help. I know many of the fishermen and their families, as all of them are Catholic, and many of them do not like the English ways and their harsh rules.'

They continued through the town to the harbour, and as it was the priest driving the cart, the soldiers paid no heed to him. A few minutes later, the priest drove the cart to the rear of an inn close to the harbour. He told Daval to stay hidden whilst he went to see the innkeeper, both Daval and Alfredo kept looking out of their cover in case any soldiers appeared. When the priest returned, he ushered them quickly out of the cart and into the inn. The innkeeper led them into the cellar, and then liaised with the priest to ensure they were not seen. In the cellar, the priest conveyed the conversation he had with the innkeeper, who was a large man with a heavy growth of beard, and wore a black leather apron over simple working clothes.

'My son, the innkeeper has agreed to help you, and he has told me that fishermen have seen your ships out on the ocean, but the storms have also caused many to be wrecked onto the rocks, with many killed or captured by soldiers patrolling the shore.'

Daval listened closely and relayed the important parts of the conversation to Alfredo.

'The innkeeper has also seen one of your smaller ships in the harbour yesterday, he believes the crew wanted to shelter from the storm, but unfortunately there was a fight with the soldiers, and about a dozen men were captured… but the rest were killed. They were taken to the coaching inn stables nearby awaiting transport to Donegal Castle in the morning.'

When Daval told Alfredo the story, Alfredo covered his eyes to mask the tears that was welling up in them, he knew that many of the men would have come from simple families like theirs. Daval placed his hands on Alfredo to comfort him.

'I am sorry my friend, but where there is war, there are always losses.'

Alfredo regained his composure a little.

'Is there anything we can do for them? Are they close by?'

Daval was torn between the easier option of escaping immediately and the more difficult option of trying to appease his friend by attempting a rescue. The latter of course, would be much more dangerous for everyone, so he turned to the priest for advice.

'Father is there anyone who could find out more about the captured men? We would like to help them ... if possible.'

The priest looked very worried at first, and having considered if there was anyone he could trust, but not endanger, he concluded.

'I will go myself to ensure that the men are safe, and offer my spiritual guidance. I am sure the guards will allow it'

When Daval explained to Alfredo what the priest was willing to do, he hugged the priest warmly.

'Thank you, Father... Thank you.'

Over the next hour or so, they waited nervously for the priest to return, and Daval was busy thinking of a plan to rescue them.

'The only advantage we will have mes amis is surprise, but we have to act quickly, and hope there are not too many guards.'

A little while later the priest returned, and the expression on his face was not what Daval was hoping for.

'The guards would not let me see them, but your men are locked inside one of the brick stables at the back of the coaching inn, and there are at least eight guards watching them. Two at the stable door, and the others are sitting at a table outside the inn which overlooks the stable, they are all armed with guns, pistols and swords.'

Daval thought long and hard as he tried to think of the best way to free their comrades.

'We need a distraction... something to take the soldiers sitting at the table away for a few seconds.'

'Father, how many entrances are there into the stables?'

'There are two that I can think of my son. The main entrance where the coaches pass through, and a side entrance for bringing supplies.'

With the help of the innkeeper and the priest, Daval

drew a plan of the coaching inn on the wall with some chalk. Then he explained the plan.

'We will need a small barrel of gunpowder with a fuse, which will be positioned outside the coaching inn on the street. Alfredo and I will wait at the side entrance. When the gunpowder explodes, it should distract the soldiers enough for us to secure the guards and release the men.'

The innkeeper looked at the priest and talked about the plan. Then the innkeeper replied.

'It could work… I will gather some men and we will get the gunpowder and light it on your signal.'

Alfredo studied the plan, and although he knew nothing of military tactics, he also agreed that it could work. Daval continued.

'We will wait for midnight, when the streets should be empty. When everyone is in position, I will give you a call like this.'

Daval placed his hands over his mouth and gave a shrieking call of an owl in distress, which was very loud. Everyone agreed that it was a good and clear signal. Daval was also pleased with his effort which he learned as a boy growing up in southern France.

'But for now, we need to know more about the ship in the harbour… Can you take me to see it?'

The innkeeper agreed, and making sure Daval wore the clothes of a local fisherman, they went to the harbour. When they arrived, the ship was pointed out to him, although Daval recognised it instantly and acknowledged his approval with a "thumbs up" signal, and they returned to the inn. He spoke to Alfredo.

'Mes amis, we are in luck because it is a Caravel which is a very fast ship, that is good and simple to sail.'

Daval spoke with the priest to make final arrangements, and Alfredo gave him another three silver coins which was to be given to the innkeeper for his troubles.

'I understand my son, and when you release your men, the innkeeper will lead you through the back streets to the harbour. I hope you succeed and that nobody is badly injured.'

The priest left them and they tried to relax as much as they could until midnight. Juan Carlos looked a little bemused.

'What shall I do Daval?'

Daval looked at Juan Carlos and replied.

'You should stay with the innkeeper, and when we free the men, we will all go to the harbour. Then you must release the securing ropes whilst your father and I prepare the sails.'

Fresh clothes were brought for Alfredo and Juan Carlos to also look like fisherman, and they waited nervously for nightfall.

At midnight, the priest returned to take Daval and Alfredo to the rear entrance of the coaching inn. Through a crack in the door, Daval could see the two guards in front of the stable, and the other soldiers were sitting further away, enjoying some free ale that the innkeeper had arranged to hopefully "dull" their senses. The gunpowder had been positioned, and when midnight came, Daval gave the signal and the fuse was lit.

'Boom!'

The street became full of smoke and fumes as the soldiers staggered to their feet to investigate, and ran through the entrance to the street. The guards in front of the stable door prepared their weapons and took a few steps towards the ruckus, and at that moment, Daval and Alfredo knocked out the guards with wooden clubs. They quickly lifted the heavy wooden bar securing the stable door, went inside and untied the prisoners, who were surprised but pleased to see them.

'Come quick… we are from the Armada, and you are free… follow us to the ship.'

The men did not need asking twice, and quickly ran out of the stable. The weapons were taken from the two guards and they followed Daval and Alfredo through the streets led by the innkeeper and Juan Carlos. As they reached the harbour, they could hear the shouts from the soldiers when they discovered the plot. Daval knew that they would be heading for the harbour too.

'We have no time to lose… release the mooring ropes and get on board.'

Fortunately, some of the men were part of the crew and knew exactly what to do, and within a few minutes the lateen-rigged sails were hoisted, and the breeze began to take the ship away from the harbour. Almost immediately, the soldiers ran onto the harbour and opened fire at the caravel, but they had to take cover as the men on the ship returned fire. Alfredo also fired at them using Daval's pistols. Soon the caravel was heading along the estuary for the open water of the North Atlantic Ocean. When they were sure that they were safe, one of the men came to Daval.

'Señor, muchas gracias… we thought that we were going to be executed tomorrow, but you have saved us… But how did you know about us, and where did you come from?'

Daval concentrated on steering the ship, but replied, 'It is a long story mes amis, but we too had to escape when our ship was wrecked. We were looking for a ship to join the fleet, and a kindly priest told us about you.'

The man looked bemused.

'Are you French? Your Spanish is good, and I don't know how you found us, but we are very pleased that you did, and we owe you our lives.'

Daval laughed.

'Si, mes amis, I am French, but I was the navigator on one the Armada ships until it was wrecked.'

As they reached the open sea, everyone gave a huge sigh of relief to have escaped from Ireland. Daval allowed the crew to sail their caravel again as he and the others kept a lookout for the two ships.

Chapter 27
Armada Reunion

September 20: Around midday on board *Napolitana*, Captain Perez and Captain Abad talked about the possibility of sighting Daval.

'I think it will be very difficult for your man to get away, as my men have seen many soldiers patrolling the cliffs.'

Abad paused before he gave his answer.

'Yes, I agree… it will be very disappointing if he cannot make it, but he is worth waiting just a little longer captain.'

Captain Perez looked up at the darkening skies, and worried that time was running out.

'I think the weather will have the last word today my friend. Look at those clouds.'

Abad looked closely at the grey clouds and agreed.

'Si, I think another storm is coming, and the sooner we can get back to more familiar waters the better.'

Captain Perez, ordered for signals to *La Trinidad de Scala* to make ready for sailing south. Upon the return signal of acknowledgement, the crews busied themselves releasing the sails.

'Sail-ho off the port beam.'

A cry came from the lookout, and field glasses were immediately trained to the direction of the call. Far in the distance, several sails were sighted coming from the north, and more came into view as the minutes ticked by. Although many ships of the Armada had been scattered across the North Sea and Atlantic Ocean, there still remained approximately 70 to 80 ships trying to sail home with *San Martin*. Although unclear as to why they arrived so late in the area, the sight of so many ships were pleasing to the eye, and as soon as the crew saw them, great cheers rang out around the ship.

'Hold fast the sails.'

Captain Perez called to his crew to stop them from unfurling the giant sails. They decided to wait and greet their commander, and to be part of the Great Armada once more.

'Sail-ho off the port bow.'

Again, field glasses were trained to the direction of the call, and a single sail could be seen heading towards them at speed, and as the ship drew nearer, Captain Abad laughed loudly.

'Ha! Ha! Ha! I knew it… I knew Daval would make it… he is one hell of a sailor for a Frenchman.'

The Caravel pulled alongside *Napolitana* and its sails were lowered and secured, a line was attached to the small ship so it could be towed at the stern of their ship, then everyone clambered aboard. By the time they made their way to the poop deck, the main fleet was fast approaching. Captain Abad greeted Daval with a great hug.

'Your timing is impeccable Daval, just look at the welcome committee for you.'

Abad pointed towards the main fleet, and Daval laughed along with the crew of the Caravel.

'Yes captain, it is a wonderful sight to see so many ships again… I thought that they had all perished in these terrible waters.'

'God works in mysterious ways my friend, and although

we have lost many good comrades and many fine ships, more lives have been saved, as you can see.'

Abad introduced Daval to Captain Perez, who ushered him into his cabin for a debriefing. Inside the cabin, Perez poured out glasses of brandy as they sat around the table. Abad could not stop smiling at Daval, and was keen to learn how he made it back safely.

'Tell me Daval, where did you find the other men?'

Daval paused to enjoy the rich flavour of the brandy, and the sudden warmth it felt as it slipped down his throat.

'It was pure chance captain, and thanks especially to one particularly friendly priest who helped us escape. He also helped us free the men, because they were going to be hanged the next day.'

He paused to take another sip of brandy which was beginning to warm his whole body.

'Their caravel went into port for shelter during the last storm, and they were attacked and captured... but thanks to the priest and the local innkeeper, we managed to release them... and so here we are.'

Captain Perez could immediately tell from Daval's almost flippant answer that he was someone special, a man who thought nothing of risking his own life to save others.

'Señor... Spain owes you a gratitude for saving its citizens, and when we return to Spain... it shall be mentioned.'

As the men enjoyed their brandy, a crewman came into the cabin.

'Captain, we have received a signal from the *San Martin*... you have been requested to go on board for a meeting.'

The men got up from the table and prepared for the meeting, and as he was leaving the cabin, Daval suggested.

'Captain... please use the caravel as it is perfect in these waters and much safer than the rowboats.'

'Good idea Daval, please inform the crew to get it ready for us.'

Daval went below deck to the galley where he met the crew from the caravel talking with Alfredo and Juan Carlos. Marcos was also there as they re-lived their tale. Everyone was huddled around the galley fire enjoying the warmth, much to the irritation of the cook.

'Amigos… the captain wants you to use your caravel to take him to the *San Martin*. They are having a big meeting today.'

The men nodded in agreement and prepared to make ready the caravel. Daval and Alfredo looked at each other with a relieved expression, that they had come through yet another harrowing ordeal. Alfredo passed Daval a cup of wine they were given, and including Juan Carlos, Daval made a wish.

'Let's hope we can enjoy a safe journey back to Spain mes amis.'

They drank the wine and laughed as Juan Carlos spluttered his out, because he had swallowed too much, and Alfredo patted his back.

'It's alright my son… you deserve to drink the wine, because you have been very brave.'

Marcos, on a more sombre note said.

'Daval, I thought we had seen the last of you, and although Abad insisted on waiting for you… we all thought you had been taken prisoner or worse.'

'It was a close call mes amis, and if it was not for the Catholic priest… then I think that we would have been killed.'

'Si mi amigo, Alfredo has told me all about him. It has convinced me that God is still looking out for us… in a strange way.'

They laughed and drank more wine, then Daval gave a quizzical "look" to Alfredo to ensure that the silver coins were not mentioned. Alfredo returned the "look", with a slight shake of his head in acknowledgement that he didn't.

On deck, the crew were busy preparing for Captain Perez and Captain Abad to disembark for the *San Martin*. They both looked up at the troubled skies as they went aboard the caravel.

'It's not looking good captain… The last time I saw clouds like that we were in trouble.'

Abad reluctantly agreed.

'Si captain, this stretch of water can produce some of the worst storms I have ever seen. We must inform the Duke and get back as soon as possible.'

With good haste, the two men were taken over the short distance to the *San Martin*. On board, the only other captain to attend the meeting was Captain Garcia from *La Trinidad de Scala*. After initial greetings, everyone made their way to the large captain's cabin of the *San Martin*. The Duke of Medina-Sidonia addressed the men.

'Be seated gentlemen and let us begin, because the weather is closing in again, and you will be needed back on your ships.'

As the men sat down, fresh wine was issued along with bread, cheese and a little fruit. The Duke continued…

'Now, as you know, bad weather has cast the fleet far apart, with many ships taking different routes to this location. For ourselves, we managed to keep most of the fleet together by going as far north as possible before coming around. We deliberately kept clear of the treacherous waters along Scotland's coastlines and islands. Unfortunately, for yourselves, that was not the case. Please explain, and most of all… tell me your experiences when on land of both Scotland and Ireland.'

Captain Abad was the first to explain his misfortune, and experiences.

'My Lord, I am Captain Abad of *La Trinidad Valencera* from the Levant Squadron, and we made our way through the straits between Orkney and Shetland Islands. Following one of the many storms that we encountered, we went to the aid of *Barca de Amburgo*, from the Urca Squadron, who was unfortunately wrecked at the Fair Isles. We rescued some of the crew from the wreck… but unfortunately, Captain Mauritio, along with many others, did not survive. We then set to port on the north coast of Scotland for repairs and supplies, where we found the local inhabitants to be very friendly. However, there was a danger of those loyal to the English Queen, would inform her soldiers, so we did not stay long.'

As he paused, The Duke interjected.

'So, captain, in your opinion… you believe that there are those in Scotland that could be supportive of Spain and his majesty King Philip?'

Abad continued…

'Si my Lord Duke… I believe there are many who would support our cause. Yet… not so in Ireland, where we ourselves ran aground following a storm. There is a lot of influence from the English Queen there, and she has many who would lend their troops to hunt our countrymen down… Fortunately, we too were rescued, by Captain Perez here from *Napolitana* of the Squadron of Galleasses of Naples.'

Abad paused to introduce Captain Perez, who nodded politely. Abad continued…

'However, other members of our crew had to escape inland, but with the help of some partisan Catholics, they were able to rescue more of our men that were captured in a separate incident. They were being taken away to be hanged, but my men managed to save them and reclaim their ship. That is the little caravel we have on tow my Lord.'

The Duke was about to take a drink of wine, but stopped when he learned of the rescue.

'Pray tell Captain Abad… what are the names of those who rescued our men?'

'Henri Daval, and Alfredo Rodriguez my Lord.'

'A Frenchman?… Really? Well, nevertheless, they deserve a reward. When we return to Spain, bring them to me.'

For the next two hours, the other officers gave their individual reports and observations, and when everyone had finished, the Duke concluded.

'Gentlemen, we have learned much from our unavoidable detour around Britain, and we know how dangerous the seas can be. The information that Scotland could be an important ally for Spain is something that I am sure, his highness King Philip will find useful. Ensure that your reports are detailed and updated when we get back to Spain, and will review them again. For now, we will sail as close together as possible, but beware of the seas and storms in this area. Do not sail too close to land or you will suffer the consequences from the storm… and myself.'

With the meeting ended, the captains made their way back to their ships, and not a moment too soon. For the weather had become worse, with heavy rain and high winds. By the time they were all safely aboard ship, the crews set sail under minimum canvas. The fleet was spread over several miles from stem to stern, but no wider than a few hundred yards apart, so they could communicate with each other. The bright light on the poop deck allowed for glimpses of each other as the ships sank and peaked between the waves. Most were pleased to be in the wide waters of the Atlantic Ocean, but others were more wary of the damage the storms could do anywhere. Through the rest of the day and night, the storm clouds gathered, with westerly winds becoming dangerously strong.

Chapter 28
Shipwreck III

A line of ships could be seen off the western coast of Ireland by its inhabitants, including English soldiers. Acting like vultures waiting for an animal to die, many people watched from the clifftops as the surviving ships of the Armada converged to make their final, and most dangerous way southwards. Many knew that misfortune had not yet finished with the mighty Armada, which was mostly felt by the soldiers and sailors who had already experienced the power of the sea. Vicious storms with gale-force winds crashed into the fleet with incredible force, and many of the smaller ships were unable to prevent themselves from being thrown towards the multitude of reefs and rocks along Ireland's rugged coast. Throughout the whole of September 1588, the Armada lost more than 20 ships to the bad weather, and many were blown off-course, sunk without trace, or smashed against the rocks. Fortunately for *Napolitana*, it remained intact, along with the bulk of the fleet sailing as close as possible to *San Martin*. Its skilled officers and navigators, had years of experience sailing in these waters. Yet the crew had to work beyond themselves to keep their ship on an even keel. Daval, Marcos and Alfredo worked side by side to assist with the deck work, and to aid the aching arms of the helmsman. They could only watch as ship after ship was being pulverised by giant waves, with some having to leave the fleet formation to prevent collision. Those individuals who managed to survive the wrecks and make it to land tried to escape across Ireland to Scotland, but the rest were captured by the inhabitants or soldiers and were brutally killed. As survivors crawled their way onto the beaches, scavengers would attack them, stab them with swords or hang them, then strip their bodies for any item of value. This unfortunately happened to ships from the Levant Squadron.

September 20: Unable to control their ship, and subject to enormous waves crashing onto their bows, three ships from the Levant Squadron became separated from the fleet:

La Lavia, a Venetian merchantman which was the vice-flagship of the Levant Squadron, with Captain Martin de Aranda on board; *Juliana*, a Catalan merchantman, with Captain Don Diego Enriquez on board; and *Santa Maria de Vision*, a Ragusan merchantman.

Captain Francisco de Cuellar, who was still on-board *La Lavia* as a prisoner, following the incident in the North Sea, was a survivor who later wrote a detailed account of the events leading to the demise of these ships, their crew, and soldiers.

Cuellar recalled:

> "We had to anchor more than half a league from the shore, where we remained for four days without being able to make any provision, nor could it even be made. On the fifth day there sprang up so great a storm on our beam, with a sea up to the heavens, so that the cables could not hold nor the sails serve us, and we were driven ashore with all three ships upon a beach, covered with very fine sand, shut in on one side and the other by great rocks. Such a thing was never seen for within the space of an hour all three ships were

broken in pieces, so that there did not escape three hundred men, and more than one thousand were drowned, among them many persons of importance, captains, gentlemen, and other officials."[1]

Captain Cuellar eventually escaped Ireland by going to Scotland, where he lived with the local people for several months. He then returned to Spain by ship, before completing a journal of his harrowing experiences.

Meanwhile, the rest of the fleet continued to have serious issues with the storm, with many having to heave-to, to repair sails, rigging and bilge pumps. Some had their masts ripped off and could only limp slowly onwards, or be towed. Others had to carry out repairs to holes in the hull, caused by passing debris, or from sailing too close to the reefs. Night after night and day after day, the fleet of the Armada slowly made their way southwards. Officers on deck watched mournfully through field glasses, as they could see the number of ships wrecked along the coastline was increasing. Powerless to go to their aide, should they themselves become a casualty, they doubled their efforts to keep their own vessel afloat. The whole fleet worked tirelessly in the knowledge that if they didn't, then they too could lose their lives. They were often reminded of this, as now and again dead bodies were brought up from the hold, wrapped in old sail cloths, and prepared for burial at sea by priests. When the storm abated, officers and crew would attend the ceremony, as the bodies were slowly entered into their watery graves.

_____

1 Extract taken from: *Captain Cuellar's Adventures in Connacht and Ulster* Author Francisco de Cuellar – translated by Robert Crawford. Funded by University College, Cork and Higher Education Authority via the CELT Project

On board *Napolitana*, Juan Carlos assisted the surgeon as best he could, although by now he had much more experience than before, and had become a valuable member of the crew. All the while, both his father and Daval kept a watchful eye on the lad. They were never more than a few yards away from him, just in case he slipped, or a wave washed him off his feet. Where possible the work on deck maintained a shift pattern so each man could have a little time to eat, sleep or relax. When it was their turn to rest,

Daval, Alfredo and Juan Carlos, who shared the navigator's cabin, tried to talk about anything else except trying to survive the storms. Daval teased Juan Carlos a little.

'Juan Carlos, now that you have experienced the life of a sailor, what do you think? Is it as much fun and excitement as you thought?'

Juan Carlos scowled a little, and realised that Daval was teasing him, but he liked his friend, so he did not react.

'I have really enjoyed working with you Daval, and you have shown me many things… but… I don't like the storms, or watching men get killed.'

Alfredo gave his son a playful hug.

'I am very proud of you my son, and you have grown these past months. I think your grandfather and mother will be very proud of you too.'

Juan Carlos, on hearing his grandfather mentioned queried.

'Papa! Do you think grandpapa saw the things that we have seen?'

Alfredo looked at Daval, and then turned to his son and rubbed his head.

'Son, your grandfather has told you many tales, but he has only spoke about the good things that happened to him… I think you now know that he will have seen much suffering too.'

Juan Carlos thought for a while and remained quiet, then he said.

'Papa… I miss home… and I miss Mama very much.'

'Mama and your sister miss you very much too Juan Carlos, and they will be very happy to see you.'

Those words provoked everyone's imagination and thoughts of home, and they spent the next few minutes in peaceful contemplation of the lives they left behind… including Daval.

At the stern of *Napolitana*, the caravel that was in tow, began to take on more and more water as the waves washed over her. With no crew on board, the bilge pumps were not being operated, and so the ship began to sink. It was having an effect on *Napolitana*, which caused the ship to lurch more in the heavy swell. One of the crew reported it to Captain Perez.

'Captain! The ship on tow is sinking… what shall we do?'

Instantly the captain ran to the stern of his ship, took one look at the caravel, and cut the tow ropes with his cutlass. The waves immediately pushed the little ship towards the rocks where it was smashed and destroyed. The officers on deck watched the caravel slowly disappear as the fleet sailed past the southern shores of Ireland. Then, looking through their field glasses, the officers sighted the remains of the last two ships to be wrecked on its rocks.

Santa Maria de la Rosa, part of the 14-strong Squadron of Guipuzcoa, was wrecked on Stromboli Reef at Blasket Sound, County Kerry, Ireland. There was only one survivor out of 297 on board.

San Juan Bautista, part of the 16-strong Squadron of Castille, and the vice-flagship. Sunk at Blasket Islands, County Kerry, Ireland.

On board *San Martin* signals were sent out, then relayed to every ship, that all officers and crew to show their respects to the fallen soldiers and sailors of the wrecks. For the next few moments, a still and quiet atmosphere permeated throughout the fleet. Quietly, officers alerted the crew and soldiers as they passed the last of Ireland's rugged coastline. Many of them took off their hats and sank to their knees in prayer, as they watched the last cliffs of Ireland drift into the distance. Almost immediately, the storm vanished, and the sea stabilised to a moderate swell, which the crew found much easier to sail. Horns blew on many ships as a mark of respect, and the order was given for everyman on board to have a tot of rum, wine or brandy to salute the fallen. The grey clouds dispersed, and the wind turned into a favourable breeze that sent the bedraggled fleet homeward.

Good weather continued to assist the Armada's return home when it left Ireland, and the fleet maintained a southerly heading across the Celtic Sea. Yet, as they had to pass the English Channel on the port side, orders were given to be on maximum alert for the English Navy. Lookouts were doubled and sent high up the masts, and officers scoured the horizon for any potential threat. Cannons, not having been used since Gravelines, were checked and cleaned, before being loaded and primed in readiness. Soldiers were ordered to check their weapons, shot and powder in case close-quarter fighting was needed. Many were relieved to be doing something, instead of always trying to survive the bad weather, or being cooped up in the stinking holds day after day. With the calmer weather, not as many men were needed to sail the ship, so the crew took a well-earned rest, and ate as good a meal as could be made from the remaining supplies.

Chapter 29
Bay of Biscay

Eventually the fleet entered the familiar waters of the Bay of Biscay, and although the weather could still be very dangerous at times, many were convinced that Ireland's waters were far worst. For late summer, the weather remained calm, with fresh winds to enable good sailing. Although the Armada fleet was still spread over several miles, each captain was within visual contact of each other should signals be sent or required. Those ships that were disabled from the lack of mast or sail, limped onwards as best they could, with repairs carried out from supplies provided by other ships. For the crew on board *Napolitana*, sailing the ship became an everyday routine, which allowed each crewman to have reasonable breaks at regular intervals.

Inside their cabin, after eating a simple meal of dried biscuits and a little soup, Juan Carlos entertained himself by cleaning his pistol, and his father leaned over to retrieve the linen pouch from the pocket of the leather bag.

'Let me take a closer look at that pouch Juan Carlos.'

Alfredo poured out the content onto the bunk, and along with 22 silver coins, there was ten gold coins, and several small coloured stones. Juan Carlos looked on with interest.

'Those silver coins papa, how much are they worth? I

have only ever seen the red ones you usually bring back from the market.'

Alfredo picked up one of the silver coins, and rubbed it until it shone brightly. At that instant, Daval walked into the cabin, and closing the door quickly, he said.

'Please, mes amis… keep those out of sight… and never show them to anyone… especially the stones.'

Alfredo put most of them back into the pouch, except for one bright red stone, one silver coin and one gold coin.

'Daval, I know about the coins, but do you know more about this … this other treasure… what are the stones?'

Daval picked up the three items, and looked closely at the stone.

'The silver coin is called a *real*, which is worth about 34 *maravedis* copper coins that you are familiar with, and the gold coin is called a *ducat*, and it is worth about 375 *maravedis* coins.'

Juan Carlos was amazed.

'Wow… that is a lot of money Daval.'

Daval tried to keep him quiet, then continued.

'Now this single red stone mes amiss, is something quite different, it is called a ruby, that is used to make expensive jewellery, and I am sure you could sell it for 10 or 12 ducats maybe more in the city.'

Juan Carlos was very excited, and tried to imagine what could be bought for such a fortune. He continued to clean his pistol with great vigour, but Alfredo suddenly became very serious as he realised just how much money there was in the linen pouch.

'It is not ours Daval… it belonged to Captain Mauritio, and we must return it to his family as soon as possible.'

Juan Carlos' excitement dropped, and stopped cleaning as he remembered his friend Paulo.

'Papa… you are right, and it also belongs to Paulo.'

For a few minutes the three of them sat quietly thinking about their options. Daval was the first to speak.

'If it wasn't for Juan Carlos retrieving the bag from the shipwreck, then it would have been lost, and after all… the pistol was used to save my life. Surely that deserves a reward of some kind.'

Alfredo tried to remember all the incidents where the contents of the bag also helped them to escape.

'You are right my friend. If it was not for the coins, then we could not have escaped Ireland.'

Daval eventually offered a possible solution.

'When we get back to Spain, you will need to purchase a horse to return home, also food and clothing for the journey, so you must use some of the coins for that.'

Alfredo and Juan Carlos thought it was an excellent solution. Daval continued.

'I will go to visit my brother in France, then when I have rested, I shall return the rest of the coins, and the stones, to Paulo's father in Germany. *Barca de Amburgo* was from there too, so it should be fairly easy to locate him.'

Alfredo shook Daval's hand warmly.

'You are a good man Daval, and both Juan Carlos and myself are very pleased to call you our friend.'

'I think we have all helped each other along the way, so it is the least I could do mes amis.'

Alfredo put the pouch back into the leather bag, and Juan Carlos replaced the pistol, before carefully hiding the bag inside the cabin. They spent the rest of the day helping the crew, and Daval liaised with Marcos and the ship's navigator for their final destination in Spain.

'Daval, we should keep clear of the English Channel because the English could be expecting us… they are not stupid and they must assume that some of our ships will return this way.'

'I agree Marcos, and I am sure the Duke is also aware of this, but it will not harm to be prepared. I will advise the captain immediately.'

The ship's navigator also agreed and added.

'When we get to the Bay of Biscay, then if the weather holds up, we should reach Spain in a few days. I will chart our course.'

The first part of the crossing over the Bay of Biscay was uneventful, which allowed many to recover their strength and for the injured to be better treated. The captain of each ship used the calmer weather to carry out much needed repairs, and to thoroughly clean their ship in readiness for entry to port. It was important for the Duke of Medina-Sidonia to have as many ships around him as possible, and so the fleet gradually manoeuvred into a closer formation around *San Martin*. He wanted to show those who would criticise him, that the Armada was still a very strong unit, but for extremely bad weather, it would have been a victorious one. Later that day, signals were sent out to every captain that all officers are to be dressed in their finest uniforms when they disembark. Plans were made between the commanders to decide on which was the better port to land, and the Duke spent time in his cabin writing his speeches. All seemed to be going well as the Great Armada reached the midway point across the Bay of Biscay. However, many experienced sailors were only too well aware of how quickly the weather in this region could change... and change it did.

On board *Napolitana*, Daval and Marcos was talking with Captain Perez and Captain Abad. Perez was interested in recruiting Daval into his crew.

'Tell me Daval, what are your plans when we land? Would you consider working with me on my ship?'

Daval was looking at the skies, and enjoying the fresh breeze as it flowed over the ship.

'Merci… Captain… thank you for your offer, but I shall be going to see my brother in France for a while… Then, who knows?'

As Perez was about to discuss more details of his proposition, Daval pointed to the westward sky.

'Captain, look… to the west… a storm is coming fast.'

Both captains used their field glasses to look closer at the distant black clouds, as they swirled and heaved towards them at great speed.

'You are correct Daval, a storm is brewing … and it looks bad.'

Minutes later, signals were sent out across the fleet, and crews prepared to reduce their sails and batten down the hatches. Ships were ordered to keep their distance from each other until the storm had passed, and not to sail too close to the shore. Within the hour the winds had gone from a pleasant fresh breeze to a storm force gale, and the sea began to surge and swirl violently. Another hour passed and the clear blue sky disappeared, only to be replaced by thunderous black clouds, with flashes of bright white light streaking out of them. Bolts of fork-lightning peppered the sea all around the ships, and the waves appeared to leap up towards them. It seemed to trigger the heavens to open up, as torrential rain began to pour down with tremendous force, making the deck of each ship more slippery than ever.

Daval and Marcos instinctively went to the aide of the helmsman, and Alfredo put on a heavy cape to assist the crew. He spoke to his son before leaving the cabin.

'Juan Carlos… do not leave this cabin, it is too dangerous out there, and I want you to be safe.'

'OK papa… I understand.'

Although Juan Carlos agreed, he thought that he was old enough to assist the crew with his father, and that he had learned many more skills as a sailor, but for now… he waited. As the storm raged on throughout the day and into the night, each ship had to fight hard to keep control as they battled against enormous 50-foot waves. Smaller ships especially were subjected more to the brutal influence of the giant waves, and were thrown about as if made of parchment. Inside the holds, men and equipment were thrown stem to stern, then port to starboard, as the relentless seas rocked their ship in many directions. Heavy cannonballs, not stowed securely enough, rolled across the deck with immense force, causing many injuries to those struck by them. Masts, weakened from all the previous storms that the fleet had to endure, snapped off then crashed onto the decks, bringing down rigging and sail. Those men below had to fight and cut their way out of the debris, or be dragged overboard as the waves washed the loose equipment into the sea. The *San Martin* experienced just that, as two topsail masts crashed and damaged the mizzen mast before smashing onto the deck. The crew worked hard to free trapped men and to cut the dangerous debris away. On board *La Trinidad de Scala*, Captain Garcia could only watch as his main mast also collapsed, which severely damaged the rest of the rigging. It was still able to sail, but it fell further behind the rest of the fleet and had to limp home.

Those ships at the back of the fleet, and still close to the English Channel, also suffered the devastation of the storm. *San Pedro Mayor*, one of two hospital ships, was driven into the English Channel, and went ashore at Hope Cove, Bigbury Bay, Devon. Fortunately, the crew and injured made it to shore safely. *Zúñiga* from the Squadron of Galleasses of Naples, was forced to take refuge at Le Havre after suffering rudder damage. In the Bay of Biscay, *Doncella*, part of the ten strong Squadron of Guipuzcoa, foundered and sunk, with many of its crew and soldiers rescued by other ships. *La Regazona*, part of the Squadron of Levant, and the flagship of Martin de Bertendona, was severely damaged, then blown off-course and eventually sunk off La Coruna, Spain.

Finally, as the storm abated, the first ships of the Armada limped across the sea towards the coast of northern Spain, and headed for the port of Santander and Laredo. Some 60 ships, and only about half the men that left Lisbon made it home. The battle with the English did little damage to the fleet, but bad weather on the other hand, caused thousands to drown at sea or to be killed in wrecks. Many others died from their wounds or from disease during the homeward voyage, and of course several were captured and killed. *San Martin* eventually limped home, where she had to be towed into port at Laredo, close to the port of Santander. *Napolitana* and other ships, also managed to make it safely into the Laredo harbour, and *La Trinidad de Scala* eventually made it safely to the port of Santander.

Chapter 30
Spain – Laredo

As *Napolitana* sailed slowly into the Laredo harbour, crowds gathered and cheered loudly, as they watched the remains of the mighty Armada appear. A mixture of sadness, anger, and relief permeated through the people, but most were impressed at the fleets impressive journey around Britain. On board, men crammed themselves on deck to get a view of the friendly port, and to wave back at the cheering crowd. Many broke down in tears at the thought of their survival. Captain Perez and Captain Abad, stood side by side in their best uniforms on the poop deck, along with as many officers. Daval, Marcos, Alfredo and Juan Carlos watched in silence from the stern of the ship, and they could not quite grasp the realisation that they were finally home. Over the next two hours the ship slowly emptied of human life. Soldiers formed a barrier in the crowd, to allow the crew off the ship, and medics were allowed to bring off the wounded and take them to the nearest hospitals. Able-bodied men were taken to refuge centres to recuperate, to bathe, put on fresh clothes and to eat fresh food.

By the time *San Martin* arrived and was moored up, the crowds had swelled and a band provided rousing music for their safe return. Civic personnel formed a reception area to greet the Duke of Medina-Sidonia and his staff officers.

With flags waving and horns blaring, the Duke, in his finest uniform, walked regally to the reception area where he was courteously received.

'Welcome… welcome… welcome my Lord. The whole of Laredo and Spain are pleased for your safe return.'

The Duke took the salutes, bows and curtsies from the civic group and spoke briefly of his voyage.

'My Lords, ladies and gentlemen… Thank you for your most generous welcome. We are pleased to have returned with so many fine sailors and soldiers from our holy quest. Had it not been for the unpredictable weather that we unfortunately encountered, then it would have been a most excellent achievement. Through the grace of our Lord God, we ensured that the superior skills of our seamen, officers and men have allowed many to return home safely, and return to Spain with the majority of Spain's most excellent ships. You should all be proud of our glorious navy. God Save the King.'

The silenced crowd erupted into a cacophony of loud cheers, banners were waved and the band played more rousing music.

The Duke of Medina-Sidonia was escorted away from the harbour and taken to suitable accommodation nearby. His officers remained to ensure that the ship's documents and treasures, were safely taken off the ship and stored under close guard, as was the case for every ship that made a safe return to port.

Hot meals were available from one the many improvised outdoor kitchens, then officers were billeted in large rooms across the city, where hastily erected sleeping cots were made available for around 20 men in each room. Other similar arrangements were made for ordinary crewmen and soldiers, who were taken to field tents on the outskirts of the city. Captain Abad had managed to secure cots in the city for Daval, Marcos, Alfredo and Juan Carlos. When they arrived at their recuperation centre, they washed thoroughly, and put on clean, simple clothes provided for everyone. Daval and Marcos went into the city, whilst Alfredo and his son relaxed on their cots. Over the next few days, all men had to report for their wages, and to compile a list of missing personnel. Detailed inventories had to be prepared for ships, crew members and soldiers brought into Lisbon. At the local townhall, civic and military officers carried out the work to identify as many people as possible, so relatives could be informed. Several tables were laid out for all the paperwork, and men filed up behind them. When they were cross-referenced with the inventory taken at Lisbon before the Armada set off, then each man was given a pouch of silver for his wages. After that, they were told which ship or military unit to report to.

As they were about to enter the townhall, Alfredo stopped Daval and took him to one side.

'Daval, there is no point in me going in there... because I am not a crewman or a soldier... you know that I stowed onboard for Juan Carlos... Also, I was a prisoner onboard *San Martin.*'

Daval laughed and tried to reassure his friend.

'Don't worry mon ami... I will explain to them, and you of all people deserve your wages... I am sure they will understand.'

Alfredo was still unconvinced and did not want to risk going to prison again.

'No... no... my friend... I will wait outside.'

Daval, Marcos and Juan Carlos eventually went inside without him, then almost immediately, two guards positioned outside the townhall, saw Alfredo lurking and grabbed him.

'Come on inside, we don't want you hanging about, do we?'

As much as Alfredo tried to object, he was forced into the building, where they took him to an empty table. The guards spoke to the officer at the table.

'Found this one outside, and he didn't want to come in for some reason?'

The officer scowled at Alfredo then began to question him, as the guards stood either side of him holding his arms.

'Name?'

Daval and the others were at a separate table providing their own details, and could not go to help Alfredo. They just looked anxiously at him. Alfredo could not think what to say, and the officer repeated more forcefully.

'Name? What is your name?'

'Errr, my name is Alfredo.'

The officer was getting a little annoyed, and the guards shook Alfredo to answer more clearly.

'What is your full name, and which ship were you on?'

'Alfredo Rodriguez, and I was taken onto *San Martin* by mistake... I... I... I should never have been on the ship.'

The officer ignored Alfredo and checked his list. After several reviews he looked up at Alfredo.

'I don't see your name anywhere on here. Explain, or I will lock you up.'

Alfredo began to sweat and get agitated as he tried to think of a good explanation. Just then, Captain Abad appeared in full uniform and banged his fist on the table.

'STOP!'

The officer at the desk was most alarmed, and dropped his quill onto the floor. Abad tore into him with an elevated voice.

'This man has saved many lives with his bravery, and prevented good Spaniards from being hung by the neck in

Ireland. With great danger to himself, he escaped from the enemy and came aboard my ship, *La Trinidad Valencera*... I will vouch for him, so go ahead and pay him.'

The officer recovered his composure, and unsure what to do, looked across at a more senior officer on the adjacent desk. The senior officer "nodded" in agreement, and so Alfredo was given one of the money pouches. The officer then asked nervously.

'Señor, could you please give me your full name and sign here for your payment, and I will mark you down as a crewman of La *Trinidad Valencera*.'

Alfredo was still hesitant to reply, but answered.

'My... my name is... Alfredo... Alfredo Rodriguez.'

He quickly signed for the money then walked outside with Abad, with the officer and the guards looking a little bewildered. Daval, Marcos and Juan Carlos quietly laughed at what happened, then completed their own information, received their reward and went to join them. Juan Carlos was registered as a cabin boy on board *Barca de Amburgo*, and he too was given a money pouch.

Outside the townhall they all met in the sunshine and laughed loudly at the event. Captain Abad's laugh was the loudest as he retold what happened.

'It was very difficult for me to keep a straight face, and I thought the officer was going to shit himself.'

Alfredo was not laughing, as he thought that he could've gone to prison again, but he thanked Abad.

'Captain, I don't know what to say... you saved me from prison... thank you.'

Abad stopped laughing and put a reassuring hand on Alfredo's shoulder.

'Rubbish! Alfredo... there was never any doubt, and they could never send you to prison... What you and Daval did for Spain deserves reward, not punishment.'

Abad paused and brought Daval and Alfredo to stand in front of him.

'Gentlemen, I am here today because… The commander of the Armada, the Duke of Medina-Sidonia, has requested your presence tomorrow in his quarters, and I can tell you that it is only good news for you both.'

Daval and Alfredo were speechless and did not know what to say. Juan Carlos jumped up and down with excitement, and Marcos congratulated them with great enthusiasm. In reality, all Alfredo wanted to do was to go home as soon as possible, and to forget about whole adventure. Abad shook everyone by the hand, and strode off.

'See you tomorrow my friends, I will collect you in the morning.'

The friends all went to an inn for some much-needed refreshment, and to quench their dry throats after such a tense, but interesting ordeal. As they sat in the cool shade of a nearby tavern, Daval tried to distract Alfredo, and to focus his mind on the next part of his journey.

'Mes amis, you are safe, and back in Spain, and now we must find some good horses for your journey back home.'

Juan Carlos was excited at this, and enthusiastically agreed.

'Si, papa. We should buy two horses, because they will be better for the journey, and I really want a horse of my own. I am almost a man now.'

Daval and Marcos rubbed their beards and mocked Juan Carlos because of his clean, fresh face. Marcos joked, 'Si Juan Carlos, I can almost see two hairs growing on your smooth chin… you really are a man now.'

They all laughed, and Juan Carlos was pleased to see that his father was joining in the fun too. Then Alfredo replied to his son.

'But Juan Carlos, I was going to buy a strong mule and a

new cart to replace our old one, and then fill it with supplies for the farm.'

Juan Carlos was not pleased at this and looked disappointed. Then Daval offered an alternative suggestion.

'Alfredo, you can buy another mule and cart when you get home... no? You will make much better time with horses than with mules.'

Reluctantly, Alfredo agreed, which brought an instant smile back onto Juan Carlos' face. Daval continued...

'Don't worry my friend, Marcos and I will find good horses for us all, and tomorrow we will buy them together and be on our way.'

The mood changed a little when Marcos enquired, 'What will happen to everyone after you have seen the Duke?' Daval spoke first.

'I will go and see my brother in France for a few days, then I must go to Hamburg to inform Paulo's father that his son is in Scotland recovering. I am sure his father will organise a ship to fetch him.'

Juan Carlos' thoughts turned to Paulo as he remembered his friend.

'I wish I could come with you Daval, and maybe go to see him in Scotland.'

Alfredo scowled at his son at the thought of him sailing in those dangerous waters again.

'No, my son... it is time for us to return home... your family needs to see you, because they miss you very much.'

Daval agreed.

'Yes, my young friend, you have had a great adventure, and maybe one day... when you are much older, then you and Paulo will meet again.'

His words seemed to calm Juan Carlos, and he was satisfied with the idea of meeting his friend again in a few years' time. He turned to Marcos.

'Marcos… what will you do?

Without hesitation Marcos answered.

'That is easy… I shall sign on with Captain Abad because he has asked me to be his helmsman, and he plans to sail to the Caribbean Islands, which will be much warmer than Britain.'

The friends all laughed again, finished their drinks, and made their way back to their billet. They decided to rest as much as possible, then head off tomorrow after the meeting with the Duke.

Early next morning, Captain Abad appeared at their billet, he looked resplendent in his full uniform including a very ornate ceremonial sword. Compared to him, everyone else looked quite drab, wearing simple clothes that was given to them when they arrived. Abad warmly greeted them.

'Are we all ready to meet the Duke?'

Nervously, they all agreed and followed him outside. Abad spoke to Marcos who was not invited and so lay on his cot to await the return of his friends.

'Marcos, you should come with us, as I know that you performed well too. Also, I have something to discuss with you later.'

It was a beautiful day with a strong, warm sun, which suited fewer clothes not full uniforms. Nevertheless, Abad set off at a brisk pace across the city, and Juan Carlos had to run at times to keep up. Ten minutes later they were at the door of the building where The Duke of Medina-Sidonia was quartered. Waiting for them was Captain Perez, who was dressed identically as Abad. Perez greeted them.

'Good morning gentlemen… I hope you have all recovered and are well rested?'

Daval acknowledged the gesture.

'Yes sir, Captain Perez, being back on familiar ground feels very good… thank you.'

Perez gathered the group together, and explained what will happen.

'The Duke is inside, and Captain Abad and myself will be with you. Do not speak unless the Duke asks you a question. Afterwards, we will give you the signal to leave.'

The group nodded in agreement, then Perez opened the door to the building and they reluctantly entered.

The building was the home of one of the civic members of the city, who had offered his house and staff for the Duke. The location was perfect as it was situated only a few minutes from the harbour. It was a very grand and opulent house, with very large oak doors, marbled floors and the walls were festooned with a variety of oil paintings. The group was ushered into one of the large reception rooms, and working at a huge mahogany desk, was the Duke of Medina-Sidonia. He was flanked either side of him with his senior officers as they perused official papers. The group stood nervously in front of him, with Abad and Perez at each flank. Captain Abad was the first to speak.

'My Lord... may I present the men to which I referred, during our recent altercations in Ireland.'

The Duke of Medina-Sidonia stopped his discussion with his officers and nodded towards Abad, who continued.

'My Lord may I present; Henri Daval and Marcos Dominguez from your imperial navy, and Alfredo Rodriguez with his son Juan Carlos Rodriguez.'

There was a pause whilst The Duke whispered with his officers. Then he spoke to them.

'Gentlemen, as you are aware, the voyage around Britain proved to be very difficult, and we experienced very unusual sailing conditions. Unfortunately, we lost more men and ships to the weather than from engagement with the English. Further, many of our men who survived the wrecks and made it to shore in Ireland, suffered at the hands of the enemy and many were killed. Yet, I am told that you not only survived two shipwrecks, but you managed to evade the enemy and free some of our countrymen from being executed. You have shown great bravery and improvisation, and especially those of you who were not part of the task force.'

Alfredo twitched nervously and did not really want to be there, but Juan Carlos held his hand tightly. The Duke rose out of his seat and came over to the group, flanked by one of his officers. He gave each one a linen pouch full of coins, together with a signed document of their bravery. He spoke to them as he gave them their reward.

'As Commander of the Armada of Spain, and a representative of his Royal Majesty, King Philip of Spain. I am pleased to reward you all for your diligence and your bravery. For those of you in the military, you will receive a suitable medal of honour in due course, but for now… please accept this small gift of appreciation.'

The Duke shook their hands and smiled, then returned to his seat. Abad nodded for the group to withdraw, and they quietly left the room and went outside.

When they got outside, Alfredo was the first to speak as he touched his shirt.

'Wow… phew! I am soaking with sweat and shaking all over my body, I … I thought that I was going to pass out.'

Juan Carlos and Daval laughed and hugged him, both pleased to have come through the ordeal. Marcos who was still in shock from being included, muttered.

'Santa Maria… I would much rather be on my ship in a storm than go through that again… I… was so nervous.'

Abad and Perez laughed too, because they knew that it would be a nervous ordeal for them.

'Well done my friends… you did very well, and that is why I came to you early so it would all be over quickly. Now come with Perez and myself, and we will have a good breakfast together before we part. As they walked away from the building, they placed their rewards into their belt pouches, then Abad took Marcos to one side to speak to him on a separate matter.

'Marcos, I have been informed that our voyage to the Caribbean has been postponed for one year, but don't worry because as soon as I get the orders to sail, then I will find you.'

Marcos thought for a few seconds then replied.

'I understand sir. It will be good to have some time to recover and relax, but be assured that I will be ready to join you in one year. Thank you for having faith in me.'

Abad acknowledged his reply and they joined the others at the inn.

They all sat around a large table except for Captains Abad and Perez. The table was situated outside the building, although in shade of the hot sun, but the inn was also full of other crewmen and soldiers from the Armada. Many were drunk and the atmosphere was becoming a little agitated. Abad assessed the situation, and following a quick look to Captain Perez, he said.

'Captain Perez and I are a little overdressed gentleman, and we have more pressing issues to deal with, so we will let you enjoy your meal.'

He placed a few coins onto the table and continued…

'This should be enough for your meal.'

He then gestured to them as quietly as he could.

'Be careful with your rewards… there are too many eyes and ears here. Hopefully we will see you again before you leave the city.'

With no time for the others to reply, Abad and Perez walked briskly away. Daval of course, understood and tried to deflect the awkward change of atmosphere.

'No matter mes amiss, we have a busy day ahead ourselves. So, let us enjoy a fine meal then we will prepare to leave.'

An hour later, everyone returned to their billet, and prepared for their long journeys. Juan Carlos was keen to see what was given to them, and pleaded with his father.

'Papa… can I look at my reward?'

Alfredo knew that it would always be on his son's mind, and so he reluctantly agreed. They sat on their cots and slowly opened up the sealed pouches. Juan Carlos' face lit up when he opened his first.

'Wow! Papa… look at this… it's a lot of money!'

He was awarded five gold ducats which shone brightly in the clear light of day. When Alfredo opened his, it was an equally amazing sight, as he was awarded 20 gold ducats.

'Alfredo, you had better give all your money to me for safekeeping. When we get home then we will decide what to do with it.'

Juan Carlos took time to enjoy the bright coins, then handed them over to his father. As they were packing up their belongings, Marcos spoke to Daval.

'Daval, Captain Abad has told me that the voyage to the Caribbean has been postponed for one year.'

Daval, turned to face his friend.

'What will you do until then mes amis… Do you have family to go to?'

'Unfortunately, I do not have any relatives alive, other than an elderly aunt in Barcelona.'

Daval smiled as a thought occurred to him.

'Marcos… I am going to see my brother in France for a few days, but then I will be going to Hamburg to inform Paulo's family about their son… you are welcome to join me.'

Marcos spent a few minutes thinking about his options whilst packing his belongings, then gave his reply.

'Yes Daval... I would like to travel with you... provided we don't sail there. Ha ha ha.'

The two men laughed, shook hands, then walked over to Alfredo to tell him of their plans. Alfredo agreed that it was a good idea.

'It will be safer for you Daval to travel with Marcos... I hope you have a good journey... And we shall miss you both my friends.'

A few minutes later the four amigos stood outside and looked up at the hot sun. Daval shaded the sun from his eyes with his hand, and looked at the clear skies that stretched forever.

'What we need now are four good horses, enough supplies for our journey and... hats!'

Chapter 31
Spain – Bilbao

After asking the whereabouts of stables with horses for sale, they made their way across the city of Laredo to the livery stables. For Juan Carlos, the smell of horses was both a pleasant reminder of home and also a terrible reminder of those animals thrown into the sea. His father understood and hugged his son and tried to distract him.

'Come on Juan Carlos which horse do you like?'

After lots of haggling, and a few heated discussions, four strong, chestnut brown horses were selected and paid for, together with full livery. After buying fresh clothes and supplies for the journey, they placed them in large leather saddlebags. They also purchased a variety of hats and rain capes, and before they set off, they went to a nearby tavern for some final refreshments. As they sat at the table, they considered the best route to travel, but Daval had already prepared a route for Alfredo and handed him a neatly drawn map.

'Alfredo, we will travel together until we reach Bilbao and then we will rest for the night. Then Marcos and I will follow the coast to France, and if you follow my route, then you will reach Madrid in a few days.'

Alfredo looked at the many details carefully written along the route, and was pleased to have the map.

'Gracias mi amigo, we appreciate this. We will stay on the main road for safety then sleep at a coaching inn… after all, we can afford it now.'

Daval smiled, then added a word of caution.

'A good idea mes amis, but you cannot be too careful and never pay with silver. Here… take this pistol.'

Daval handed Alfredo a new pistol, shot and powder he had purchased along with the supplies. He also gave Juan Carlos a sharp dagger with belt.

'Keep your weapons hidden and only use them if you have to. Be alert at all times, because you have a long journey ahead and there could be many problems.'

Alfredo understood the warning and remembered the dangers he experienced during the search for his son.

'Of course, Daval, I fully understand and we will be careful.'

They set off on the road out of Laredo and headed east towards Bilbao. The sun was high and hot, so they rode their horses slowly, stopping now and again at streams or horse troughs to refresh them. To protect themselves from the sun, Daval and Marcos chose black, wide brimmed hats, pinned on one side. Alfredo and Juan Carlos opted for more traditional farmer's hats, although Juan Carlos really wanted one the same as his friends.

By late afternoon, they arrived on the outskirts of Bilbao, but they did not go into the town. Instead, they travelled to the crossroads on the outskirts of Bilbao where the road divided, east to France and south to Madrid. Marcos sighted a coaching inn.

'Daval, we should stay here for the night, it will be better for the horses.'

Daval agreed, and they made their way over to the coaching inn stable around the back. Daval gestured to Alfredo.

'Come with me my friend. You and I will get the rooms…

we can leave Marcos and Juan Carlos to see to the horses.'

After dismounting the horses, Marcos and Juan Carlos led the them into the stable where a young man assisted them. Daval and Alfredo walked to the bar inside and spoke to the landlord.

'We would like two rooms for the night señor.'

The landlord looked at the men, and not recognising them asked.

'Of course, señor. Have you come from Laredo? We have seen many men come this way since the navy landed in the port.'

Daval did not sense any hostility in his demeanour and happily obliged the question.

'Si, many of us are going home for a well-earned rest. It has been a long voyage.'

At the other end of the room, a group of local men were drinking, and overheard them talking. One particularly obnoxious man, spoke to his friends in a loud voice so Daval and Alfredo could hear.

'I heard that the 'great Armada' ran like cowards when the English attacked.'

The men laughed and jeered, but Daval and Alfredo chose to ignore the comment and continued to pay for the two rooms.

'Thank you, landlord, we will fetch our belongings and go to the rooms.'

As they picked up the large heavy iron keys, the landlord added.

'Let me know when you are ready to eat, we will be serving hot stew tonight sir.'

Daval acknowledged the gesture and they returned to the stables. Although the men continued to taunt them, they were ignored, and as they approached the stables Daval commented.

'Always ignore those kind of people mes amis… they are nothing but trouble, and are only cowards.'

'Si Daval, I understand only too well, but I was ready for them should if you wanted to teach them a lesson.'

The two friends laughed as they walked towards Marcos and Juan Carlos.

'What are you two laughing about?'

Marcos enquired as he heaved the saddle off the last horse, then Juan Carlos led it into the stall with fresh hay and water. Daval picked up his belongings and flippantly replied.

'Oh, nothing really mes amis… we were just laughing at some local idiots.'

Inside one of the rooms, all the bags were placed onto the floor, and Alfredo handed Daval the leather satchel containing Juan Carlos' pistol and the linen pouch of coins and stones. Daval took the leather bag, and before he placed the pouch into it, he checked the contents. Without anyone noticing, he placed three rubies into the secret pocket of Juan Carlos' leather satchel and kept a single ruby in his hand. Then he placed the pouch into his own bag hid it under the bed. He walked over to Alfredo and gave him the single ruby.

'Alfredo, take this ruby for your farm, and when you get to Madrid look for a quality jewellery merchant, who will purchase it from you for a good price, and if they are unsure if you own it, then show them the document from The Duke… it will convince them.'

Alfredo was a little concerned.

'But it is not ours, and should go back to Paulo's family.'

Daval explained how Captain Mauritio would have originally received the jewels.

'Mes amis, I worked with Captain Mauritio, and he was a very shrewd man, he was in charge of the King's treasure on his ship and I am sure that he secured a little for himself. Anyway… the treasure is lost in the sea now, and these few stones do not really exist.'

Daval placed the jewel into Alfredo's palm and closed his fingers around it.

'My friend… take this single stone as a reward for all you have done for Paulo. I will explain to his father, who I am sure will understand. Besides… there are many more rubies left for him in the pouch.'

Reluctantly Alfredo agreed, and placed the ruby securely in his own bag, then Daval handed Juan Carlos the leather satchel he had been looking after since their first shipwreck.

'Juan Carlos, I know Paulo would want you to have this, and you may need to use the pistol again one day. So, look after it and keep it clean and oiled.'

Juan Carlos was pleased to own the pistol at last and thanked Daval.

'Thank you… thank you, it will always remind me of our adventure… of you Marcos and Paulo. Maybe someday… when I am older, we can go on another adventure together.'

Daval smiled, and rubbed Juan Carlos' head.

'Oui, mes amis… of course… of course.'

They soon settled into their rooms, with Daval and Marcos in one room with the bags and Alfredo and Juan Carlos in the other room. Then they went to the main bar which was busy, but with plenty of spare tables. As soon as they sat down, a busty barmaid came over, rubbed Juan Carlos' hair in a friendly manner, then placed her bosom on his neck.

'What can I get you gentleman? Are you eating or just drinking?'

Juan Carlos shrugged away the attention because he considered himself not to be a boy any longer. The others laughed, then Alfredo interrupted them.

'We will all have ale, and one small, weak wine for my son, and the stew por favor.'

The barmaid looked at the three men and gave an encouraging wink to Alfredo, which made Daval and Marcos roar with laughter, causing embarrassment for Alfredo. The meal was good and as the evening wore on the crowd began to disperse. Juan Carlos yawned loudly from a full stomach and a warm room, and Alfredo stood up.

'We will go to bed now my friends, so we can get an early start tomorrow.'

Daval and Marcos nodded in agreement.

'Si mes amis, we will not be far behind you… it has been a long day, and I am looking forward to sleeping in a real bed for a change.'

As Alfredo and Juan Carlos departed for their room, the men from earlier walked up to Daval and Marcos. They were more drunk than before and therefore bolder, so the big obnoxious man brazenly challenged them.

'Why did you come back to Spain when you were so easily defeated? You should be ashamed of yourselves.'

Marcos was getting agitated, but Daval tapped his arm and tried to remain calm.

'Marcos… ignore him, he does not understand.'

Ignoring them made the man angrier, and he continued with his tirade. He noted Daval's accent and prodded him with his finger.

'You… you there… you are not even Spanish… no wonder you ran away… no wonder we were defeated.'

He continued to prod Daval, who looked at Marcos and "winked".

In an instance, Daval turned, grabbed the man's finger and broke it, sending the man sprawling to the floor in agony. As the other men came towards him, Daval swiftly used the heel of both hands to smash them on their noses, and their blood sprayed like a fountain, with both noses broken. The fourth man stood, rooted to the spot, and on seeing his friends bloodied on the floor, he turned and ran out of the inn. The broken men helped each other to crawl away, and they stumbled out of the inn to join the other man. Marcos, who was still sat at the table, applauded Daval.

'Fantastic mi amigo… I have never seen anything like that. You are a very talented man indeed.'

Daval simply brushed himself down and turned to Marcos as he headed for the stairs back to their room.

'Come on mes amis… we have a long journey tomorrow.'

Daval "flicked" a silver coin towards the innkeeper for their food, and although he caught it, he, and the rest of the inn were in shock at the speed with which Daval dealt with the drunks.

Next morning, Daval and Marcos woke early, and washed in turn out of the plain white bowl and water jug on the bedroom dresser. Once they were dressed, they gathered all the saddlebags and headed for the stables. Alfredo and Juan Carlos were already there preparing the horses, and Juan Carlos was very pleased to see them.

'Hola mes amis.'

Juan Carlos had decided to use Daval's words, and everyone smiled at his attempt at a French accent. Alfredo also greeted them but more quizzically.

'Good morning gentlemen… I have paid for our rooms and the stable fees for the horses, but the innkeeper acted very strange towards us… did anything happen when we left you last night?'

Daval gave Marcos a quick glance and tried to keep himself from smiling.

'No… no mes amis, nothing happened last night. We finished our drink and went to bed… the same as you.'

Alfredo was not convinced and with a knowing grin on his face he continued preparing the horses.

When everything was ready, the horses were led out of the stable into bright sunlight. Daval, then Marcos, hugged Juan Carlos and shook his hand in a manly way. Then Alfredo shook Daval and Marcos' hands.

'Daval, Marcos it has been very interesting meeting you both, but I must tell you that I don't ever want to repeat that experience again.'

Daval agreed and understood what Alfredo had to do to find his son.

'Alfredo, I really admire you, and the way you persevered with everything to find your son. I am very proud to call you my friend.'

Daval turned to Juan Carlos and hugged him again, then he placed his hands onto his shoulders.

'Juan Carlos… you should be proud of your brave father, and you must do everything you can to repay the debt you owe him. Now return to your family, and it has been a plea-sure knowing you. I am sure that we will meet again mes amis.'

Juan Carlos was lost for words, and tears started to well in his eyes. The men took that as a signal to get going, and everyone mounted their horses. As they rode away in differ-ent directions, Daval waved his wide brimmed hat as a ges-ture of goodbye, and the others repeated the signal. Daval called from the distance…

'Au revoir mes amis… au revoir.'

Chapter 32
Long Journey Home I

Miranda de Ebro

Having parted from Daval and Marcos at Bilbao, Alfredo and his son headed south towards Madrid. The route was on a winding, dusty track, passing over many hills, through valleys and woodland. Daval considered it would take them between 12 and 15 days to get there, and that he should assess each small village they came across to see if they were friendly or not. Alfredo realised that, and as he did not want to push the horses too much, they would sometimes have to camp outside before reaching a coaching inn. The summer had ended, and although it could be very warm during the day, the temperature could drop at night. He was pleased to have bought blankets with the supplies, and some basic cooking pans, which he placed in two sacks tied and straddled at the back of his saddle. He was thinking to himself how much more supplies he could have brought home in a cart, and he was regretting the horses, so he grumbled a little to his son.

'If we had bought a cart and two mules, then we could've carried much more equipment.'

'But papa, I have always wanted a horse, and I know you have often complained how slow the farm mule is.'

Alfredo continued to grumble under his breath, but he

knew that his son was correct, and that he too wanted a horse to get around the farm more easily.

Unknown to Alfredo, as they left the coaching inn, the men who caused trouble for Daval and Marcos watched them leave from the shadows. Although they wanted revenge for what Daval did, they decided that the easier target would be Alfredo and his son, and so they followed them on their horses. When they were sure which direction Alfredo was taking, they took a shortcut to ambush them. Alfredo and Juan Carlos rode slowly along the well-worn track, which was dusty and dry in the hot sun. Every now and then a coach and horses galloped by, sending plumes of dust into the air which made them cough. They quickly remembered to cover their faces when they saw the next one approaching, but Juan Carlos felt sorry for the horses having to put up with the dust and the noisy carriages. After two miles, they came upon a copse by the side of the track, where a small stream from the nearby hills trickled its way down the valley. Alfredo and Juan Carlos dismounted their horses so they could drink the water. The shade of the trees allowed for a respite from the hot sun, and as the horses drank, Alfredo and his son also drank water from a pouch, and snacked on a little bread and cheese purchased at the inn.

The men following them, sneaked up and startled them, and one held a pistol to their faces.

'Stay where you are and place your weapons on the ground... Now!'

Alfredo slowly took the pistol out of his belt and tossed it towards the big man with the broken finger. The man angrily shoved his hand close to Alfredo's face.

'See this... that Frenchman did this... and you will pay for what he did because he has run off again, just like the rest of the Armada cowards.'

The three other men jeered and backed up their colleague,

which made Juan Carlos afraid for his father. The big man took a knife from his belt and waved it over his head, and the others grabbed Juan Carlos.

'I think it is time you two felt a little pain… give me your hand boy.'

As the big man was about to cut off a finger, a shot rang out from nearby trees.

'Bang!'

The knife flew out of the man's hand as a pistol shot passed through his hand, sending the man sprawling to the dirt in agony. Daval and Marcos rushed at the three men who were still wondering what had happened, in less than a minute they were knocked out and lay in the dirt next to their friend. Alfredo picked up his pistol, and as he kept a close eye on the big man, he asked…

'Daval? Marcos? Why did you come here? How did you know we were in trouble?'

Daval and Marcos quickly stripped the clothes off the men and tied their hands behind their backs.

'I am sorry Alfredo, but Marcos and I had a disagreement with this rabble last night, and when we left the inn this morning, I saw them lurking in the shadows. At first, we thought they were going to follow us, then we soon realised that you were going to be an easier target. We got here as fast as we could mes amis.'

Both Alfredo and Juan Carlos were amazed at the speed with which Daval and Marcos dealt with the villains, but were also very relieved they arrived in time. Marcos scared away the men's horses and Daval kicked the naked men back towards Bilbao. They scuttled away bumping into each other, and yelled when they stood on a stone with their bare feet. Marcos tossed their clothes into some bushes and then retrieved their own horses. As Marcos and Daval mounted their horses, Daval waved his hat again.

'Maybe now it really is au revoir mes amis, and don't worry about the men because Marcos and I will push them back to Bilbao.'

Alfredo and Juan Carlos mounted their own horses and bade them farewell yet again.

By nightfall, they had reached a small village nestled in a valley, with wooden farm buildings and small stone houses. Alfredo thought it reminded him of his home villages, and he knew that the people there would be similar. He went up to one of the farm houses and asked if a few small coins would allow them to sleep in their barn for the night. His instincts were correct, and when they saw Juan Carlos, the farmer and his wife insisted on feeding them before leading them to his barn. As the night air cooled, it felt good to be warm and comfortable inside the barn and Juan Carlos enjoyed brushing the horses down with straw.

'Papa, did you see how quickly Daval dealt with those men? It was amazing.'

Alfredo smiled.

'Si my son, he is a very talented man indeed. I know he has worked as a soldier for many countries… So, he will be used to dealing with men like that. Now get some sleep as we have a long journey ahead of us.'

After a good night's sleep, they rose early, thanked the farmer and set off on their journey. They followed the track as usual, and Alfredo noted that Daval had marked a larger village called Miranda de Ebro on his map, which he thought they could reach before nightfall. The mountain stream followed the track, making it easier to keep the horses watered, and for the last few miles it meandered gently downhill into the village. The sun was setting as they rode into the village, where a coaching inn provided a welcoming sight for the weary travellers. Although it was not as big as the one at Bilbao, they were able to secure a room for the night. When they had seen to the horses, Alfredo and his son washed the dust off their bodies, changed into clean clothes and then went for a meal at the inn. After a welcoming tankard of ale, which Alfredo allowed Juan Carlos to drink, they looked around the room at the patronage. No one stood out as being villainous or suspicious, although one man, who looked like a fellow traveller, sat on his own enjoying a bowl of hot broth. The man noted Alfredo's glance, and acknowledged it with a nod of his head. He was a man in his fifties with receding grey hair, and wore the clothes of a merchantman. When Alfredo and Juan Carlos had finished their meal, the man came over to their table and sat down. Alfredo was immediately wary about the stranger's reactions, and gave him a cautious glance, and the man apologised.

'Forgive me for intruding, but I assume that you are a fellow traveller, si?'

Alfredo was reluctant to answer, but because his son was there, he did not want to be too alarmed.

'Si señor… my son and I are travelling to Madrid.'

The man sensed a little tension in Alfredo's voice and tried to explain his situation and that he was not a threat.

'Again, forgive me for the intrusion, but I am just a simple merchant returning to Madrid myself, and I was hoping to travel with others for safety.'

Alfredo relaxed a little, and Juan Carlos was interested in the man's explanation. The man continued, 'I travelled to Laredo when I learned that the ships from the Armada had returned… You see, I am the owner of two of the ships that were commandeered by the King, and naturally, I was hoping to get them back.'

Both Alfredo and Juan Carlos' ears pricked up at the mention of the Armada ships, and Juan Carlos asked interestingly.

'Señor? … What are the names of your ships?'

The man noted a sudden air of enthusiasm, and explained.

'Well, the smallest one is a patache that we use for sailing around the coast, it is called *Santa Christa*. The other ship is much larger that I use to sail across the continents, and it is called *La Trinidad Valencera*.'

Juan Carlos' jaw dropped and was speechless for a few moments. Alfredo grabbed the man's arm, and whispered.

'What was the name of the captain of *La Trinidad Valencera*?'

The man was startled and found the question a little strange.

'Why do you ask? Do you know of the ship and its captain?'

Alfredo shook the man's arm and insisted.

'Tell me please… I need to know if you are telling the truth.'

The man thought the questioning very strange, but reluctantly answered.

'The name of the captain is… Abad… Captain Armando Abad.'

On hearing his name, Alfredo and Juan Carlos looked at each other in disbelief. The man queried their expressions and reactions.

'Do… do you know of him?

Alfredo was now convinced that the man was telling the truth and not a fraudster or trickster, and so he explained.

'We have just returned to Spain with the Armada, and we have sailed with Captain Abad, whom we know very well indeed. Unfortunately for you… *La Trinidad Valencera* was wrecked off the coast of Ireland, and we sailed back to Spain on board *Napolitana* with Captain Abad. I also think your smaller ship sank too as we did not see many small ships return to port… You see, the storms were very bad'

The man's heart sank, and he spent the next few minutes contemplating what he had been told, then he said, 'I must've left Laredo just as you sailed into port, because I did not see my ships I decided to return to Madrid and wait for news. Thank you for letting me know, and now I can make arrangements to claim the loss of my ships from the King. I am sure Captain Abad will contact me soon with the paperwork.'

Alfredo was pleased to provide the man with news of his ship, but sad that such a fine ship had been lost. The man introduced himself.

'My name is Luis Ortega… please… may I buy you a drink in return for your information?'

Alfredo looked at Juan Carlos, and as it was getting late, he refused the offer.

'Muchas gracias señor Ortega, and my name is Alfredo Rodriguez… but we have to be up early, and my son is very tired. We are travelling on horses, and you are welcome to join us.'

Ortega understood, and gave Alfredo his business card.

'I understand, but I will be travelling on the first coach in the morning… I don't ride horses. Please accept my card, and when you get to Madrid come and visit me because I would like to know more.'

Ortega shook Alfredo's hand, and Alfredo left with Juan Carlos to go to their room.

Next morning, Alfredo and Juan Carlos walked across the yard to the stables, just as the sun was rising. Once they had saddled their horses, they set off along the well-worn main road to Burgos, their next stopping point according to Daval's map.

'The man from last night papa… do you think he was telling the truth?'

Alfredo thought for a few minutes before answering.

'Mmmm, I am not sure? He seemed genuine, but we must always be careful just as Daval had warned us. I will only be really happy when we have reached familiar sights near home.'

Over the next two days, they travelled across the beautiful countryside of Montes Obarenes-San Zadornil, a mountainous region in Northern Spain, where the dusty road weaved its way around rocky outcrops, as it followed the natural flow of the mountain streams. It was very pleasant and easy riding their horses, as they seemed to follow the road without guidance. Apart from the occasional coach passing, they saw no one, and it felt very comfortable in the warm sun, breathing fresh country air. Juan Carlos was happy to be with his father and that they were going home, and he realised that he missed his family.

'Papa, I am pleased to have met some very good people, but I don't want to be a sailor anymore... I like our country and working on the farm. I am truly sorry for running away.'

Alfredo smiled at his son, and in his heart, he was pleased to bring him back home safe, despite the feeling of anger he had at first.

'You have had your adventure Juan Carlos, and now you realise how dangerous the world can be. Your mother and I only ever wanted you to be safe.'

'I understand now papa, and I will not be so stupid in future.'

Alfredo did not reply, instead, he stopped the horses at the stream for them to drink, and in the distance, he saw the village of Miranda de Ebro, their next stop according to the map. Alfredo was pleased that Daval had taken the time to prepare the map because it proved to be a very accurate, and valuable guide through central Spain. Before the search for his son, Alfredo had only ever travelled to Malaga city or Granada city to trade and buy supplies. He had no need to venture any further, as he had everything he needed at the farm with a good and happy family, and hopefully, that would include his son. As they rested and thought more of their home, a coach came rushing past them leaving great plumes of dust, but inside was the merchant from last night. He waved at Alfredo and his son as the coach flashed by, and Alfredo returned the gesture.

Over the next few days, the journey to Madrid continued to be uneventful, with the only annoyance being the dusty road, and the endless hours sitting in the saddle. Juan Carlos was beginning to think that sailing back to Malaga might have been the better option, although he was pleased with his horse, as they were gradually become good friends. To ease the boredom of the journey, they often stopped to cool their muscles in the larger streams and pools. They also passed through many interesting towns, such as Burgos which was a place of pilgrimages, where many people came to hear about miracles, and to see the many stunning churches. Further south was Aranda de Duero, another ancient town famed for its magnificent buildings. Alfredo had heard about these places but had never seen them, and for that reason alone he was pleased to have travelled by horse.

When they were within two days ride of Madrid, rain-clouds formed, and as the day wore on, the skies became blacker with rumbles of thunder. A crack of lightening flashed through the clouds which seemed to open the floodgates for the heavy rain to lash down. The horses were startled and it took Alfredo and Juan Carlos several minutes to calm them down, and then they put on capes from their saddlebags and tried to continue the journey. An hour later, with the rain relentlessly pouring down, they approached a ravine with a large stream running through it. As the road crossed over the stream, Alfredo decided to see if it was safe to cross. Satisfied, they entered the stream just as a cascade of water, broken tree branches and boulders came rushing down from the hills. Alfredo kicked his horse to move quickly across the river, but Juan Carlos was too slow, and the power of the water knocked him off his horse and into the raging torrent. His horse galloped off towards Alfredo who managed to stop it, but it cost him precious time to save his son. By the time he had calmed the horses and secured the horses under a nearby tree, there was no sign of Juan Carlos.

Alfredo followed the river of raging water from the bankside as it continued along the ravine. Frantic with worry, Alfredo ran over the rocks on the side of the bank, trying to prevent himself from slipping into the fast-flowing water. He called Juan Carlos' name as loud as he could, but the noise from the torrent was too much for his voice to carry. As Alfredo made it round a sharp bend in the ravine, he saw the river disappear over a ledge, before dropping into a deep gorge. He despaired at the thought that his son would never survive such a drop. Then he noticed a large tree hanging over the river just before the ledge, and its roots were anchored deep into the earth. He could see that Juan Carlos was hanging from one of the branches, held by the strap of his leather satchel. The boy was unconscious, and although his head was out of the water, his body was limp, and the rushing water was trying to drag him away from the tree. Desperately, Alfredo scrambled closer to the tree, trying not to fall in, but the bank was wet and slippery, and he had to claw onto whatever hand and foothold there was available. Clinging onto one of the roots of the tree, that had spiralled itself around a large rock, Alfredo held on with one hand, and swung round to grab his son. After several failed attempts he heard a loud "crack" as the branch holding Juan Carlos broke. With one last swing, Alfredo leaped as far as he could, and managed to grab his son as the branch fell into the river and over the ledge. He hung on for a few seconds trying to gain enough strength to swing them both back again, if he failed, then they would both be swept into the gorge below. Juan Carlos suddenly regained consciousness, and clung onto his father's neck, as Alfredo tried to keep them both calm.

'Son, you are OK… Now… grab whatever you can when I swing back towards the bank… are you ready?'

Juan Carlos, although dazed, understood and tried to regain his senses.

'Si… papa, I will try.'

With a final burst of strength, Alfredo groaned as he swung back towards the bank, and Juan Carlos was able to grab onto one of the tree roots. Eventually, after slipping on the wet bank and being drenched by the spray from the river and rain, they managed to clamber up the bank to safety. They lay exhausted on the bank to recover their strength, oblivious to the rain soaking their entire bodies. When they had recovered enough strength, Alfredo and his son carefully made their way back to the horses. Alfredo found a large overhanging rock with which to shelter from the rain, and using dried grass and fallen branches from under the rock, he managed to light a fire. As night fell, the warm glow of the fire brought their strength back, and they fashioned a hot meal from their supplies. That night, they slept on blankets next to the fire, and exhaustion made them drift quickly off to sleep.

Chapter 33
Long Journey Home II

Madrid

The following day, Alfredo woke to the sound of birds singing in the trees, and the sun shining through the branches, as the last of the wet ground slowly dried up. The horses were happily munching on the long grass close to their rocky shelter, and Juan Carlos slumbered on. By the time Juan Carlos woke up, his father had prepared the horses and cleared the camp ready for the next part of the journey. Alfredo went over to him.

'Juan Carlos, how are you feeling?'

The boy rubbed the sleep from his eyes and assessed his body.

'I... I... feel fine papa, but I am very thirsty, and my neck hurts.'

Alfredo looked at his son's neck and noticed a nasty burn mark where the strap had held him in the tree. Alfredo gave him some food and water, and then took out a piece of cloth and wet it in the stream, before placing it onto the wound.

'You have a nasty graze on your neck from your strap... when we get to Madrid, we will seek a physician. Now drink this water and eat some bread and cheese, and I will find some herbs to put on your wounds.'

Alfredo searched the area for herbs using his skills as a farmer where they were used to treating themselves in the countryside. He gathered the herbs and mixed it into a paste with the juices from a cactus plant. By the time he returned to his son, Juan Carlos had removed his shirt to bathe and wash the wound in the stream. Alfredo noticed the mark of the strap was also across his chest, back and under one arm.

'Juan Carlos dry your body, because I have prepared this potion for your wound… and there a more marks across your body.'

As Juan Carlos dried himself, Alfredo laughed as a thought occurred to him.

'Ha! Ha … I could not have gathered these herbs when we were at sea… I am much happier on land where I can look after you better.'

They both laughed, and once his father had tended his son's wounds, they were ready to set off on their journey. Alfredo looked at the sky to see if the storm had cleared, and satisfied that it was going to be a fine day, he encouraged his son.

'Come on Juan Carlos, let's get home as soon as possible so we can both relax… and I hope the journey is very boring with no further incidents.'

As they approached the outskirts of Madrid, they noticed that there were more coaches, people on horseback, and more stone houses, farms and inns. Juan Carlos was pleased to see that there were more children playing, and women working outside their homes. With so many people around, Alfredo felt a little safer, and began to relax as they wandered closer into the heart of the city. However, the problem for Alfredo was that the city was huge and very busy. He wondered what his best option would be, and so they decided to stop at one of the coaching inns along the roadside. Hitching their horses to a rail, Alfredo spoke to his son.

'Juan Carlos, you wait with the horses while I get some ale and information.'

Alfredo went inside the inn and ordered two small tankards of ale, when the innkeeper returned with the drinks, Alfredo gave him the merchants card.

'Señor. Do you know the address on this card?'

The innkeeper looked at the card, and scratched his head, then he went to talk to a well-dressed man in the corner, then he returned.

'Señor. I am advised that this address is in the centre of the city, which is about 30 minutes from here. Follow the road you have come on and look for the church of St Sebastian in the middle of the city… it is the same location as the address you seek.'

Alfredo thanked the innkeeper and nodded his appreciation towards the gentleman, then as it was getting late, he added.

'Do you have a room for myself and my son, and a stable for our horses.'

The innkeeper confirmed that he had and Alfredo took the ale to his son outside the inn. As they sat in the shade of the inn porch drinking their ale, Juan Carlos asked his father what his plan was for the city.

'Papa, are we going into the city, or should we go around it? It looks very busy.'

Alfredo sipped on his ale and thought about his plan.

'We will stay here tonight, then try to find the merchant in the city, and also a physician for your wounds… I also have something else that I want to do, but we should be out of the city as soon as possible.'

As soon as they finished their ale, the horses were stabled and they settled into their room, taking all their belonging s with them as Alfredo did not trust being in the city. After a hot meal, they relaxed on a bench outside of the inn and watched the busy streets, before going to bed.

Early next morning, after a breakfast of bread and cheese, Alfredo paid and thanked the innkeeper, then helped his son saddle the horses. Following the directions given to them, they set off slowly into the city, and marvelled at all the buildings both old and new. Alfredo enquired along the way as to the location of the church of St Sebastian, as he was keen to complete their business and get back to the countryside as soon as possible. Eventually, they found the church, and then looked up and down the street for the merchant's address. When they found it, an archway at the address led into a courtyard, so they walked their horses into the courtyard and looked around.

'Wait with the horses Juan Carlos, and I will look for Ortega.'

There was a horse trough in the courtyard, so Juan Carlos watched the horses drink as his father went into the building. The courtyard itself was neatly set out with arches on one side leading to stables, where a boy, a little younger than Juan Carlos, was busy cleaning and feeding the stock. Other arches, at right angle to the stables led to offices and other rooms. Ornate ceramic pots festooned the walkway under the arches, they were filled with beautiful and fragrant flowers. Alfredo enjoyed their pleasant perfume, which made a change from the smelly streets they had just travelled on. He knocked, and entered through an oak door with large ornate hinges, and the room looked like an office with shelves full of books and papers. In the corner behind the door a voice spoke.

'Si, can I help you?'

A woman was seated at a desk organising paperwork. She was heavy-set, with dark, tied-up hair and wore a white, high collared blouse and long dress. Alfredo felt a little uncomfortable, but managed to compose a reply.

'Yes… I hope so, I am looking for Señor Ortega… he gave me his card.'

Alfredo handed over the card to the woman, who looked at it, then got up and walked through another door leading to a hallway and stairs. A moment later the woman and a man came back to the office, and the man greeted Alfredo warmly.

'Ah! Señor Rodriguez, welcome to Madrid. Please come to my office.'

They shook hands and Ortega led Alfredo out of the office, up the stairs, to a very large and well decorated room with many shelves filled with books and files. His large, mahogany desk was covered in paperwork and writing material, and two grand leather backed chairs were positioned either side of the desk. Two large windows allowed for lots of natural light which also overlooked the courtyard.

'Please... please be seated, I am very happy to see you... How is your son?'

Alfredo was amazed at the quantity of papers on the desk and on the floor.

'Err... my son... yes, he is fine... he is with the horses in your courtyard. How was your coach journey?'

Ortega looked out of the window and could see Juan Carlos talking to the stable lad.

'Ah! He is with my grandson Roberto, who loves horses... My journey? Oh, my journey was very hard and uncomfortable... I hate those coaches... they are not good for long journeys.'

Then he shuffled some of the papers away from the desk to get a clearer view of his guest.

'The horses out there belong to my son and business partner. As I said when we last met, I do not ride horses, but it keeps the boy out of trouble... But please, forgive all the papers, I am trying to prepare all the documents for my claim for the ships lost with the Armada. I have not seen some of the documents for many years.'

Alfredo sat calmly and watched Ortega juggle the papers.

'I understand señor… if you are too busy then I can call back later.'

'Nonsense my friend… I am pleased to see you and I need to take a break from this work. Please tell me more of what you know, and how I can be of assistance to you?'

Alfredo began to relax and told Ortega the story of his ships and how *La Trinidad Valencera* met its demise. He concluded with his own request, and took out of his pocket the single ruby stone given to him by Daval.

'As part of my payment for the Armada voyage, I was given this stone… I was told that there could be an honest jeweller in Madrid that might buy it from me for a reasonable price. Could you advise me on this matter? Also, my son was hurt in an accident and has a minor wound, but I would like a physician to take a look at him.'

As Alfredo placed the stone onto the desk, Ortega picked it up and took out a jeweller's eyepiece from a drawer, then he studied it carefully.

'Mmm… yes… mmm yes.'

Alfredo was bemused and wondered if he had done the right thing, and was just about to leave, when Ortega returned his stone and smiled.

'This is indeed a nice stone, and the quality is very good. I think that I may be able to help you my friend. I know of one or two good jewellers that will pay a good price for this beautiful ruby.'

Alfredo was amazed and pleased at the same time.

'Oh! oh… thank you señor, I was hoping to make a little money for my farm near Granada.'

Ortega became interested in the location of Alfredo's farm.

'We trade at all the ports and cities, and I am sure the wagons pass nearby your farm in Granada. Tell me, what do you grow or produce on your farm?'

'Just a few simple crops of mixed olives, oats, maize and goat grazing fields, and I produce my own ibérico ham to sell at the local markets.'

Ortega smiled and imagined the peaceful scene.

'Ah… it sounds very nice. You produce ibérico ham? it is very popular in Spain, and in other countries too. I have been looking for other producers… I will purchase all you can supply my friend, and you will not get a better price than I can offer you.'

Alfredo was stunned into silence.

'Ugh! O… OK… yes, I agree.'

Ortega rose out of his chair and went to a tall mahogany cabinet, and brought a bottle of fine brandy and two glasses to the desk.

'Come my friend… we shall toast to our new enterprise.'

In the courtyard, the stable boy was busy working inside one of the stables, and Juan Carlos stood outside the stable door and called in quietly.

'Hello, my name is Juan Carlos… what is your name?'

The boy was completely engrossed in his work cleaning out one of the stables, and did not hear him, so Juan Carlos went further into the stable and tapped him on the shoulder.

'Hello?'

The boy was startled, and jumped back a little.

'Oh! I… I… didn't hear you come in… What can I do for you?'

Juan Carlos pointed back towards the building and to his horses.

'My name is Juan Carlos, and my father is in the office over there, so I am waiting for him… these are our horses… what is your name?'

The boy recovered quickly and walked out of the stable.

'My name is Roberto… Roberto Ortega.'

On hearing the familiar surname, Juan Carlos was enthused a little.

'My name is Juan Carlos Rodriguez, and we met someone called Ortega at a coaching inn near Laredo.'

Roberto smiled, stopped working, and leant on his brush to reply.

'Si… he is my grandfather; he and my father own these buildings. They are merchants and do a lot of trading all over Spain.'

He sighed a little then continued.

'I am supposed to be part of the business soon and to work in the office, but I like working with horses more than trading.'

It was Juan Carlos' turn to smile.

'Si, Roberto… I also like being with horses, and I would not like to work inside a building… this is my horse… do you think she is beautiful?'

Roberto went over to both horses, and cast a good eye over the creatures, and eventually agreed.

'Si, Juan Carlos you have two fine horses, but it looks like they have travelled a long way, and one of the them will need new horseshoe soon.'

Juan Carlos was impressed by Roberto's knowledge and made a mental note of his recommendation.

'Wow! Roberto, you know a lot about horses, and you are correct because we have travelled a long way. I will ask my father to take the horses to a blacksmith as soon as possible.'

As the boys enjoyed talking about horses, they were quickly becoming friends. A few minutes later, another boy about the same age as Roberto, walked into the courtyard. He was very skinny, scruffy, and looked like a street urchin. He knew Roberto, and acted "cocky" and overconfident as he ate an apple, that he had most likely stolen. As he leant against a wall close to Juan Carlos' horse, he spoke to Roberto.

'Hola Roberto, how are you today and who is your friend?'

Roberto answered sluggishly as he did not really like the boy.

'This is Juan Carlos, and he is travelling with his father... he is talking with my grandfather in the office... they will be here soon.'

Juan Carlos did not like the look of the boy either, because he was looking at their saddlebags, so he stepped closer to his horses.

In an instance, the boy grabbed at Juan Carlos' leather satchel that he had placed on his horse until his wound felt better. Juan Carlos reacted quickly, and he lunged forward to cling on to the strap, jerking the other boy to the ground. As the two boys pulled against each other with the strap, the satchel opened and its contents spilled out onto the floor. The boy noticed the bright pistol, then picked it up and ran off, Juan Carlos got up quickly and gave chase.

'Stop... Stop! Thief!'

Roberto was shocked and initially rooted to the spot, then he tried to follow, but it was too late as they had disappeared out of the courtyard. On hearing the commotion, Alfredo and Ortega looked out of the window to see two boys running out of the courtyard. Alfredo called out in alarm.

'It's my son... he is chasing another boy... I must go.'

Alfredo ran outside to the courtyard and looked at Roberto.

'What happened?'

Roberto, struggled to explain at first, and pointed to the main street, just as Alfredo rushed up to him, he stuttered.

'I... I saw the other boy take something from your son's bag, and he is chasing him.'

Alfredo looked at the satchel on the ground and began to

replace its contents. It was then that he noticed the pistol had gone, and as he replaced the pouch of coins into the secret pocket, he saw three rubies similar to the one Daval gave him. As he didn't have time to understand it, he placed them in his pocket, secured the satchel onto the horse and ran after his son.

Although Juan Carlos was bigger than the boy, the little street urchin was very fast and agile, and he skipped around the busy streets with ease. Juan Carlos was not far behind, but with so many people and unknown streets, he was afraid of losing sight of the boy. Juan Carlos ran as fast as he could to keep up and was beginning to tire, but as he came to an alleyway, he saw the boy had stopped. Thinking he was safe, the boy stopped running and walked slowly along the alleyway looking at the pistol, so Juan Carlos caught up with him and tried to grab him. The boy instantly jumped onto a low wall, before climbing onto the roof of an outbuilding. The chase continued along roofs, back onto walls and then onto more roofs until eventually, the boy came to a roof with no means of egress. The two boys stood panting and facing each other, as the urchin looked at his options. As they were now several feet off the ground, jumping down could have been problematic, and he looked at the pistol. Juan Carlos raised his hands out to show that he was not a threat, but the boy was beginning to panic and raised the pistol. Juan Carlos tried to calm the boy.

'All I want is my pistol back and you can go free… I don't want to harm you.'

The urchin continued to shakily point the pistol at Juan Carlos as he looked for an escape route, but it was of no use. Down on the ground, Alfredo appeared, having been directed by people knocked down by the urchin. He pleaded with his son to let the boy go, and to forget about the pistol, but Juan Carlos did not want to do that, and firmly replied to his father.

'No papa!… this is my pistol and it means a lot to me… He cannot have it.'

The urchin felt that he did not have any alternative, and pulled the trigger. Yet nothing happened, as the primer in the pistol was rendered useless when Juan Carlos nearly lost his life in the water. The boy lost his footing, and as he fell down the roof, he dropped the pistol, but Juan Carlos caught his flailing hand, and stopped him from falling. As he pulled him up, the boy pushed Juan Carlos and ran away. As he recovered, Juan Carlos looked down to see his father had picked up the pistol, and with no sign of the boy, Juan Carlos climbed down from the roof and returned to the courtyard with his father.

Back at the courtyard, Ortega was talking to his grandson to understand what had happened, and Roberto explained as best he could.

'I have seen the boy a few times, and I know he is a thief, but he has never stolen anything from me. It happened very quickly, and I think he saw the bag on the horse and tried to run away with it, but Juan Carlos was too quick for him.'

Satisfied with the explanation, and that his grandson was not involved, Ortega turned to go inside his office, just as Alfredo and Juan Carlos returned.

'Alfredo… is your son alright? Did you find the boy?'

'My son is fine, and the boy ran away.'

With no one injured, Alfredo walked with Ortega into the office, and Juan Carlos resumed his conversation with Roberto.

'Juan Carlos… What happened? Did you catch the boy?'

Juan Carlos was just pleased to have his beloved pistol back and he began to clean it, then gave a very sincere reply.

'Si Roberto, the boy dropped the pistol and then ran away. I am pleased that he was not injured, but I hope he learns from this.'

Inside the office, Ortega poured another brandy for them both and tried to put the incident behind them.

'Alfredo, please accept my apologies for what happened, but the city is full of homeless children trying to survive.'

Alfredo began to understand that living in a city has many disadvantages.

'Si, Luis, that is why I will be very happy when I get home to my little farm in the quiet countryside.'

They finished their brandy and Ortega and Alfredo went to see the jeweller that Ortega knew. They left Juan Carlos and Roberto talking, and walked about 200 yards to the jeweller's shop. As they entered the shop, Alfredo was amazed at all the fine quality of items on display, and felt that his small stone surely cannot be worth much. However, the jeweller examined the ruby closely, and then spoke privately with Ortega in a separate room. When they returned, Ortega spoke to Alfredo.

'My friend has examined your stone, and agrees with me that it is of good quality, and as I have given him a legitimate reason why you own it, then he is happy to offer you 20 ducats for it.'

Alfredo tried not show any emotion, but inside he was pleased that it was worth more than Daval had said.

'Thank you, señor, for your guidance and advise, and I would like to sell it so I can improve my farm and provide more ibérico ham for your business.'

Ortega was just about to prepare a bill of sale document with the jeweller, when Alfredo placed two more stones onto the counter. He had decided to keep one in a safe place at home as a kind of insurance for the future. Both Ortega and the jeweller were surprised, but then agreed to include the other stones. On inspecting them, they agreed that they were from the same source.

An hour later, Alfredo and Ortega were celebrating with

yet another brandy in the office, when Juan Carlos and Roberto appeared at the door.

'Papa, it is getting late… and I am hungry. Where are we going to sleep tonight?

Without any forthcoming reply from his father, Ortega intervened.

'You shall be my guests tonight. My house is outside the city to the south, and it is on your way home, so you must stay with me.'

Alfredo was a little overwhelmed, but very grateful.

'I cannot thank you enough Luis, you have helped us beyond my expectations.'

As they prepared to leave, Ortega waved away his politeness.

'Nonsense, Alfredo, I shall make a little commission on the stones, and the information you gave me about my ships will allow me to get some recompense. Also, we have a new business venture together… so all is well my friend.'

As they stepped out of the office, Ortega summoned a carriage, and he entered it with his grandson.

'We will wait here for you until you get your horses, then please follow us to my house Alfredo.'

After they had travelled about 20 minutes, Ortega stopped the coach, got out to speak with Alfredo, and pointed to a building.

'Alfredo, this building is where my family physician works, and he will look at Juan Carlos' wounds.'

Inside, the physician inspected the wounds, and observed the poultice that his father had used.

'Where did you get the poultice from?'

Alfredo explained about his old countryside traditions, but was a little wary of what the physician's reply would be.

'I can see that it was a nasty abrasion, and that normally it would take many weeks to heal, but your poultice has reduced the inflammation, and the wound is healing very nicely... I can do nothing to improve this.'

The physician washed the wound and placed a dry cloth over it, then explained to his father.

'Now you must make a fresh batch of the poultice as soon as possible, and I will give you more cloth for regular dressings. Now tell me... what herbs did you use?'

Alfredo smiled, and gladly gave the physician a detailed list of country herbs, as his son got dressed. Ortega gave some coins to the physician before they left the building and entered the carriage. Forty minutes later they were at Ortega's home, and the carriage turned off the main road onto a tree-lined avenue. It led to a magnificent house, set apart from part of a large farm, and Alfredo rode in silence as he could not believe the opulence of the property. There were separate stables and farm buildings where several farmhands busily worked with horses, cattle and goats. When the carriage pulled up outside the house, Ortega and Roberto stepped out, and to greet them was his wife, together with Roberto's father and mother.

'Welcome to my home.'

Alfredo rubbed his grubby hands onto the back of his breeches and politely greeted Ortega's family. One by one he shook the hands of each member as they were introduced to him. Ortega began.

'May I introduce my wife, Sofia... My son, Jose... and his wife and mother of Roberto, Angelita. My dear... these are our guests Alfredo and his son Juan Carlos.'

'Very pleased to meet you... señora... señor... señora.'

Sofia was very warm and welcoming towards them, and especially towards Juan Carlos.

'Please come in and we will arrange for you to bathe and refresh yourselves... Your son must be very hungry and tired.'

Alfredo was feeling very inferior at such a grand building, and in the midst of such elegant, civilised people, and he really wanted a little time to come to terms with it all.

'Thank you very much, my son and I are looking forward to your kind hospitality… but first we must stable the horses.'

Sofia looked at Ortega and nodded to him, to which he reacted.

'Err… no Alfredo… I will get my men to do that… please come in and relax,'

Alfredo was reluctantly about to accept, when Juan Carlos interrupted.

'Sir, I really enjoy putting my horse to bed, and I would like my father to help me.'

'Of course, of course, no problem. I fully understand, and I will meet you when you return to the house.'

Ortega understood, and quickly accepted the request, then he ushered his family into the house.

Alfredo followed his son who was leading the horses to the stables. He smiled and patted his son on the head.

'Thanks for that son… I didn't want to go into the house just yet.'

Juan Carlos laughed as he too felt the same way.

An hour later Alfredo and Juan Carlos gathered all their bags and returned to the house. Ortega saw them coming and met them at the door, then led them up the stairs to their room. Alfredo noticed how wide the stairs were, with many portrait paintings hanging on the wall, positioned in such a way as to allow each painting to be inspected closely as they walked up the stairs.

'Are these paintings of your family?'

Ortega smiled and nodded with pride.

'Si, there are seven generations of my family, as we have lived in this region for many years.'

Their bedroom was large and lavishly decorated, and two huge beds with dark oak headboards dominated the room. A separate smaller room held all the washing and ablution facilities for guests, and a grand bay window looked out onto the fields beyond the farm. As they were trying to come to terms with the room, Ortega left them in peace, and smiled to himself.

'Enjoy the room my friends, because you are our welcome guests… see you later for dinner.'

Ortega closed the door and Juan Carlos was about to jump onto the bed, when someone knocked at the door. Sofia opened the door slowly with a small pile of clothes.

'Forgive the interruption Alfredo, but here are some fresh clothes for you, as I think Roberto is the same size as your son, and you and Jose are similar too.'

Alfredo gratefully accepted the clothes.

'Thank you very much señora… you are too kind to us.'

Sofia left the room with a contented smile, and Alfredo tried to keep his son from messing up the neat room.

'Juan Carlos, this is not like your room at home, and you must respect how neat and tidy it is… so please no jumping on the bed.'

Juan Carlos reluctantly agreed and they washed and changed into the clean clothes.

Chapter 34
Long Journey Home III

After a hot meal and a good night's sleep, Alfredo and Juan Carlos felt refreshed and ready to make their final journey home, and they couldn't wait to get going. Ortega had given them extra food supplies, and advised that he will arrange a visit as soon as possible. After saying their goodbyes to Ortega and his family, and thanked him for all that he had done, Alfredo and his son set off on the long road south. There were still many days of travelling to do, but they did not want to tire the horses, and agreed to rest as much as possible. The road continued to be hot and dusty with many carriages, carts and riders passing, so they rode in single file for most of the time with little time to discuss the events in Madrid.

At the end of the first day, they reached the Tagus river, which Alfredo remembered passed through Lisbon, in Portugal on its way to the ocean. He recalled the magnificent sight of all the ships as they gathered, before sailing to England. The land either side of the river looked to be very fertile, and farmers were growing many crops. Alfredo thought that being so close to the large city of Madrid, there would be more market opportunities, and he considered relocating. They paused before crossing the river, as it seemed to be a little deep, but as others were riding through it with no problem, they slowly made their way across. The water felt cool and refreshing as the horses splashed across the river, which they too seemed to enjoy. Alfredo decided that it was a good place to camp for the night, so they moved away from the main road, and found a quiet location around the first bend of the river. As Juan Carlos settled the horses close to the river, he noticed fish swimming, and there were so many that he wished he had his fishing rod, as it was one of his favourite pastimes. Alfredo started a fire, then he gathered fresh herbs to replace the poultice on his son's wounds. When they had both washed the dust from their bodies, Alfredo changed Juan Carlos' dressing and prepared a meal. They lay their blankets on the soft grass, and although the evening was becoming cooler, it was good to be outside under the stars, listening to the flowing river. As they ate their meal Juan Carlos mentioned the river.

'Papa, this is a good place to go fishing, I would love to come here one day.'

His comments reminded Alfredo of his own observations.

'Si, my son… this valley is very good indeed and the land is good for growing many crops.'

The conversation triggered more thoughts into their heads, and Juan Carlos added.

'It is not too far from Roberto and we could become good friends… Because we both like horses.'

Alfredo also thought that relocating to the area could have more positive than negative reasons, but then he thought of the rest of his family.

'But what would mama and grandpa think Juan Carlos, they might not want to move?'

They lay on their blankets in silence and looked up at the stars, thinking about the possibility of relocating. Alfredo was trying to calculate in his head how much it would cost, but now he had the money from the stones and from the Armada payment, then it was indeed possible.

Back at the farm south of Granada, Alfredo's wife Francesca, thought about her husband and son every minute of every day, and the worry was beginning to cause her problems. She was not eating properly and doted more than ever on daughter Maria, who had now turned six years old. She also got a friendly dog for Maria to play with, although it was a poor substitute for her missing brother. However, it was also acted as an alarm for the family, should anyone approach the farm. Yet she worried that her father Emile was getting older too, and although he was restricted, he managed to keep the farm going. Relatives, friends and neighbours called in to see them now and again, but the farm was too remote for them to be of any real assistance. She contemplated moving into the city of Granada, or to the port of Malaga, but for now she would wait a little longer, just in case they came home.

Emile returned to the farm from Malaga, in the family cart pulled by their ageing mule. He seemed a little excited when he brought their meagre food supplies into the house. Francesca was preparing a meal of thick vegetable broth, including the bones of one of their ibérico ham joints, which they stripped for selling at the market. She was using a large iron pot which hung over the fire, and she hoped the meal would last them at least a week.

'Francesca… Francesca, I have news!'

She continued to stir the pot as her father placed the supplies onto the table and hobbled over to her, sceptically she asked.

'What stories have they been telling you now father?'

Emile tried to get some positivity from his daughter, but she only ever expected bad news.

'There is news about the Armada… and that many of the ships have returned home to the north of the country.'

Francesca could not get excited about the news.

'Father, we really don't know if they were with the ships… Manuel only told us that Alfredo was going to Cadiz… I cannot think any further than that or I will die.'

She began to weep, and Emile realised that his daughter could not begin to have hope, just in case the reality was opposite. As she gathered her composure, Francesca turned to her father.

'Papa… I have been thinking, and we should move into the city before the winter comes, or stay with relatives in Malaga… But we cannot stay here, it is too much for you and I to manage… I … I have to think what is best for Maria.'

After several days travelling, and either camping by the roadside, or staying at a coaching inn, Alfredo and his son eventually arrived at the outskirts of Granada. Alfredo could not stop himself from smiling and waving his hat in the air.

'Whoooopeee! At last, Juan Carlos… we are in country-side that I know.'

It all looked the same to Juan Carlos, but he trusted that his father knew the familiar sights of his youth.

'Does this mean that we are not far from home papa?'

Alfredo looked around, and although he had not been to this part of the countryside since he was a boy, he still recognised it.

'I know that there is a shortcut around the city which will save a little time, and if we push the horses, then we should be home by nightfall.'

Juan Carlos could not believe that they were nearly home.

'Really papa… how wonderful. Let's go now.'

Following worn tracks across the countryside, where Alfredo could never take his old cart, he rode his horse at a brisk pace followed closely by his son. It felt good to be riding faster, and the air was cool against their faces as they rode across fields, through woods and across many streams. They stopped periodically for the horses, and themselves to eat and drink, and walked the horses occasionally to keep them cool. After four hours, they eventually came upon the hills above their farm, but as it was getting dark, they decided to slow down to walking pace. Both Alfredo and Juan Carlos were a little nervous about meeting their family after such a long time away.

It was very dark when they approached the family farm, but they were guided by the light coming from the farmhouse, which looked reassuringly familiar. A dog started barking, and they stopped the horses, unsure if their family was still living there, or if they had moved away and another family now lived there. They dis-mounted and walked the horses up to the farmhouse and tied them to a rail, then the door slowly opened a little. Emile pointed a pistol through the opening, as the dog continued to bark loudly behind him.

'Who… who's there?'

On recognising his grandfather's voice, Juan Carlos shouted as loud as he could.

'Grandpapa… it's me! Juan Carlos. We have come home!'

The door flung open and Emile lurched himself out of the doorway, then Juan Carlos ran up to him and leapt into his arms. Alfredo rushed into the house and enveloped Francesca within his strong arms. Francesca burst into tears and almost collapsed on the floor, but Alfredo picked her up and kissed her. Emile and Juan Carlos went back inside the house, and everyone was in floods of tears. The noise eventually woke up Maria, and rubbing her sleepy eyes, came into the room. When she saw her father and brother, she too burst into tears, and everyone comforted her, including the dog. Francesca cast her eyes to the sky, and thanked the Lord for answering her prayers.

A little later, Alfredo and Francesca prepared some food together, taking turns to hold Maria. Then Francesca looked a little pensive which her husband noticed.

'Que pasa carino? What is the matter?'

Francesca paused preparing the food and wrapped her arms around her husband and daughter.

'Alfredo... you have been away a long time, and I don't want to know what happened. All that matters is that you are both home safe... Never do that again because this place is too remote for me without you, and it is too much work for my father.'

Alfredo nodded in agreement and kissed his wife and daughter.

Meanwhile, Juan Carlos was sitting with his grandfather next to the fireplace, staring at the stories in the flames.

'Juan Carlos, I hope you have learned a valuable lesson, adventures are wonderful, but the most important thing in life is to be with your family.'

Juan Carlos hugged his grandfather.

'Si, Grandpapa, but even though there were many dangers, I enjoyed my adventure, and I always thought about you and what you would have done.'

He hugged his grandfather, and added with a big grin.

'But now grandpapa... It is my turn to tell you many stories.'

THE END

Chapter 35
What Happened?

In the end, 67 ships and fewer than 10,000 men survived. It was reported that, when King Philip II of Spain learned the result of the expedition, he declared, 'I sent the Armada against men, not God's winds and waves.' The conflict between Spain and England continued, and in 1589, Queen Elizabeth I launched a failed "English Armada" against Spain. King Philip II, later rebuilt his fleet and dispatched two more Spanish Armadas in the 1590s, but both were scattered by storms. It wasn't until 1604 that a peace treaty was finally agreed.

The 7th Duke of Medina-Sidonia, Alonso Pérez de Guzmán suffered badly with his health as a result of the campaign, and after his return to Spain the King finally relieved him of his command. Yet, royal favour was not withdrawn from him, and in 1595, when Philip III became king, he was appointed captain general of the Ocean where he remained in practical control of the Spanish navy.

The route taken by the Spanish Armada of 1588 can be seen in the map below, which highlights its starting point at Lisbon in Portugal, to their return to Santander and Laredo in the north of Spain.

As for the ships of the Armada themselves, many thanks go to Laurence Flanagan whose valuable information allowed for the location of many of the wrecked ships, during the cruel voyage around Britain.

Donald R. Wraith

1588 Spanish Shipwrecks around Britain.

July

30 July – ***Bazana***: Part of four-strong Squadron of Galleys of Portugal – Damaged during a storm in the Bay of Biscay.

30 or 31 July or 15 November — ***San Salvador***: Said to have been wrecked off Chesil Beach, Dorset in July, or sank in Studland Bay while en route to Portsmouth in November.

August

6 August — ***São Mateus***: Part of the 12-strong Portuguese Squadron of the Armada, *São Mateus* ran aground between Nieuport and Ostend.

6 August — ***Santa Maria Rata Encoronada***: Part of the ten-strong Squadron of Levant and part of the Armada, may have sunk after colliding with the galeasse *San Lorenzo* off Erria, Ireland. Alternatively she grounded and was set alight in late September 1588 in Blacksod Bay, Co Mayo, Ireland.

8 August — ***São Filipe***: Part of the 12-strong Portuguese Squadron of the Armada, *São Filipe* ran aground between Nieuport and Ostend.

8 August — ***San Juan***: Part of the 14-strong Squadron of Biscay and part of the armada, was wrecked at Dunkirk, France.

251

8 August — **San Lorenzo**: Part of the 14-strong Squadron of Galleasses of Naples and part of the Armada, the galleasse collided with the *Santa Maria Rata y Coronada* and was stranded in Calais.

10 August — **Maria Juan**: Part of the 14-strong Squadron of Biscay and part of the Armada, was damaged during the Battle of Gravelines and sank two days later.

Unknown date — **Capitania**: Part of the 12-strong Squadron of Galleys of Portugal and part of the Armada, *Capitania* foundered off Bayonne in the Bay of Biscay.

September

1 September — **Barca de Amburgo**: Part of the 23-strong Squadron of Urcas (Hulks) and part of the Armada, the sailing ship sank during a storm southwest of Fair Isle, Scotland. Her crew were taken aboard *El Gran Grifon* and *La Trinidad Valencera*; both were later wrecked.

4 September — **Castillo Negro**: Part of the 23-strong Squadron of Urcas (Hulks) and part of the Armada, the sailing ship foundered off Donegal, Ireland.

15 September — **La Trinidad Valencera**: Part of the 16-strong Castile Squadron of the Armada, she ran aground at Kinnagoe Bay, Ireland.

15 September — **San Nicolás (Sveti Nikola)**: Part of the ten-strong Squadron of Levant, the carrack was wrecked during a storm off Toorglass, Ireland.

15 September — ***São Marcos***: Part of the
12-strong Portuguese Squadron of the armada, she was
wrecked on the coast of County Clare, Ireland.

20 September — ***Anunciada***: Part of the ten strong Levant
Squadron of the Armada, she was anchored in the mouth of
the River Shannon at Scattery Roads and was burnt and abandoned by her crew who were rescued by other armada ships.

20 September — ***San Esteban***: Part of the
14-strong Squadron of Guipuzcoa and part of the Armada,
near the mouth of the Doonbeg River, western Ireland.
The survivors were either killed as they reached the shore
or later hung.

21 September — ***Santiago***: Part of the
23-strong Squadron of Urcas and part of the Armada,
she ran aground near Mosterhamn in Hardanger
Fjord, Norway.

21 September — ***Santa Maria de la Rosa***: Part of the
14-strong Squadron of Guipuzcoa and part of the Armada,
she was wrecked on Stromboli Reef at Blasket Sound,
Ireland. There was only one survivor out of 297 on board.

22 September — ***Ciervo Volante***: Part of the
23-strong Squadron of Urcas (Hulks) and part of the
Armada, she was wrecked off the west Irish coast while
attempting to return to Spain.

22 September — ***Gran Grin***: Part of the
14-strong Squadron of Biscay and part of the Armada, was
partially burnt in the English Channel and finally sank
south of Clare, Ireland.

25 September — ***Concepción de Juanes del Cano***: Part of the 14-strong Squadron of Biscay and part of the Armada, sank during a storm at Spanish Point, Ireland.

25 September — ***Falcón Blanco Menor*** :Part of the 23-strong Squadron of Urcas (Hulks) and part of the Armada, sank during a storm off the island of Freaghillaun, Galway, Ireland.

25 September — ***Juliana***: Part of the ten-strong Squadron of Levant, she was lost near Spanish Point between Streedagh Point and Black Rock, Ireland.

25 September — ***La Lavia***: Part of the ten-strong Levant Squadron of the Armada, she was grounded near Streedagh Strand, ten miles north of the town of Sligo and near to Spanish Point.

25 September — ***San Juan Bautista***: Part of the 16-strong Castile Squadron of the Armada, she was lost at Streedagh Strand, Ireland, near Spanish Point.

25 September — ***Santa Maria de Visión (de Biscione)***: Part of the ten-strong Levant Squadron of the Armada, she was lost at Streedagh Strand, Ireland.

26 September — ***Duquesa Santa Ana*** : Part of the ten-strong Andalusia Squadron of the Armada, she was wrecked at Loughros Mor Bay, County Donegal with the loss of 223 lives.

28 September — ***El Gran Grifón***: flagship of the 23-strong Squadron of Urcas (Hulks) and part of the Armada, went ashore in the cove of Stroms Heelor on Fair

Isle, Scotland. Her three hundred sailors spent six weeks on the island and the wreck was discovered in 1970.

October

27 October (or 26 October) — ***Girona***: Part of the four-strong Squadron of Galleasses of Naples and part of the Armada, wrecked at Lacada Point, County Antrim, Ireland. There may have been as many as 1295 casualties due to survivors from *Santa Maria Rata Encoronada* and *Duquesa Santa Ana*.

28 October — ***San Pedro Mayor***: One of two hospital ships or hulks which followed the Spanish Armada. She navigated the British Isles and was driven into the English Channel, and went ashore at Hope Cove, Bigbury Bay, Devon.

Unknown date — ***Doncella***: Part of the ten-strong Squadron of Guipuzcoa and part of the Armada, the hulk foundered when she returned to Santander, Spain.

Unknown date:

Maria de Aguirre: Part of the 14-strong Squadron of Biscay and part of the Armada, the patache wrecked.

San Antonio de Padua: Part of the 16-strong Squadron of Castile and part of the Armada, the patache sank off the west coast of Ireland.

Information taken from: https://en.wikipedia.org/wiki/List_of_shipwrecks_in_the_16th_century